Consequences

This paperback edition published in 2025 by Tweedlecoate.
tweedlecoate.co.uk

Cover Design by The Tweedle

Printed and bound by CPI Group (UK) Ltd, Croydon, CR0 4YY

ISBN 978-1068644573

FSC www.fsc.org MIX Paper | Supporting responsible forestry FSC® C013604

Consequences

Edwina Jones

Tweedlecoate

For Hefin, with thanks for his
support and encouragement
in everything I do.

Thank you to my children,
Ian and Angela, for always listening
to me and for giving their advice.

I'm also grateful to my friends and the writers at Write On and Copper Writers for their help, and for their confidence-inspiring nagging!

Chapter 1

Ellie Harris sang along with the radio as Kylie Minogue belted out her latest catchy hit 'The Locomotion'. She glanced around her large kitchen one last time. The kitchen was filled with delicious savoury aromas from three slow cookers on the worktop which had been turned down low: chilli con carne in one, chicken curry in another and a vegetarian curry in the third. The table was almost groaning under the weight of plates of cold meats, salads, pasta dishes and a selection of cheeses all covered with plastic wrap. Another worktop held various bottles and glasses. On a side table covered by a cloth was Tom's eighteenth birthday cake. He hadn't seen it yet and Ellie hoped he wouldn't be embarrassed but, knowing her good-natured son, he would laugh at the photograph of himself lying naked on a rug as a one-year-old which she'd had transferred onto the icing, and which was surrounded with the requisite number of candles. The party was for family and a few of their friends. Tom's friends were taking him out to a club later that evening but it wouldn't be until everyone else was going to bed, knowing the youngsters.

Matt came in and gave a low whistle of appreciation as he put his arm around his wife's shoulders and gave her a gentle squeeze.

'Wow! Everything looks good, haven't you been busy!'

'It wasn't just me, Fiona helped too. She brought the cheese and arranged some grapes on it,' she laughed as her next-door neighbour was well known for her lack of culinary skills.

'Well it all looks fantastic. Organising and preparing a party for thirty guests is no mean feat and you should be proud of yourself. I hope Tom appreciates it.'

'I'm sure he does. He's a good boy. We've been so lucky, haven't we, Matt? He's been absolutely no trouble, not like some teenagers we could mention!'

'I know. What will we do without him when he goes to uni in the autumn?'

'Don't bring that up tonight. You'll only set me off. I can't bear to think of my baby leaving home!'

The unmentioned teenager was Gina, next door. Greg and Fiona Clark had become their neighbours shortly after Matt and Ellie had moved in to Chestnut Grove. Over the years, a friendship of sorts had built up between them. They babysat each other's children occasionally, shared the odd evening meal and generally helped each other out when necessary. Greg was a partner in a high-end garage business and the car on his drive was always top of the range. He needed to earn a large salary in order to keep Fiona in the luxury she expected, although she also worked part-time in something she vaguely described as events organisation. They were certainly a high-flying, glamorous couple but they never seemed to have time for their children. When she was small, Gina had been looked after by a succession of *au pairs*. She had never been an attractive child and at eighteen she hadn't lost what her mother called her 'puppy fat'. She didn't appear to be a happy young girl and always seemed to be whining about something. Twelve years after her birth Ben had arrived. At the time, Ellie was surprised as Fiona had hinted that all was not well in the marriage. Things seemed to have improved after that because they were still together and they doted on their little boy.

'I don't want to rush you, darling, but it's 5.30 and Fiona and Greg will be here in half an hour or so and you need to change,' Matt smiled.

'Okay. I'm all done here. I just need to get out of these clothes and slip into my new dress. I'll be five minutes. Will you organise the children?'

Kissing him quickly, Ellie left the kitchen checking that the hall was clear of children's paraphernalia, straightening the large flower arrangement on the hall table as she went upstairs. From the bedroom window she could see that the garden was looking good. It had been a glorious summer's day and the evening was going to be pleasantly warm. The tubs were overflowing with brightly-coloured flowers and the borders throbbed with colour. Neither she nor Matt would have been able to manage the large garden without help so they paid a gardener to come in one day a week and, looking at it now, she felt it was money well-spent. Matt and Greg had laid out tables and chairs in small groups and had strung some fairy lights on the trees for later on.

At the far end, the garden extended up a wooded hill to the boundary. It was here that Ellie had her own little sanctuary where she did her work. It would be unfair to call it a wooden shed; it was far too grand for that. It was large, with lined walls and had water and electricity connected. As she worked from home she felt it was important to be able to cut herself off from family life while she worked. When people asked her what she did for a living she said she worked in publishing. It was true to say that most of her income was derived from her editing work but Ellie thought of herself as a writer. She had had several articles published, and a few short stories in women's magazines. The sums she was paid for these brought her far more pleasure than her income from her editing work. She glanced towards her office on the hill. Sighing deeply she turned away. After slipping into her new dress she sprayed herself liberally with perfume and left the room.

When Ellie walked into the sitting room joining Matt and the boys. Matt and Tom both gave a wolf whistle. As she gave them a twirl Will, her sixteen-year old said, 'Yay, Mum!' which she took as a compliment. Oscar and Hugo, the seven-year-old twins, studied her briefly then went back to their game. She was an attractive woman and although she shunned the gym, a combination of healthy genes and busy lifestyle kept her figure trim and, with the assistance of her hairdresser who streaked her naturally blonde hair, she looked younger than her thirty-nine years.

'You don't look bad yourselves,' she returned the compliment. It wasn't often that the whole family was so well turned out. The twins looked adorable in their new shirts and trousers with their fair hair slicked back neatly. Will, who normally lived in his sports clothes, looked grown up in his best clothes while Tom managed to look smart and trendy at the same time despite the slightly too-long hair and low-slung trousers.

The three younger boys were reminded about their duties of walking around their guests to offer nibbles and not to eat them before the guests had a chance and, more importantly, to behave themselves.

'Uncle Greg, Aunty Fiona, Gina and Ben will be here soon,' Ellie reminded them.

'Why do they have to come first?' grumbled Will.

'We thought it would be nice for both families to have a little drink together before everyone else arrives,' said Matt. 'They have helped prepare and we have been friends since we moved here fifteen years ago. Everyone else will start to arrive at seven so it won't be long.'

'Well I don't like Aunty Fiona,' went on Will.

'We don't either, she's mean,' said Oscar, speaking on behalf of his twin, as always. 'And we don't like Uncle Greg.'

'Now that's enough! Just be nice to everyone this evening. Mummy's gone to a lot of trouble to make sure that we're going to have a pleasant time celebrating Tom's birthday. He'll be leaving home in September so things are going to change for us all.'

As he spoke the doorbell rang. Preceded by the scent of expensive perfume, Fiona came in, make-up expertly applied, stylishly dressed and shrieking her greetings to everyone. She was followed by six-year-old Ben who was as spruced up as the twins and carrying a small parcel which was beautifully wrapped. Then, rather more quietly, came Greg followed by a sulky Gina, scruffily dressed in black from head to toe.

Fiona did her rounds, bestowing kisses on everyone which were borne patiently by Matt, avoided by a last minute turn of the head by Will, and suffered with grimaces by Oscar and Hugo.

'You smell ...' said Hugo pulling a face.

'...nice,' finished Oscar, nudging his brother.

Not that Fiona had noticed as she had moved on to Ellie. Greg was shaking hands with everyone, including the twins, which made them feel important. Gina stood silently, leaning against the wall just inside the door with her arms folded watching everyone with a surly expression. She was very much into the Goth look at the moment: her hair was dyed black, eyes heavily lined in a pale face. She looked totally out of place in Ellie's elegant sitting room.

Turning to her young son, who was looking a little bit uncertain, Fiona said, 'Ben, are you going to give Tom his present?' Embarrassed that everyone was looking at him Ben ran up to Tom and thrust out the gift.

Kneeling down to the little boy, Tom took the gift and said gently, 'Thank you, Ben. Will you help me open it?' Curiosity getting the better of them, Oscar and Hugo sidled up to watch. Gina remained standing, leaning against a wall, saying nothing but watching everything.

'What about you, Gina, are you coming to help me too?'

For a moment she looked as if she was going to join them but she sneered and stayed where she was.

The three youngsters lost interest when the parcel was opened to reveal a leather wallet and ran off.

'Thank you very much, Aunty Fiona and Uncle Greg,' smiled Tom.

'You're welcome, darling,' replied Fiona. 'There's a cheque inside but we wanted you to have something to keep as well.'

Matt turned to a tray which was laid out with a bottle of champagne in an ice-bucket and some crystal glasses. He poured out the frothy bubbles of gold. He had even thought of the little ones and handed them sherry glasses of sparkling apple juice so that they could feel part of the occasion and he warned them not to drink any just yet. Taking the tray of glasses round everyone, he turned to Gina.

'Are you going to come over here and join us?' he invited with a smile.

'No thanks, I'm fine here.'

Tom patted the seat by his side. 'Please – come and sit by me and protect me from the oldies and the speech which I can feel coming on any minute!'

Gina, who had harboured a crush on Tom for as long as she could remember, blushed but obstinately remained where she was so Matt took her a glass of champagne.

Matt stood in the centre of the room with his glass in his hand and spoke. 'As Tom has so accurately predicted, I would like to say a few words.' Tom laughingly covered his face with a cushion and the others laughed. 'Ellie and I have been blessed with four wonderful sons and Tom, our eldest, has now reached the grand age of eighteen. He has been a delight to us since he was born on a day as hot and sunny as this one in 1969. When he was small, one of his favourite sayings was "When I'm a big boy I'm going to be..." One week it was a fireman, the next week it was a policeman and I've lost count of how many different things he was going to be. Then, one day, he said "I'm going to be a doctor." He has worked hard to enable himself to take the first steps to realise his ambition and he will be leaving us in September to start university which will take him along that road. Please raise your glasses and join me in a toast. Happy birthday Tom and good luck in the future.'

Gina snorted from her position by the door but said nothing.

As they raised their glasses Ellie looked at their handsome boy who was almost a man with tears in her eyes. Tom smiled his thanks at everyone and asked innocently, 'Now that I'm eighteen can I have my first sip of alcohol?'

Amid much laughter and knowing glances from the adults Matt once again raised his hand, smiling, 'Before you all polish off this highly expensive champagne and demand another glass can I just make another toast to our friends and neighbours and to thank them for their assistance.'

No-one's lips had a chance to touch their drink before Gina stomped across the room. They all paused and turned to look at her as she stood there and, to everyone's astonishment, she smashed her glass onto the coffee table, shattering the crystal into hundreds of tiny pieces. There was a moment of silence before she said loudly, looking between Ellie and her father.

'Crap! What a load of crap! Friends? Happy families! Who are you kidding! What sort of man shags his friend's wife?

Eh? What sort of woman welcomes her friend's husband in her shag-shed or...' sarcastically, 'should I say "office".'

She turned and stalked out of the room leaving a stunned silence behind her. Matt looked from Greg to Ellie in amazement. Greg flushed a deep red and, in contrast, Ellie's face was blanched white. Their guilt was written all over them without a further word having been spoken.

It was little Ben's voice that broke the silence when he said, 'Can I drink my champagne now?'

It seemed to galvanise everyone into action. Greg put down his glass and turned to Matt and said, 'Sorry, mate' and left the room.

Matt went to follow but Tom put his arms around him to restrain him, calling over his shoulder to Will, 'Take the kids upstairs, NOW, and stay with them.'

Fiona struggled up from the depths of her armchair and flew across the room at Ellie striking her on the head and pulling at her hair. 'You fucking bitch! BITCH! How could you?'

Ellie covered her face but did nothing more to protect herself from the onslaught. Matt and Tom dashed over and pulled Fiona off.

'That's enough!' said Tom.

'Enough? I could kill her for what she's done.'

'Fiona, we're all in shock at the moment,' said Matt. 'Believe me; I know exactly how you feel. You're not the only one to be suffering.'

'Well it's her fault. She's the one who got her claws into my Greg. She's always fancied him.'

Tom stepped in front of her. 'I think you'd better go, Aunty Fiona. Now isn't the time for this.'

'You Harrises have always thought you were better than us. Just wait until people hear all about you. There's a messy divorce on the way and you are right in the middle of it. I'm not moving from here until you tell me how long this has been going on.'

Fiona continued ranting and making threats and throughout it all Ellie just sat as if she was unable to take anything in. Eventually Fiona ran out of steam and turned to leave with a final threat, 'I'll be back – you haven't heard the last of this – not by any means.'

Chapter 2

The second I dropped my bombshell I regretted my words. The euphoria and sense of power that sent a buzz through my veins when I delivered my killer speech had dissipated rapidly. I hadn't thought any further than letting everyone know that I had the upper hand: that I was someone to be listened to, to be taken notice of, that I was as important as anyone else, that I deserved some attention too, dammit. What had I done? I felt a bit sick. I sat on my bed in the silent house. Thinking. Waiting. My stomach churned when I thought of Tom's face. Kind, gentle Tom who had always been nice to me and whom I had hero-worshipped for as long as I could remember, pretending to other girls in my year that he was nobody important but secretly pleased at their jealousy because he was my friend. I'd even dreamed that he could be more than a friend one day. Fat chance now. I shouldn't have spoiled things for him. But I hadn't done anything wrong; that was all down to Dad and Aunty Ellie.

The front door slammed shut and I stood, tense, as I heard footsteps coming upstairs but they went into Mum and Dad's room. I could hear drawers and wardrobes being opened and then the bleep of the access code to the safe. I sat down on my bed again, still and quiet. The low rumble of Dad's voice making a telephone call came to me and I went and stood in my bedroom doorway chewing my nails, wondering what to do. Eventually he came out onto the landing, suitcase in one hand and a bag over his shoulder. He stopped in front of me, looking at me as if I were a stranger. His pale blue eyes seemed to look straight through me.

'Dad,' I put my arms out towards him, longing for him to tell me off and then say it didn't matter but I knew how futile that was. 'I...'

'Well done, kid. That was typical of you wasn't it. I always thought you were a stupid misfit and this proves it. Anyway, you probably did me a favour in the long run.'

Stunned, I started to whisper 'I'm sorry...'

'Yeah, tell that to your little brother. He's a great kid and doesn't deserve a sister like you. Just you remember to tell him that it's your fault his Dad doesn't live here any longer.'

With no hint of hesitation, he hoisted the bag further on his shoulder and walked lightly down the stairs and out of the house. I heard his car start and listened to the sound of the engine taking my father further and further out of my life. My dad. Gone. And it was my fault. He had never been a hands-on type of father so the rare times he had taken notice of me were precious and now I knew what he thought of me: a misfit. I threw myself on the bed and cried great racking sobs which shook my whole being, consumed with guilt and shame at being so stupid and unlovable.

Chapter 3

Greg was one of those people who didn't appear to have a conscience but he didn't like being in the wrong and now that he had been caught out he was furious. So, once that stupid girl had let the cat out of the bag, there was no point in hanging around. Yes, he and Ellie had had sex. It was just a quick shag, nothing more. There was no romance involved. The opportunity came up and he took it. Goodness knows why – just because he could. It just made things a bit complicated living next door. He understood the saying now that you should never foul your own doorstep. Anyway, it was done now, and maybe that was no bad thing.

He'd had enough of Fiona for some time. She was past her best and she was turning into a proper nag. Nothing was good enough, there was never enough money; she always wanted more, to be better than everyone else. Well he'd had it with playing happy families, there was no such thing. His parents had never liked each other and never liked him much either. They were both drinkers and he grew up with nothing, making him all the more determined to fight for the better things in life. The biggest favour they had done him was to die when he was in his early twenties. With the money he had inherited from the sale of their house he had been able to set himself up nicely with a small garage. In the early days not all the deals he'd made had been strictly above-board but it didn't matter, they brought in the money.

Nowadays, everything was legitimate, more or less anyway, and he was the managing director of a huge dealership and doing very nicely thank you very much. Not that Fiona had any idea of that; he had always been careful to underestimate things to her. He'd led her to believe that the pittance she brought in with her silly part-time job was essential to the family finances.

The best thing now was to call it a day. He'd clear out, taking all the details of his various accounts with him so she wouldn't know the half of it. He couldn't face her begging him to stay which he knew she would as soon as she'd got the temper out of her. She would be especially furious because he'd been with Ellie for a start, someone she'd always looked down on for not being glamorous enough. She could never see that Ellie's natural beauty was far superior to her own which came via the beauty salons she frequented so regularly and which cost a fortune. When the penny dropped and she understood that he wasn't coming back he knew the divorce would be vicious, but he'd get his lawyer to drag things out as long as he could. He'd have to pay eventually, he knew, but he'd try to make sure it was the minimum he could get away with.

It didn't take long for him to clear out anything important from the safe; most of the confidential stuff was kept in the safe at work. Flinging a few things into a suitcase, he rang Charlotte to see if she was home. He had just started seeing her. He'd never had any difficulty in attracting the girls. He knew he wasn't classically handsome but he must have something, he kept himself trim and dressed well. In fact, he didn't know why he had stuck with Fiona for so long, apart from the fact that he'd been able to make it conveniently clear to his occasional girlfriends that he was a married man and wouldn't leave his wife because of the kids.

Charlotte was particularly lovely, a bit out of his league if he was truthful. He wasn't sure exactly where he stood with her. She seemed to be a bit like him in that she didn't want any commitments, just an occasional night out and a dinner date once in a while. She certainly wasn't after him for his money. Wealthy in her own right, thanks to a fabulously rich father, she also ran her own successful design business. They had met at a charity function which Fiona had been unable to attend. When he was at home on the rare occasions that she telephoned about the charity work he'd reply 'Hi, Charlie' with Fiona having no idea that he was listening to his girlfriend, as he liked to think of her. Childishly, it amused him. Over the years he'd sometimes felt that Fiona had her suspicions about him but she never came out and said anything.

He had occasionally wondered about Fiona. Did she have anyone on the side? Vainly, he never entertained the thought for long, as she gave the impression that she was besotted with him, especially when she wanted something. She had only been sixteen when they met but hardly the sweet sixteen and never been kissed type. Looking back, she'd been out to get him from the start. When she told him she was pregnant he'd stood by her. That was what you did in those days, so they got married when she was seventeen. At twenty-six he'd thought it would do him good to present himself as a family man. No, he told himself with arrogance, Fiona had never needed to look at another man when she had him. She could do what she liked now though.

He would only stay with Charlie for a couple of nights because he didn't want her to think it was a permanent arrangement, not that Charlie would, being such an independent spirit. Also he wasn't absolutely sure that Charlie would want him there. He might just have led her to believe that his marriage had been over for a while. Then, maybe he'd go away for a few weeks. Yeah, that would be a good idea. Put a bit of distance between everything and then, a few weeks down the line, things would have blown over a bit and tempers would have cooled. It might be nice to have a place abroad, he mused. Not Spain, everyone went there. Maybe France? Then he could just come over now and again to see that things were ticking over at the garage.

With that idea bringing a smile to his face, he snatched up the keys to the Mercedes and left the bedroom. Not once had thoughts of his children, and how they would be affected, entered his head.

Chapter 4

When she had first stormed back home and thrown open her front door Fiona was consumed with fury, not hurt or sorrow, but a rage that filled her entire being. She knew what Greg was like, had always known – they were two of a kind.

She stalked into the lounge before marching upstairs. 'Where are you, you bastard?' When she opened their bedroom door and saw the open wardrobes and empty hangers she roared like some wild animal and threw things around, not caring what was smashed. How dare he, how dare he leave *her*! If anyone was leaving it would be her that would leave *him*. Who the hell did he think he was?

She stomped her way downstairs and made for the drinks cabinet. Pouring herself large vodka she sat there and seethed. What had he seen in that mousy Ellie? What was remotely sexy about her? She'd had four kids for Pete's sake so she must be a mass of stretch marks! Fiona spent a fortune on her glamorous image, never missing an appointment with the hairdresser, beauty parlour or gym.

Rising to pour herself another drink she caught sight of a photo which fuelled her anger again. It was of her and Greg on holiday. She drew back her arm and swept it to the floor along with all the other photos and ornaments on the shelf, smashing most of them. She went even further and ground her heel on Greg's face until there was a hole through the photo and the backing of the frame.

Restlessly, Fiona went into the kitchen and was pouring a glass of wine from the fridge when she became aware that someone was behind her. When she turned and realised it was Gina she was filled with an icy anger. This stupid girl had ruined her life. Maybe she had been a means to an end to start with but once she'd hooked Greg she'd had no use for her. She watched Gina step slowly across the kitchen. Like all the other occasions in the past, she couldn't connect with the child who was again reaching out to her, and whom she normally ignored. This time she saw red and meted out a ferocious attack on her daughter.

Breathing deeply, she stepped over Gina who was lying on the floor, and moved back into the lounge. Once again her thoughts returned to Greg. She'd make the bastard suffer. If he thought he could creep back home with a bouquet of flowers and tickets for some holiday or other he had another think coming. Oh no! She wasn't going to roll over as quickly as that. It would take a lot more before Mr Greg Clark could crawl his way back here. She'd show him that he wasn't quite the Mr Wonderful he thought he was. Yes, he'd be very sorry indeed.

Fiona poured herself another drink. Her mind went back to the scene next door. Poor Matt. Poor stupid Matt. His face had been a picture! He didn't seem able to understand at first. He must have been a bit thick not to realise what was going on. Mind you, she hadn't realised either and she wasn't thick. Oh yes! Ellie and Greg had been very clever and very sly. She would never have thought that Greg would have wanted Ellie rather than her. What had the damn woman got? She was older than her by about four years for Christ's sake! Matt, the poor fool, was slavishly devoted to her. He must be feeling a right idiot now.

Fiona knew that there were other women in Greg's life. It had bothered her at first but then he always came back to her didn't he? It kept him happy as, basically, Greg was a lazy man and their life together was convenient for him. Occasionally when they were at some function or other she caught the sympathetic looks of the vacuous girls Greg had dallied with and hid a smile, wondering how long they would be on the scene.

Then that stupid lump of a girl Gina had to go and open her big fat mouth. She despaired of her; she'd been nothing but a nuisance since the day she was born.

She wasn't surprised that Greg had gone. It wouldn't be for long. Yes, she could read Greg like a book. He'd be back in time. It wasn't as if she was an angel either. She'd been a bit more discreet than Greg, a bit less obvious, but there had been many men over the years; it was only lately that they had been getting younger. She felt a frisson of unease for a moment... but just for a moment.

Chapter 5

When Tom went to open the door for Fiona to leave he was never so relieved to find his friend Adam walking up the drive, arriving early for the party.

Tom grabbed his arm and said, 'Look, mate, I need your help. We've got a party to cancel and people will be arriving in...' he glanced at his watch and saw that it was only 6.30. Half an hour since the whole world had tilted on its axis. He couldn't think about it now. 'We've got half an hour to get in touch with everyone to say the party's off. Some might have already started off, so come on – please, mate, I really need your help.'

'OK. Let's get started. What reason are we giving?'

'Err... I don't know.'

'Shall we say family illness? Nothing serious but we've had to cancel the party.'

'Yeah, great. Go and shut the gate and we'll put a sign on it to say the party's off. While I'm making a list of who to phone can you give the lads a ring.'

After half an hour on the telephone all guests had been contacted. It was inevitable that questions were asked but Tom had breezed over them by apologising and saying that he had to get in touch with everyone so he were keeping the phone calls short.

'Anything else I can do? Adam asked.

'Yeah, Will's with the little ones. Will you go and see if they're OK? I suppose they'll be hungry so we'll get them some food from the kitchen but, whatever you do, stay away from the lounge.'

They were all in the playroom with the television on, but they weren't watching anything as Will had organised a game of cowboys. He had found a blanket and draped it to make what he convinced the boys was a tent. Will, who normally didn't have much patience with the twins, was joining in. Tom went to turn the television off but changed his mind when Will said, 'I put it on to... um... mask any noises.'

Tom squeezed his shoulder. 'Good thinking.'

Adam came in with a tray laden with food for the cowboys to have a picnic while Tom quietly told his brother what had happened since he'd asked him to leave the room with the younger boys.

'What's going to happen now?'

'I honestly don't know, Will. Some birthday, eh!'

'What about him?' Will nodded towards little Ben who seemed happy enough playing with Oscar and Hugo.

'Shit, I forgot about him! Poor little bugger. Perhaps he should stay with the twins until someone comes looking for him.'

After they had finished their picnic the younger boys started to become restless.

'When are we having the party?' asked Oscar.

'We're not. We've had to cancel it for now.' Tom knelt down and ruffled his hair.

'Is it because Gina was naughty? She said a bad word, I heard her.' Hugo chipped in.

'Yeah,' nodded Oscar, 'she said "crap".'

'Where's Mummy?' asked Ben, eyes round with apprehension.

Tom was out of his depth and didn't know what to say or do. The best thing he could come up with was to let the boys choose a video and put it on which gave him an hour or so.

'Stay with them for a bit longer eh, Will? I'll get you a beer.' Tom knew his brother was only just sixteen but he didn't think a small bottle would do him any harm considering the grown-up situation he was in at the moment. 'We don't want them wandering...' he nodded towards the downstairs lounge

Tom went downstairs, listening quietly at the lounge door as he went past but hearing nothing. He put some beers and some soft drinks on a tray and took them upstairs. Realising that Adam hadn't any idea of what had happened, and hadn't asked either, he beckoned to his friend to go with him to his room. He sat on the bed and drew his fingers through his hair, 'Jesus, what a mess.'

Opening the beers he handed Adam a can and told him how the day that had been so long planned, had disintegrated into chaos. He had been dry-eyed as he spoke but when he thought of his father's face, he broke down himself. His father, his hero, to whom he had always looked up, had seemed so broken and helpless.

'Hell, mate, I don't know what to say,' Adam was concerned for his friend. 'That Gina is a prize bitch, no wonder nobody can stand her.'

'Yeah, she sure chose her moment but the other stuff isn't her fault.'

'What will happen now?'

'I just wish I knew. The whole thing is bound to come out. But don't tell the lads for now, will you?'

'Course not, what d'you take me for? I guess these things happen all the time. My mum and dad are divorced.'

'Sorry, mate, I didn't think. It's bad when it's your family isn't it?'

When they went back to the playroom some time later the boys had finished watching their video and were getting tired and grumpy. Once again Will made an adventure out of things. He and Adam had fetched the mattresses from the twins' room and with a toy sword with a pillowcase on it had decreed that it was a pirate ship. Meanwhile Tom took the three young ones to the bathroom and helped them change into pyjamas, giving Ben a pair too. He made them brush their teeth and soon they were in bed, each with a small glass of water, or "grog" as it was now called.

It wasn't long before they were asleep. Will disappeared to his own room and plugged himself into his computer game as if he could shut out the world. Tom turned to Adam,

'D'you want some food or something?'

'Nah, mate. I'll get off unless you want me to stay?'

'No, it's okay thanks. I'll just... Look, thanks for everything. I'll give you a ring.'

They gave each other a clumsy man-hug and Adam left.

In the lounge Ellie and Matt sat looking at each other as if they were total strangers.

After Tom had left the room earlier Matt turned to Ellie, asked, 'Why, Ellie, why?'

She shrugged.

'Answer me, dammit, don't sit there shrugging. Don't you think you should say something to me?'

She jumped at his outburst after so much silence.

'Sorry. I don't know what to say,' she said in a small voice.

'Well make an effort. It's the least I deserve,' snapped Matt.

Ellie twisted her hands, 'I... I...'

Matt got up and poured himself another brandy, pouring one for Ellie too. She took a gulp and choked briefly. Conversations were started and aborted and occasionally the silence was punctured by a shuddering breath from Ellie.

'Are you in love with him?'

'No. Gosh no.' She shook her head vehemently.

'What did I do to drive you to him?'

'You did absolutely nothing, it's my fault.'

'I always thought we had something special, you and I.'

'We have...'

'How long has it been going on?'

'There's nothing going on. Not really.'

'So what was that all about earlier?' Matt shouted, jumping up out of his chair and pacing around the room. 'Tell me dammit! I don't think I've ever hit anyone in my life but I certainly feel like hitting someone now and I'm just fighting the urge to go and thump Greg and slap you too, if I'm honest. So, how long has this affair of yours been going on?'

Ellie drew a long shuddering breath. 'There is no affair. I don't love Greg but we have had sex. Once. I regretted it as soon as it happened, and I've regretted it ever since. I hate myself for what we did.'

'Did he force you?'

Ellie shook her head, guessing that she was dousing a glimmer of hope in Matt which would help him make sense of things.

'Eleanor, I think you had better start talking. You're not being fair with these half answers. What has happened between you?'

Ellie looked up sharply at Matt's use of her full name, something he never used, and his voice was so cold. She drank the rest of her brandy and moved to the sofa where Matt was now sitting. She tried to take his hand but he snatched it away.

'I promise you Matt, there is no affair and there never has been. Yes, we have flirted together but no more than the way you and Fiona have flirted in a light hearted and jokey way. Recently he has been talking to me more seriously. Not about anything romantic. He has just been asking my advice about things.'

'Such as?'

'That Fiona and Gina don't get on and wondering what to do about the situation. I told him that I'm a mother of boys and I always got on with my parents so I couldn't really offer anything constructive. He also hinted that he and Fiona weren't getting on but I said I didn't want to hear any more because Fiona was my friend and that he should talk to her. I swear that's all there was.'

'So how did this innocent flirting and agony-aunt advice end up in the bedroom?' Matt hesitated. 'Please don't tell me that you slept with him in our bed!'

'No, of course not. It happened as Gina said, in the shed.'

'In your office, where you work so hard – apparently.'

'Please, I'm trying to tell you.' Ellie got up and poured some more brandy, taking a sip before continuing. 'It was about a month or so ago, on a really hot day and I was working in the shed and I had the door open. I had been there since first thing that morning as I had a deadline to meet. Greg was home that afternoon and he was sitting in the garden with a bottle of wine. He noticed that the shed door was open and he came over the fence and offered me a glass. I was a bit annoyed at being interrupted, but I stopped to be polite. He insisted that I had a glass of wine, which I did and then he asked me what I was doing. I told him that I was editing a book and it was quite erotic. He started reading it out loud and I sat back with my eyes closed listening to his voice, my head feeling lighter and lighter because I hadn't eaten anything since breakfast. Then he kissed me. Do you want me to go on?'

'I want to know everything.' Matt was looking at her as if she were a total stranger. 'Everything.'

'I was surprised but... I kissed him back. Then the next thing I knew we were having sex. There was just a spark between us that emptied everything out of my mind. Afterwards, I was horrified, and I think he was too. Gina must have seen us. It was exam time and she must have come home from school early. I'm so sorry, Matt. I never meant it to happen.'

'Oh! Ellie! Tom was taking his exams too; it could have been him that had seen you both. Wasn't there just a split second when you hesitated before crossing that invisible line, when you could have drawn back and said no? You aren't a couple of teenagers after all.'

'I just got carried away. I'm so sorry, Matt.'

'Did you enjoy it?'

'What?'

'Did you enjoy the sex? Was it good?'

'Why are you asking me that!'

'Tell me, Ellie, was it better with him than with me?'

'Oh, Matt, it was nothing like us. We make love together, with him it was just sex.'

'You have the advantage of me. I've only ever slept with you. We were kids when we got together and I've never even looked at anyone else. But, do you know something? It isn't just the sex, adultery is more than that, it's about destroying trust and loyalty, but you never thought of me did you? It was all about you and what you wanted in that instant. I never meant enough to you for you to stop and draw back.'

They heard a loud knocking at their front door, then Fiona's voice. Then the low rumble of voices as Tom once again took charge.

'Where is he? Where's my little boy?'

'Ben's fast asleep with the twins.'

'Well get him then. I don't want him in this bitch's house a moment longer,' she slurred.

'Look, Aunty Fiona. It's been an awful day for us all, especially you. Why don't you leave him here with Oscar and Hugo? I promise he'll be OK with them until the morning.'

When they heard the door close, Matt and Ellie looked at each other, guilty that they were allowing their young son to take charge of the situation. Ellie broke the tense silence.

'I'd better go to Tom,' Ellie moved to get up off the sofa.

'You stay where you are. I don't want you anywhere near any of them.'

'What do you mean?'

'We've got to think of the best way to handle this.'

'I'm not leaving the boys, there's no way I'm going anywhere.'

'I really don't think you've got much say in what happens, Eleanor. Do you think the boys will want to have anything to do with you? You heard what Fiona said earlier, this story will be around the town before you know it. How will the boys cope with that? And what about everyone who was supposed to be here this evening? What will they be thinking?'

Ellie buried her face in her hands, 'What have I done? I'm so sorry, Matt. I don't want to go anywhere and I don't want you to leave me. What am I going to do?'

'We've been talking for hours and we're just going round and round in circles. I don't know what we're going to do. I don't even want to look at you at the moment never mind have you around. I'm going to see Tom and then I'm going to bed.' Without a backward glance, Matt got up and left the room.

Ellie sat there for a while, too shocked and nauseous to cry. Ironically she just wanted to feel Matt's arms around her. He was the one she always turned to, the one who made everything all right. And now, nothing would be all right ever again. Eventually the tears came and she cried until she ached.

Upstairs, Matt and Tom wept in each other's arms. Will, with his earphones on, was playing his game and shooting everything that moved, tears running down his face. Three little boys were huddled together on their mattresses, now and again giving deep sighs in their sleep.

Chapter 6

No sooner had Dad left than I heard Mum crashing her way into the house.

'Where are you, you bastard,' she shouted.

I choked on my tears and held my breath, listening to Mum's high heels pecking their way along the wooden floor, first to the lounge and then stomping upstairs to their bedroom. I heard the sound of things breaking and glass smashing. I was scared, expecting her to come into my room but she stormed back downstairs and there was some more smashing. There was silence for a while and I listened. I realised that I had to face the music sooner or later, so I took a deep breath to try and compose myself and went downstairs. How was I going to apologise for this? In the kitchen Mum was gulping down a glass of wine. She didn't notice me standing in the doorway watching her pour out another glass. I must have moved slightly and caught her eye. She stood there, expressionless, as I walked slowly towards her, my mouth dry as my brain tried to formulate something to say.

'You stupid little bitch,' she said quietly. 'Why did you have to do that?' Before I could reply, she put her glass down and grabbed me, shaking me violently. 'I could have handled it,' she screamed in my face, 'if it wasn't for your stupid interference, you evil little bitch.' She drew back her hand

and I braced myself for the slap that was to come. What I didn't expect was the vicious punch in my face that sent my head reeling against the marble worktop before I fell to the floor. I curled myself up in the foetal position as she kept on hitting and kicking me and shouting. 'Do you think she's the first one? That poor cow is only one of many but I've put up with it so that you and Ben can have the life you lead. And now, you stupid, stupid moron, you've ruined everything by announcing it to everybody. How dare he leave me, I should have left him years ago.' She turned away from me, grabbed the wine bottle and went into the lounge.

I lay there, aching from the beating and too shocked to cry. When I eventually moved I realised that my face had been lying on the shards of glass that Mum had smashed. I struggled upstairs to the bathroom, holding my side against the jarring pain that came with every step, some ribs no doubt cracked. When I looked in the mirror I almost didn't recognise myself. I was deathly pale apart from the bleeding cuts on one side of my face and the redness of my eye and cheekbone on the other. One eye was swollen and it was starting to bruise.

'Well, Gina,' I said to the battered face looking back at me. 'You definitely know what they think of you now.' The certainty of how unloved I was and always had been, it seemed, felt far worse than the physical pain. Why? I'd never been really bad, not even that naughty when I was small. With this thought came the knowledge that there was nothing left for me in this house any more. I cleaned myself up and went back to my room.

I dug out my rucksack and, as I gathered my clothes, I realised that I hadn't particularly liked the Goth look. Had I adopted it as a way of trying to be noticed? I left everything but the bare essentials. Fortunately, I hadn't spent much of the money I'd been given for my recent eighteenth birthday so I scooped it up from the drawer together with all the other personal papers I kept there.

I stayed quietly in my room, not knowing what to do next. All my senses were alert and I could hear every creak of the house. The sounds of singing birds and the scent of garden flowers drifted in through my window. I listened to Mum moving around for a while but everywhere was quiet now.

I went downstairs and, through the open lounge door, I could see Mum lying comatose on the couch, an empty wine bottle on the floor and another on its side which had spilt on the rug, staining it red. She had a bottle of gin in her hand. I looked at her dispassionately, clothes askew, make-up smeared. She had never been the loving mother that I'd craved but, apparently, I'd never been the kind of daughter she had wanted either. As I turned away I caught sight of a photograph frame on the floor. Ben smiled at me through the cracked glass. I took the photo out and put it carefully in my rucksack. With a final glance at my mother I turned and left, shutting the front door quietly – the second person that evening to leave that house for ever.

As I headed towards the main road I kept my head down, not wanting anyone to see or speak to me. With so little time to plan my leaving I had no idea where I was going or what I was going to do. I guessed that hitch-hiking was as good an option as any, where a random passing car could choose my destination. I walked until the houses on either side of the road started to thin out but the traffic was fairly busy. It wasn't quite mid-August so it wasn't very dark and the air was still warm from the heat of the lovely summer's day. The scent of flowers and barbecue smoke lay on the air, reminding me of the evening I had ruined for so many people. Regret brought tears to my eyes and a sob to my throat which caused my side to hurt. It served me right.

I leant against a wall to rest for a moment watching the passing cars while trying to pluck up the courage to stick out my thumb in the universal, unspoken language of someone wanting a lift. It was a simple enough thing to do and people could stop or not as they wished. A couple more cars passed and then another but still I stood with my hand in my pocket. I heard the pounding beat of a car radio before I saw the next car. The driver noticed me and slowed down. He clearly thought he was worth a second look in his souped up Ford Escort and, lowering the passenger window, he looked at me. I turned away and headed back into town, knowing that I was no hitchhiker. I just didn't have the courage, some of the warnings from my parents and schoolteachers had obviously taken root.

I hadn't realised how far I'd walked and I was tired. My feet hurt and my bag seemed to be getting heavier as I shifted it from hand to hand and shoulder to shoulder. I heard a car slow down behind me but didn't turn my head and strode on. I was aware that it was keeping pace with me and then it stopped a little way ahead of me. A police car! My heart thumped. The window was lowered and one of the police officers asked, 'Are you okay, love?'

'Yes, fine thanks,' I replied with some bravado while thinking that my parents had called the police. I'd done nothing I could be arrested for had I? They couldn't make me go back, I was eighteen after all.

'Where are you off to then?'

'I'm going to the station.'

'How have you done that? Has someone hurt you?'

'Done what?' What was it with the police I wondered? Were they programmed to question everything and everyone they see?

'Your face.' The young officer looked at me with concern.

'Oh! That. It's nothing. I banged it on the wardrobe door as I was getting my bag down.' Even I was surprised at how quickly and smoothly the lie had come out of my mouth.

'We're on our way back to the police station now. We'll give you a lift if you like and drop you off as long as you don't tell the sarge,' he smiled. I debated with myself for a brief moment but I was so tired. I smiled my acceptance but at the same time was determined to keep my wits about me in case the questions continued.

They dropped me off at the entrance of the railway station but I could see that they were watching to make sure I went inside. There was no train for hours and the next one was going to Liverpool. I'd never been there before and didn't know anyone who lived there so no-one would know me. It was as good a place as any so I bought a single ticket.

I found a bench in a quiet part of the platform where no-one could find me. Who was I kidding? Who was looking for me? I tried to think of what I was going to do but strangely enough my mind wouldn't go any further than catching the next train. The dusty smell of the warmth of the evening lingered on the platform blended with the smell of diesel, and I must have dozed. I jumped when I heard someone shout and woke up to find someone with their hand on my rucksack. A scruffy looking man was turning away, empty handed, after having been spotted by one of the station's staff. He ran off as the man approached.

'Did he take anything?'

'No,' all the zips are shut anyway. I fumbled to check. 'Thank you.'

'You want to be careful. You never know who's around. Where are you going?'

'To Liverpool on the next train.'

'Won't be long now. Take care,' he added as he moved away.

As the train moved north I looked out of the window catching glimpses of other people living their lives in the glow of their lighted windows. Families enjoying each other's company. Or were they like mine? A false veneer for the outside world with nothing solid underneath.

The train sped through several small stations before it stopped at Crewe and a group of girls got on. They had obviously been to some sort of function and had been celebrating all evening. They were noisy and loud but in good spirits. One or two people looked disapproving and moved to the next carriage but I didn't. I didn't mind, they were only having fun. I think I was a bit envious of the camaraderie between them. Several miles later they eventually realised that it was only me and them left in the carriage and they insisted that I joined them. It wasn't long before they all knew my name and I was trying to remember which girl was Tracy, Carla, Elaine, Nicola and Sarah.

The girls had been to a wedding. One of their friends had married a "boring old git" but he had loads of money.

'She's got a bit toffee-nosed now,' according to Tracy (or was it Sarah?) because she had looked down her nose at her erstwhile friends who had become more drunk and raucous as the evening reception wore on. So, before they were thrown out of the posh hotel, the girls had "nicked a few bottles and legged it", as Nicola had put it as she passed the contraband bottle between them. Nicola then decided to make an announcement. 'I'm going to give you all a present,' she said with a hiccough, lifting her handbag on to her knee. She took out several boxes each containing a chocolate and handed them round.

'But these are favours for the guests, they were supposed to have one of these each,' laughed Tracy.

'Yeah, well, they didn't eat them did they, so it was a shame for them to go to waste,' she giggled. 'And for you, 'cos you're our new friend,' she turned drunkenly to me, 'I've got a special present. Digging again into the bag she brought out a model bride and groom.'

'Oh! Gosh. She's only nicked it off the top of the cake,' squealed Tracy and they all screamed with laughter. By this time, because of the wine I'd shared on an empty stomach, I also thought it was funny and I accepted the gift with due ceremony. How nice to have friends like these, was my woozy thought. When the train stopped at Lime Street station it struck me that I had nowhere to stay.

'Hey girls, d'you know of a cheap B&B where I could spend the night?' I asked.

'You can doss down at ours.'

'Yeah. It's no problem,' they insisted.

And so it was that the first night of my new life was spent in Liverpool, on the sofa of some girls I had only just met.

Chapter 7

Ellie had cleared the kitchen before Matt got up. There was no sign of the previous night's feast. The back door was open and she was sitting outside with a cup of coffee, still wearing the clothes she'd had on for the party. Matt joined her; she seemed to have aged ten years overnight.

'I've spoken to Tom. He handled things admirably last night. He told everyone there had been illness in the family so I think we'll go on with that story. We'll say it was you that was ill and because you had prepared the food we didn't think it wise to continue with the party. People will talk but we can't do anything about that. Tom and Will know better of course, but Hugo and Oscar don't really know what's happening for the moment. As for Ben, that's up to Fiona and Greg.'

'Thank you.'

'You don't need to thank me,' he snapped. 'I'm not doing any of this for you, it's our children I'm thinking of; it's just a shame you didn't. I'm going to see Fiona and Greg later and I'll try and make Fiona see that by making everything public, it will be as embarrassing for her as everyone else.'

'I'll go and shower and change and then I'll make breakfast for the kids.' She turned to Matt as she left. 'I'm sorrier than you'll ever know. I love you with all my heart and I don't know why I did what I did.'

He said nothing, just looked at her, and she had never felt so cold and alone.

Ellie had just finished setting out the breakfast when the youngsters came downstairs slowly.

'Are we allowed to come downstairs now?' asked Oscar.

'Of course you are. Come and have some breakfast.'

'Tom wouldn't let us come down last night but we had a midnight feast instead.'

'That was exciting.' Ellie was surprised at how normal she sounded.

'We didn't have a party, though, because everybody was cross,' said Hugo looking at her with his huge blue eyes, bringing a lump to her throat.

'It was a shame that I was sick so we had to cancel everything,' Ellie tried out the lie for the first time.

'Are you sick now?' he asked.

'I'm a bit better today,' she reassured him and then noticed Ben still standing in the doorway. 'Come and have some breakfast, Ben.'

'Where's Mummy?' asked the little boy.

'We'll go and find her after breakfast shall we?' She tried to smile even though her stomach churned at the thought of seeing Fiona.

Tom walked into the kitchen, his expression blank. 'I've just plugged the phone back in and Gran and Granddad have rung wanting to know how everyone is this morning. They've been trying for ages but I'd forgotten that I'd unplugged it last night. They were going to come over but I told them that you were still under the weather. I said you'd phone them later.'

'Yes, thanks. I will. Thank you for everything.' She wanted to say more but she was aware of three pairs of eyes looking at her. Before she had a chance Tom turned on his heel and left.

It wasn't only her parents who had been trying to phone. Now that the phone had been reconnected several friends rang to see how she was and, before long, the practised lie was tripping off her tongue as she reassured everyone that she felt much better now, but they suspected food poisoning and thought it better to cancel in case anyone else should suffer. When anyone asked she was vague about the idea of rearranging another date in the future. Her parents wanted to come over immediately and she had to be firm in telling them that it was better for them not to come and that she would call and see them in a day or so. She knew their feelings were hurt but she couldn't face them at the moment.

It was later in the morning that she realised that Will had not come down for breakfast. Of her four boys Will was the deeper one, the thinker, the independent spirit and the one who kept his thoughts to himself. *I must go to him*, she thought. *What must he think of me?*

She knocked gently on his bedroom door and when there was no reply she opened it to find him lying on his bed, earphones in, playing a game. The curtains were still drawn so she closed the door quietly and moved to open them. 'Will,' she said gently. He completely ignored her, carrying on with what he was doing as if his life depended on it. 'Will,' she tried again, louder this time. Still there was no reaction from him. 'William. Will you please put that down and listen to me.' At his continued dismissal of her presence she snatched the headphones off his ears. 'Dammit, Will, I want to talk to you.'

With one fluid movement he got up off the bed and opened the bedroom door for her. 'You've got nothing to say that I want to hear. Get out of my room please.' His voice was quiet and cold.

Ellie trembled. This wasn't the way she had meant to handle things. As she walked past him she was surprised at how tall he was, when had he grown to be so much taller than her? He might look like a young man but he was still a boy really. She put out a hand to touch his cheek but he flinched away from her, the look on his face chilling her to the marrow. As she stepped out on to the landing she fully expected him to slam the door but he closed it with a gentle click.

She realised that Tom was standing nearby, leaning on the doorframe of his bedroom. 'That went well then,' he remarked.

'Tom, can we talk. Please.'

'Not now, Mum.' And with that he opened the door to Will's room, and closed it firmly behind him.

Ellie went downstairs slowly, aware of how she had excluded herself from her beloved family.

Matt was determined to be civilised, despite his smouldering anger, when he went next door. He was shocked at Fiona's appearance when she answered his abrupt knock. She was still in the same clothes she had on last night, her face was bloated and she smelled of stale alcohol. 'Is Greg here?' he asked shortly.

'No. He left last night – but he'll be back when he's ready and if he thinks...'

Matt lifted his hand to silence her and stepped inside. Despite the way he felt about her, he couldn't help feeling sorry for her so he gave her a hug. This set off her tears and she latched on to him until he prised her arms from around his neck.

'Go and have a shower, Fiona, while I make us some coffee, and we can have a chat about where we go from here.'

'Where we go from here? I'll tell you...'

'Not now, Fiona. Off you go.'

Making his way to the kitchen Matt stepped over the results of Fiona's tantrum of last night. It took some time but, by the time Fiona was finished in the shower, he had done a fair job of clearing up the mess and there was a pot of coffee on the go. He shouldn't have been surprised when Fiona came back looking fresh, smartly dressed, make-up on her face not quite disguising her bloodshot blue eyes, but he was. Could he hide his own heartbreak so well?

They sat at opposite sides of the kitchen table, each wondering how to start until 'Look...' they both said at the same time. They talked for a long time. Initially Fiona was hell-bent on revenge. Revenge on Ellie in particular.

'Your wife is a slut and I want the world to know that. Whether you stay with her or not is your business. I know Greg will be wanting me to take him back eventually but we'll see about that!'

Matt let her talk through her anger and then in his quiet voice he made some suggestions. Did she really want everyone to know that Greg had, however briefly, preferred Ellie to her? He certainly didn't want people to think that Ellie thought Greg was better than him. If she told everyone, wouldn't that make it more difficult for Greg to come home? And what about the children? The little ones were too young to understand what had happened last night, but if Fiona announced things to all and sundry they would soon understand. Was it fair on them when they were still so little? He explained about the so-called food poisoning being given as the reason the party was cancelled and if people were sceptical, so be it. They wouldn't know otherwise if nobody said anything. Eventually, Matt convinced her it would be best to remain silent.

'Shall we get everything done in one fell swoop?' Matt said. 'Come back home with me to fetch Ben and then you and Ellie will have faced each other rather than dreading the encounter.'

'What? You expect me to come and be nice and friendly to her?' Fiona appeared close to being speechless.

'No. I think being civil is the best we can hope for. I don't think there is any chance that any of us can resurrect any kind of friendship. I think we should allow the boys to be friends though. They've known each other since they were born and it would be cruel to stop them seeing each other. That means we have to be adult about the situation. As time goes by I can see both sets of families moving from here can't you?'

'As soon as possible I would have thought,' replied Fiona. Matt guessed that Fiona would insist on a move to somewhere even bigger and better as part of Greg's coming back home package.

'Talking of the kids, how's Gina? I bet she didn't expect such repercussions from her little bombshell.'

Fiona looked at him blankly. Clearly, she hadn't given Gina a single thought.

'I don't know. I haven't seen her since last night.' Fiona failed to mention her violent attack on her daughter.

'She's probably hiding out in her room, ashamed of her behaviour and too embarrassed to show her face. Why don't you pop up and fetch her? She'll be scared to face everyone and I'd like a word with her. I want to tell her not to discuss the matter with Tom and Will.'

A few minutes later Fiona came down looking slightly bemused. 'She's not there.'

'Gone out you mean?'

'No. Gone. She's taken her things and she's gone.'

'Oh! That's all we want. A missing teenager. Do you think she could have gone to one of her friends? Or do you want to ring the police?'

'The police? No. She's gone somewhere for a few days. She's like her father. They'll both be back with their tails between their legs sooner rather than later. She is eighteen after all so the police wouldn't be interested.'

'Are you sure?' Matt was somewhat perturbed at Fiona's casual dismissal of Gina's disappearance.

'Mummy,' Ben yelled throwing his arms around Fiona's knees as she entered the kitchen behind Matt. He started chattering about the pirates' picnic and the midnight feast he had shared with Oscar and Hugo.

Ellie turned and started to say, 'Fiona...' but Fiona held up her hand.

'We're going back home now Ben. Are you going to say thank you to Aunty Ellie?' Her words sounded genuine but the look she gave Ellie was chilling.

'Thank you for having me,' said the polite little boy, waving at his two friends.

Chapter 8

I woke up on my first morning in Liverpool after sleeping surprisingly well. The flat was quiet. I found the small kitchenette, put the kettle on, and was opening cupboard doors to find some tea when one of the others walked in.

'Who the hell are you?' she asked.

I didn't blame her as I couldn't remember her name either. Over a cup of tea we renewed our acquaintance while the other four slept.

I learned from Carla that she worked in a shop, three of the girls were nurses and one was a university student. According to Carla, the girl whose wedding they had all attended the previous day was also a nurse and had shared the flat until she had snared her doctor husband.

'I think they've found someone else to share, though. Shame, you could have moved in.'

'What about you or Tracy. Didn't you want to move in?'

'Tracy couldn't afford it as she's only got her grant and what she earns from her part-time job and anyway, she's sharing a house with some other students next term. As for me, I'd love to have moved in because they're great girls, but my boyfriend and I have just got engaged so I'm still living at home. My mum and dad take hardly anything for my keep so I can save. I live over the water so the fare to come to work is my biggest cost.'

I looked at her in puzzlement, 'Over the water?'

'That's what they say around here about someone who lives on the Wirral – on the other side of the Mersey,' she laughed. She stifled a yawn and took another sip of her tea. 'What did you do to your face?'

I lifted my hand to my cheek. I didn't want to lie but I didn't want to talk about the events of yesterday evening. Was it only yesterday evening? It seemed like an age ago. I stood up and looked in the mirror above the fireplace and was surprised to see that I now had a black eye as well as one or two little cuts and a bruised jaw. 'It's a long story,' I sighed.

Elaine walked in wearing her pyjamas. She stopped short when she saw me. 'Oh! Hi, it's err –'

'Gina.'

'Yeah, of course. I'd forgotten you were here. I'm gasping for a cuppa.'

My bruised face caught her eye and she put out her hand to turn it to the window and looked at it with a professional eye. 'Someone did this to you.' It was a statement.

'Yes, but it was probably my fault.'

'No-one deserves to be hit,' she said quietly.

I turned away. 'Let me make you a cup of tea,' I said. 'I'm so grateful to you for letting me stay last night. I don't know what I would have done otherwise.'

After returning with a pot of tea I asked if I could use the bathroom. Feeling much refreshed after a quick shower and a change of clothes, I returned to the lounge. The conversation stopped as I walked in.

'Carla tells me that you're looking for somewhere to stay,' Elaine said.

'Yes, that's right, do you know of anywhere?'

'Well I could ask around... I'm not being funny or anything... but we don't know anything about you and we don't want any trouble for us or anyone else.'

'I do understand but I promise you I'm not in any trouble at all. I'm just making a new start without any ties. Obviously I do need to find a job but I can pay my way for a couple of months, so if you do know of anything I'd be very grateful.'

Maybe Elaine saw the honesty in my eyes and maybe the desperation. She held up her hand. 'Don't say anything more for now. My head is thumping after last night, and I know the others won't be any better. Why don't you stay here again tonight? We can have a proper chat tomorrow. The new girl is on holiday and won't be here for another week or so. I'll have a word with the others to see if they mind you staying until then. I'm not making any promises, though. I'll see what the others say.'

'That would be wonderful. It would give me some breathing space. Thank you. Thank you very much.'

'Don't thank me yet.' She stretched and yawned again. 'I'm going back to bed for an hour or so. See you later.'

Carla also got to her feet. 'I'd better get dressed and go home. Darren's picking me up later.'

'I think I'll go for a walk if that's okay. Will I be able to get back in without disturbing anybody?'

Elaine gave me a spare key and, grabbing my handbag, I set off to explore Liverpool. Twenty-four hours ago the thought of Liverpool had never entered my head and yet, here I was, about to look for work and live here. The only thing I knew about the place was that the Beatles came from here.

A couple of hours later I arrived at the flat with bread and milk. I heard movements in the bedrooms and bathroom and by the time Elaine, Sarah and Nicola came into the room I had prepared a plate of toast and a pot of tea. Tracy was still fast asleep.

'Wow,' exclaimed Elaine, 'someone's trying to make a good impression.'

'I thought it was the least I could do after you kindly let me stay. I'm really grateful.'

Sarah and Nicola fell on the food, 'I'm absolutely starving,' Sarah said with her mouth full, 'and as far as I'm concerned the answer is yes.'

'Me too. By the way it's yes as far as I'm concerned too. You're welcome to stay until Amy, the new girl, gets back from her holiday.'

'Ugh! How can you two eat?' Elaine asked. 'I just want a couple of aspirin! Anyway Gina, we all agree that we're happy for you to stay until Amy moves in.'

Chapter 9

Ellie knew she had to face her parents at some point. It had been several days since the planned party and her mother's comments were becoming increasingly barbed whenever she phoned, as if she knew something was being hidden from her. Parking her car outside the neat dormer bungalow her parents had bought when they retired, she sat with her hands on the steering wheel eyes fixed on the window until the curtains twitched. Her mother had opened the door wide by the time she walked up the short drive, dread in every step.

'Oh my dear, you do look ill! How are you feeling by now?' Ellie felt her mother's hand on her shoulder and was grateful that she made no comment about her straggly hair, or her bloodshot eyes.

Ellie started. 'Mum...' and, much to her surprise, she broke down and sobbed. She thought she had drained all the tears out of her body over the past few days.

Her father came into the hall from the lounge. 'Whatever's the matter, Ellie, darling?'

She drew a shuddering breath. 'Dad...' but once again she was racked by sobs and she threw herself into her father's arms. She breathed in the smell of him, his cologne, his warmth, relishing the roughness of his sweater on her cheek and the feeling of being safe, as if he could make everything better for her like he did when she was a child.

'Come through here and sit down while your mum makes us all a cup of tea,' he said muttering soothing words as he led her to sit beside him on the sofa. He allowed her to sob until, by the time her mother came in with the tea tray, she was reduced to hiccoughing and scrubbing away at the tears with her father's handkerchief. Such distress came from more than an upset stomach

'What is it, darling? Have you had bad news? Is someone ill?'

Ellie took a deep breath; she knew she had no choice. She focussed on the patterned rug at her feet as if she was fascinated by the intricate pattern, and gazed at it as if she'd never seen it before.

'Ellie?'

She raised her eyes briefly before looking down again. 'I've done something stupid. Something I will regret for the rest of my life. Something that will probably mean the end of my marriage.' There, she'd said it. She knew they would be hurt. No longer would she be the wonderful, perfect daughter who did everything right.

'You mean you're having an affair?' Elizabeth's voice was hard.

Eventually she lifted her head. She hated seeing the shock on her parents' faces. They were both looking at her and she knew she had disappointed them, disappointed them badly and she couldn't stop herself from crying again. Her father knelt in front of her and put a mug of tea in her hand.

'Come on, drink. We've been so worried. We guessed that there was some sort of problem but we didn't expect this.' He patted her knee. Ellie gulped down her tea and took a few deep breaths before sitting up straight.

'I'm not having an affair, I've been an idiot but I love Matt truly and deeply.' She then went on to tell them everything. Elizabeth and Anthony sat there listening without uttering a single word until she had finished. There was complete silence for a moment. Ellie trembled.

'Poor Matt,' said her mother 'and those poor boys.' It was her turn now to mop her own tears.

'What happens now? Are you going to separate?'

'Oh! I *do* hope not, Dad. I love Matt so much. At the moment he hates me. He barely talks to me and he won't even look at me if he can help it. I've hurt him badly. Maybe in time he can forgive me, I don't know. I'm hoping we can work something out for the sake of the boys.'

'Yes, of course. They are the primary concern for the moment. Eleanor, how could you have done such a thing? If you love Matt as much as you say you do, that is.'

Again, the use of her full name as another form of censure had not gone unnoticed and Ellie dropped her gaze from her mother's angry face. She'd always felt special, doted on by her parents, chosen by Matt to be his wife and loved by her children, but now she felt as if she were no-one.

'Now is not the time for recriminations, Elizabeth. Ellie knows full well what she has done and it's something that she and Matt have to sort out between them.'

Ellie got to her feet and gave her father a hug. She had always been close to him and valued his wisdom and advice. 'Thanks, Dad. I'd better go,' she said and turning to her mother, 'I'm so sorry, Mum.'

The hug given to Ellie by her mother was stiff and perfunctory rather than her usual warm embrace. 'These things happen I suppose. You know where we are if you need us. Shall we give you a few more days before we pop over and see the boys? And tell Matt that we love him and are thinking of him,' she added with what Ellie thought was a touch of defiance.

Anthony and Elizabeth stood at the door watching Ellie walk down the path to her car, raising their hands to wave as she drove away. Anthony went to the kitchen to make a cup of tea which he put in front of a pale-faced Elizabeth.

'What on earth's got into the girl? I'm stunned that our lovely Ellie, who slipped so easily from being our perfect daughter to Matt's perfect wife, has done this. I never took her for a fool before. And with that smarmy Greg from next door of all people! I never liked him, or that wife of his – common, that's what she is. Matt's just too soft with her. Anything she's wanted she's had. She doesn't know how lucky she is. A beautiful home and four lovely boys and then she goes and does something like this! It's unbelievable.' Anthony sat in silence until her anger was spent. Eventually, she asked, 'What do you think will happen, darling? Do you think Matt will leave her? Poor Matt, we couldn't blame him I suppose.'

'I wish I could deny that possibility, but I can't.'

They sat, lost in their thoughts. Theirs had been such a charmed life. Anthony and Elizabeth enjoyed good health and had a lovely home. They had been saddened that they could only have one child but they rejoiced in their daughter. Beautiful and clever, she hadn't given them a moment's worry as she grew up. They had delighted in her choice of husband and they truly loved Matt as if he were the son they never had. They became even closer when he lost both his parents in quick succession shortly after he and Ellie had married. When the first two of their grandsons had arrived they'd thought their world was perfect. They were even more delighted when the twins were born all those years later, even though Elizabeth secretly hoped that one of them would be a girl.

Though it was warm in the lounge, Elizabeth shivered. The foundations of her perfect world had been shaken. What would happen now? What had Ellie done?

Chapter 10

Tom looked around his bedroom. His belongings were arranged in neat piles and, not for the first time, he wondered if he had forgotten anything. He couldn't wait to get away and start his new life, or rather, leave the old one behind.

It had been six weeks since his eighteenth birthday, six weeks since everyone's lives had changed. It was as if they were living as other people, over-polite and without any spontaneity. They were like actors playing themselves and not getting it right. He hadn't minded too much about the aborted birthday party, after all that had only been for the sake of his parents and other relations. His friend, Adam, had made sure that he celebrated, taking him out and making sure he got back home safely after trying to drink himself into oblivion. He knew that he and Adam would always be friends even though they would be living at opposite ends of the country. As predicted, they had both excelled in their exams allowing them to take up their first choice of universities: Tom was going to Durham and Adam to Exeter.

Adam had told no-one about what happened on that awful night. There had been rumours but the unfuelled gossip had remained speculation until nothing was mentioned now. There had been a flurry of comments when Gina hadn't turned up to collect her A level results. Where was she, her classmates wondered. Had she run away from home? Several people questioned him, even some of the teachers. It saddened him to realise how few friends Gina had. He supposed he was the closest. They would hang around together and were familiar with each other as only a friendship formed over a long period of knowing each other could be. He often thought that he was the only person who worried about her and he knew that he had feelings for her. He had hoped to tell her how he felt on the night of the party but events had overtaken him. Now, his emotions were in turmoil and he didn't know how he felt about her. He was a bit hurt that she hadn't got in touch with him, but guessed she was embarrassed about spoiling his birthday and was afraid that if she rang, his mum or dad would answer the phone. Or worse of all, maybe she didn't feel anything for him. Could there ever be a future for them now? He'd asked Aunty Fiona about her but she'd shrugged and said she knew nothing.

It was strange not having Aunty Fiona drop in at all hours of the day and Tom wondered what Dad had said to prevent her from muddying Mum's name to all and sundry. Ben was still a regular visitor as he often came to play with the twins. He noticed that Uncle Greg still hadn't come back home. For the life of him he couldn't see what his mother had seen in him. Even in his youth Tom could see that Uncle Greg was shallow, vain and selfish.

Mum had certainly paid the price for her infatuation or whatever it was. It was clear that the relationship between his parents had changed. There was an artificial politeness between them and his father slept in the spare room. She was very jumpy and there was a false brightness about her.

His dad, too, was a changed man, quieter than usual and no longer his jokey self. Their relationship seemed to have become closer. Dad now treated him as an equal; the shared experience of seeing him heartbroken at his lowest ebb, drawing them together. He hoped that his dad and mum could work things out between them and give his three brothers as secure a childhood as he had. Could they? It was something beyond the scope of his experience but he hoped so. He could do nothing but leave them to it.

Tom's main concern was Will. He had barely been home since that night. He treated his mother with disdain and rudeness. Whenever she asked where he was going he invariably replied "out" and slammed the door as he left. She seemed to be at a loss as to how to handle him. Tom had brought him home drunk on more than one occasion but had been able to hide the fact from their parents. There had been the odd occasion when he suspected that he had taken drugs and he knew that he had to confront him before he left for uni.

As if on cue there was a light knock on the door and Will stuck his head round.

'Hi, bro, are you nearly good to go?'

'Hi. Come in. I was just thinking about you. Will you come up to Durham with Dad and me, to see me off?'

'Whoa, I thought you didn't want anyone except Dad to take you up there.'

'Well...'

'I get it. You just don't want Mum there.' He curled his top lip into a sneer. 'Can't say I blame you.'

For some inexplicable reason Will's attitude towards their mother made Tom feel protective towards her. 'Look, Will, she's messed up and messed up big time. We all know that, but let's face it, it's none of our business – it's between her and Dad. So how about cutting her some slack eh?' Will looked uncertain and shrugged. 'I mean it, Will. I'm not going to be here to act as a peacekeeper or whatever, so it's up to you now to try and help keep this family together. The way you act can make or break the family so, for the sake of the twins, I'm trusting you to be grown up about things.'

Through narrowed eyes, Will looked at the brother he'd looked up to for as long as he could remember and gave a slight nod.

'There's something else, Will. I won't be here now to hide the fact that you've been going out drinking. And I know you've been taking other stuff too. It's got to stop, mate.'

'It was only a bit of weed. Nothing more, honestly.'

'Do me a favour then and stop taking it. I know I'm asking a lot of you but I'll be so far away and if I can't depend on you, I don't know how I'll cope.' Tom knew he was using emotional blackmail on his younger brother but he didn't care if it helped him to get on track. 'And while I'm pulling the big brother act, work hard at your exams eh? Not that I'm preaching or anything but they are your way out of here to do whatever you want.'

'It's OK for you to say that but I'm not clever like you.'

'Yes you are. Just keep your head down for the next couple of years, get the grades and you can be out of here. I know that's what you want.'

Will smiled. 'WOw! You've turned into an old man! Does that happen to everybody after their eighteenth birthday?' Laughingly the two brothers hugged knowing they'd miss each other very much.

The car was packed and it was time for the final goodbyes. Tom's grandparents had been over earlier in the day and had slipped him an envelope with some generous pocket money. Much to his surprise, Aunty Fiona had given him a good luck card with some money in it too. He couldn't get the measure of the woman but he accepted her kind gesture. He'd asked her to tell Gina to get in touch when she eventually made contact. She still seemed strangely unconcerned about her daughter, and if she was beginning to feel some slight unease about her she kept it well hidden.

The twins were bouncing around him dying to give him their packages.

'We've got some presents for you because you're going to un-i-ver-si-ty.' Oscar pronounced the word by breaking it up into many syllables as it was the only way he could remember it.

'We know what un-i-ver-si-ty is,' said Hugo, not to be outdone by his brother. 'It's a school for grown-ups.' Tom smiled, realising he would miss these two little boys, knelt down by them and accepted his presents graciously. He pretended he didn't know what was in them but the boys couldn't keep a secret to save their lives, and they had told him several times he would need a nice new pen for his homework at university. When Hugo handed him the package he exclaimed, 'What can this be?' Before he had a chance to open it Hugo said excitedly, 'It's a pen!'

Tom was still showing delight at his gift when Oscar struggled to hand over his parcel. 'It's a dictionary,' said the little chap before Tom even had a chance to play a guessing game with him. Tom thanked him very much for the medical dictionary, including his parents in his smile for their thoughtfulness.

If his mum was hurt that Tom had asked Will to go to Durham with him and Matt instead of her, she didn't show it. She stood uncertainly on the pavement. Now that he was actually leaving Tom realised that he had a huge lump in his throat and he felt sorry for her. Who the hell was he to judge her? He went over to her and gave her a hug. She held on to him tightly and started to cry.

'My lovely boy. I love you so much and I'm going to miss you. I'm sorry for everything and so grateful for all you've done. Just remember that I'm proud of you. Write soon and let us know how you are getting on. Love you lots. Good luck.'

He drew away and, putting his hands on her shoulders, looked down at her and said, 'Good luck to you as well, Mum. Love you.' And with a further peck on her cheek he got into the car beside his dad.

As they went back inside the house Oscar looked up at her. 'Why are you crying, Mummy? Is it because Tom's going to uni?'

'Yes,' she replied with a tremulous smile. 'We're all going to miss him aren't we?'

Hugo looked up at her and his bottom lip trembled slightly. He patted her hand gently. 'Don't worry, Mummy, I'm not going to go to uni. I'm going to stay here with you.'

Chapter 11

Although I had loved living in the flat with the girls, I'd always known it was a temporary arrangement, not that any of the other girls said or did anything to make me feel uncomfortable. In fact, to the contrary, they were friendly and familiar in a way I had never experienced before and such openness made me slightly uncomfortable. While I had always hidden my shapeless body under layers of loose clothing they thought nothing of wandering around the flat in next to nothing. The way they shared each other's possessions was something I was not used to, probably because I had no-one to share with. The way they hugged each other easily or sat on the sofa leaning on each other as they giggled about something or other was alien to me. I had never experienced this level of friendship obviously or it wouldn't have seemed so strange. For a while I wondered what they wanted of me but they never seemed to expect anything. The only person I thought of as a true friend was the one whose birthday I had ruined and totally destroyed his family life. My face prickled with shame whenever I thought of dear, dear Tom. I didn't allow myself to think of Uncle Matt and Aunty Ellie.

I scoured the pages of *The Echo* trying to find somewhere to rent. I had seen a couple of places but they weren't available for another month and I didn't have the nerve to ask the girls if I could sleep on the couch. Eventually, with days to spare, I saw an advertisement for a bedsit in the local newsagent's window. I'd got to know Ernie from my regular visits to buy milk and bread.

When I asked him where it was he asked, 'What do you want to go there for?'

'I need somewhere to live.'

'Those nice girls thrown you out?' he joked, 'what have you gone and done?'

'It was only temporary but I need somewhere for myself now.' I didn't want to go any further than our usual conversations about remarking on the weather.

'It's not very nice but it should be cheap – make sure that feller doesn't overcharge you.' He suggested a figure which he thought would be reasonable. I had no idea. I had absolutely no clue about the cost of living so I was grateful for all his advice.

I went to the address and my heart sank. The steps leading up to the front door of the three-storey-house were crumbling with a rusty handrail on one side. There were steps leading to a basement which were strewn with rubbish. The front door hadn't been painted for many years, neither had any of the windows and the net curtains were grey and grubby. My knock on the front door was answered by a fat, unshaven man in a vest with a cigarette, ash drooping, dangling from his lips.

'I've come about the room.'

He turned back towards the dark hall without a word, taking a key from his pocket. I followed him up the stairs to the first floor. There were four doors opening on to the landing and he turned the key in the lock of one on the right and ushered me in while he stood in the doorway, showing me his yellow teeth in what I assumed to be his effort at smiling.

'This is it?' I couldn't keep the surprise out of my voice. The carpet was dirty and fraying in places, the wallpaper was yellowing and the curtains hung by only three or four hooks each. It was permeated by a musty smell.

'What's wrong with it? It's a nice room, shared bathroom is down there. What did you expect? If you want a fancy penthouse go to the Albert Dock and pay their fancy prices. Who do you think you are, turning your nose up at my house?'

I realised my options were limited. 'How much is it?' I asked and when he named a figure I sent a mental thank you to Ernie, the friendly newsagent.

'I'm not paying that. I'll look elsewhere.' I was about to turn away when he reduced his figure. 'That's still too much.' I told him how much I was willing to pay and he scratched his fat belly as he thought.

'Go on then. I'm a fool to let it go for that but you look decent enough and I don't want any trouble.' He held out his hand and said, 'I'll be wanting a deposit.'

'And I'll be wanting a receipt and a rent book.' Again I mentally thanked Ernie because the deposit was never mentioned again.

A couple of days later I had moved in. The girls seemed sincere enough when they said they were sorry to see me go and made me promise to stay in touch. They bought me gifts for my new room and their kindness touched me.

Elaine drew me to one side and asked quietly, 'If someone comes looking for you are we to say where you are?'

I was a bit taken aback but I should have known that she was no fool. 'Don't worry, no-one will go to the bother. I promise you, I haven't done anything wrong; something stupid, yes, but nothing wrong.'

After I had carried the last of my things upstairs and shut the door behind me I sat on the bed and looked around. It wasn't the fact that I had been brought up in what many would think of as luxury, and had been reduced to living in a scruffy bedsit that made me cry. It was the fact that I was completely alone. I had no-one. I cried for ages until I felt cleansed by my tears. Eventually I gave myself a mental talking to and told myself how futile tears were and to damn well get on with my life. 'This is how it is now,' I said out loud.

I spent the rest of the day sorting out my room. I almost gagged when I saw the state of the bathroom so I went out and bought cleaning materials and rubber gloves. When I came back staggering under the weight of my purchases the landlord came out of his room on the ground floor.

'Settling in are we?' he asked.

'Trying to but the place is filthy. I've been out and bought these to clean that disgusting bathroom and I'll be taking the money for them out of my rent.'

'You what?'

'This is how it is now,' I replied with my new mantra, surprising myself with my newfound confidence.

By bedtime I was exhausted but the communal bathroom stank of bleach and my room was passable. It was clean and it smelt fresh, or fresher than it had been. For someone who had been brought up in a house with a cleaner and who had never done a hand's turn with the housework I felt I had done well. It had taken ages even though the room was small. It had a single bed for which I'd bought some new bedding in St John's market. I'd taken down the old curtains and bought some new ones to match the bedcover. They were hanging complete with their creases as I didn't have an iron. There was a wardrobe which had a set of drawers inside so my things were neatly put away. I had covered the one easy chair with a throw given to me by the girls. The stained and wonky table which held a rusty kettle I had covered with one of the old curtains, and a television stood on another small table. I'd cleaned the window and it let in the evening sun which shone weakly. No matter how good a job I had done, it was still a dive – but it was my new home. I would need to find work before long after spending so much money today. I was hungry and thought I deserved a treat so I set off to buy something to eat. No sooner had I left the house than the sun disappeared and it looked like rain so I retraced my steps to fetch my raincoat. As I arrived at the top of the stairs I noticed that my door was slightly open so I walked quietly along the landing and pushed it open. There was a stranger standing in the middle of the room.

'Hey, what are you doing here?' I shouted, making him jump. He stood there awkwardly.

'I just popped in to say hello and welcome you to the house. My room is over there.' He pointed across the corridor.

I was furious. 'You didn't hear me say "Come in", did you? And I didn't open the door for you so how the hell did you get in?'

'It wasn't locked.'

'It damn well was. Now get out or I'll call the police.' He laughed at my words.

With my appetite gone I stayed in my room and, until I could get a padlock and bracket, I vowed to carry all my money and valuables with me.

When I was getting myself ready to go to bed I thought I heard someone outside my room and when I put the light out I could see a thin gleam of light from the landing through a split in the door panel, then nothing, then the light again. It dawned on me that there was someone standing there so, as quickly as I could, I snatched open my door.

Not quickly enough though, because by the time I stepped out onto the landing I heard one of the other doors close. I remained on the landing and looked closely at my door. Yes, there was a crack in the panel. Had someone been watching me undress? I returned to my room, slamming the door shut behind me. I was upset and disgusted. The creep. I covered the door with the musty curtain I had taken down from the window hammering nails into the door and not caring who I disturbed. I sat on the bed, hungry, tired and a bit scared. Did I want to go back home? Did I have a choice? This was how it was now.

I had been in the bedsit for several weeks and still hadn't found a job. I was starting to get anxious. My money was getting a bit low. I needed to find work very soon but so, it seemed, did everyone else in Liverpool. Carla said I would have to think of going to 'sign on' but I hadn't got a clue how to go about that. I had thought of myself as such a rebel when I had styled myself as a Goth with those ridiculous clothes and make-up but I wasn't really. When I looked back I could see that I had led a sheltered life, living in an affluent home with my needs catered for and I never had to lift a finger to look after myself. I might have been unhappy but I was protected from the knocks of poverty and need.

I had called to see the girls as promised and they said they were asking around for me. Elaine said she was making enquiries at the hospital and would bring me some application forms. I'd filled in so many already but they all wanted to know what qualifications I had – I wondered that myself. How had I done in my A levels? Nicola and Tracy had been teasing me saying they were looking forward to my housewarming party but there was no way I would bring anyone back to the dump which was now my home.

I had enough money for my rent but I hated taking it down to the landlord. He stood far too close to me and took every opportunity he could to touch me. It was under the guise of friendliness but it was enough to frighten me. He told me he was going to have to put my rent up and it was just too bad if I didn't have enough money. I could either be nice to him or get myself down to Dock Road. I wasn't stupid, I guessed what he wanted. Was I desperate enough to go back home? It was getting that way.

I counted out the money in my purse carefully. I was meeting Carla for lunch because she had a half day and she was going to help me find a job. She had told me she worked in a shop but she didn't say it was at George Henry Lee's which was a smart department store. When we met she handed me a cushion which she'd bought me for my room.

Touched and surprised I thanked her profusely.

'It's nothing, I get a staff discount and I thought you'd like it.'

We traipsed the city looking for staff vacancy cards laughing as we walked arm-in-arm window shopping. I can't remember when I enjoyed myself so much. Eventually it was clear that Carla expected me to ask her back to the bedsit and there was no way I could refuse so, as we headed home, I bought a couple of cream cakes to have with our cup of tea. I was nervous as we turned into the street. Carla said nothing until we reached my room and she praised everything with a false brightness as I made us a cup of tea. She didn't stay long and I felt strangely deflated after she left.

The following evening I had an unexpected visitor.'Can I come in?'

'Of course.' I was surprised to see Carla again so soon. She had come straight from work and seemed a bit nervous.

'Listen,' she hesitated, 'is it important for you to live and work in the city?'

'Not really. Why?'

'I told Mum about you. She works as a cook in an old people's home in Meols and they're always looking for carers. I said you mightn't be interested. I can't think of anything worse than looking after a bunch of old fogeys and wiping their bums but, if you're desperate, I suppose it's a job of sorts. And it would be easier to find a room on the Wirral, I think.'

'Wow, I don't know what to say.'

'In a good way or not?' Carla asked nervously and as I hesitated, she went on 'I know I'm interfering and...'

'No, not at all. That's so kind, thank you so much. I don't know anything about old people or how to look after them. I never even had any grandparents. But I'll give anything a try.' I couldn't believe that someone would be this concerned about me. I'd only known Carla and the other girls such a short time and yet I felt closer to them than any of my friends from my old life, as I thought of it now.

'Why don't you come to ours for your tea tonight? I'll ring Mum to say you're coming and you can ask her about it. You don't have to decide anything straight away.'

'Hello, Mrs Layton,' I said, feeling a bit nervous.

'Call me Carol,' was the reply as I was warmly welcomed to Carla's home which was a cosy terraced house. 'This is Bill, he works at the docks, and Karen's a trainee hairdresser and, last but not least, that's Mark. He's still at school.' They all acknowledged her with a smile or a 'Hi'.

'Come and sit down. It's only shepherd's pie but there's plenty.' Carol wasted no time in serving everyone. The meal was noisy with everyone talking about what sort of day they had had and plates being replenished. By the end of the meal I was full and felt I had known the family for ages. I helped Carol with the dishes and thought Carla would do the same but she made an excuse to disappear to her room so Karen was made to help. Not that she did much, she leaned against the kitchen cabinets and chatted and put away the dishes as I dried them. At one point she took hold of my hair and rubbed it between her fingers.

'Why did you put this colour on your hair,' she asked turning up her nose.

'I don't know really, to be different I suppose.'

'Doesn't do much for you though.'

'Karen, don't be rude!' Carol admonished.

'It doesn't matter, she's probably right.'

'I'd love to get my hands on it. I'd like to cut it as well. This long straight style is okay for some people but it doesn't suit you.'

Carol rolled her eyes and sighed at her daughter's directness.

'Okay then, you're on. As long as it's not going to cost me a fortune you can do what you like to it.'

Karen's face lit up. 'Really? In that case I'll do it for free because I'm only a trainee. I'll fix it with the salon and make arrangements with you.'

'Are you sure you know what you're letting yourself in for?' Carol joked. 'Don't worry, our Karen's really good and she's nearly at the end of her training. You'll be in safe hands.' She then went on, 'Carla tells me that you're looking for a job. The home I work in is looking for carers. D'you think you could do that sort of work?'

'I don't know but I'm willing to give it a try.'

'You do realise that it's only some skivvying don't you? If I put in a good word for you I don't want you to let me down, mind.'

'I wouldn't do that, I promise.'

'If I'm any judge of character I can see that you wouldn't. I'll have a word tomorrow then. You're also looking for somewhere to live? I might have one or two ideas on that as well. Leave it with me.'

A few weeks later, as I was starting a new life on the Wirral, I guessed that Tom would be embarking on his new life in Durham. I never doubted that he would gain the grades in his exams to be able to go to his chosen university to follow his dreams.

As the weeks went by, I didn't remember a time when I had been happier. It was an odd time for such a thought to strike me as I was struggling to dress an elderly lady who, like a stubborn two-year-old, was refusing to put her arms through her sleeves. But it was true.

I laughed encouragingly, 'Come on, Cynthia. We don't want George the Man seeing you in your undies, do we? And we can't leave these empty sleeves flapping about all day.' I waved them about. Cynthia giggled and her arms were through the sleeves before she realised.

Having worked in the care home since October, thanks to Carol putting in a good word for me, I realised that I had a real affinity with elderly people. It surprised me as I had never known anyone of significant age, but I enjoyed their company. Whenever my duties allowed I spent time chatting to the elderly residents, often spending my free time with them as well. I didn't find it difficult to treat them with the respect they deserved. It came naturally because I was genuinely interested in them and their lives. Of course, as with any job, there were some aspects I didn't like. I'd never changed a baby's nappy in my life and changing an adult's took some getting used to but it had to be done and that was it. But on the whole I loved it.

There were nineteen people in the private home, eighteen of them women. When George had joined them a couple of months ago most of them had exclaimed "But he's a man!" resulting in the title "George the Man". A widower,

George had found living alone very difficult having been completely spoilt by his wife, and he took to life at the home with pleasure. He was a real gentleman. Although no longer able to get to his feet when a lady entered a room, he was always ready to greet them with a smile and sometimes a cheeky comment, but they lapped it up. Having a man around seemed to have a good effect on the ladies, as the staff noticed with amusement when they made coquettish comments back to him.

It was thanks to Carla and her family that I not only had a job, but somewhere to live. Carol had found me somewhere to stay: a neighbour whose son had emigrated to Australia. Mrs McIntyre had never taken in lodgers before and the sum she suggested charging was so ridiculously low that I insisted on paying more. So, it was with no regrets that I had packed up what few belongings I had and left the bedsit in Liverpool. The landlord had tried to charge me for not giving him notice so I said I would check with the council if I had to do so. I took his muttered reply of “Good riddance” to mean that there was no need! And here I was happily settled in the house a few doors down from Carla and thoroughly spoiled by Mrs Mac, as everyone called her. The little terraced house didn’t hold a candle to the luxury of my childhood home but there was a welcoming warm heart here which made it easier to put my past behind me and ignore the sudden longings which occasionally overcame me, but these were mainly when I thought of Tom.

Chapter 12

Greg had known when he walked out on Fiona, leaving his home and his children, that he wouldn't be going back. It wasn't the way he would have chosen to leave but, in a way, Gina had made it easy for him by blurting things out the way she had.

Charlotte had been surprised to see him when he turned up on her doorstep that summer evening and not, initially, as delighted as he expected. Perhaps he had presented himself as someone she would be grateful to share her flat with. Obviously he gave her his own version of why he had left home, suggesting that his dalliance with Ellie had been several months before the two of them had met.

'Why did you come here? Did you have nowhere else to go?'

'You were the first person I thought of, and as a good friend...'

'I suppose you could stay for a few nights, until you get yourself sorted. Your wife might want you to go back?'

'I'm sure she will but...'

'Hold on, Greg, you're sure are you? Not all women need a man. These days women can hold their own with any man. This is 1987 after all, and Mrs Thatcher has won her third election so don't make any assumptions. Look at me, I love being a free spirit with no attachments.'

With that, she showed him into the spare bedroom. This was not the way things were supposed to be and Greg's confidence took a bit of a knock. He made himself as unobtrusive as possible while trying his best to be helpful.

Even though the flat was spacious Greg felt strange there as it was so different from his home. It was sophisticated, functional and tasteful, with sleek, Scandinavian furniture and plain muted colours, the style of which was becoming the latest trend. Ornaments were few and far between, and expensive; there were none of the crinoline lady ornaments that Fiona favoured. After reassuring each other that his stay was temporary they settled down well together as they learned to share the flat on a daily basis. Charlie was often away or working late so there were several days at a time when they didn't see each other.

Eventually, for the first time in his life Greg felt as if he had found solace. The act of leaving Fiona had left him more bruised than he had expected, but only because he didn't expect to miss his children so much. Not that he'd ever had much to do with them. With distance from what had happened, he felt sorrow for Gina rather than any anger at her. And also guilt. The end of the marriage hadn't been her fault, she had only precipitated it in her clumsy way. She had looked so wretched on that awful day as he left and he had been so cruel. And his little boy Ben. When had he last played with him? He could see that he had subconsciously taken on his father's attitude to parenthood?

Greg loved his new living arrangements but he did occasionally contact estate agents, leaving the information around so that Charlie could see that he was making some sort of effort to find alternative accommodation.

'If I find something I like,' he asked her, 'will you come with me for a second look to give your seal of approval?'

Apparently nothing proved to be suitable as a second visit didn't happen. As the months passed, Greg and Charlie began to feel comfortable together and gradually Greg's hunt for a flat had become perfunctory rather than purposeful. Fiona still hadn't found out where he was living which pleased him as he didn't want the sanctuary he had found with Charlie tarnished by her.

She had been surprisingly quiet for the first few weeks after the split. The relief he felt at leaving her turned into anxiety as he awaited the explosion of her temper which he knew would come when she eventually realised that he wasn't going back. To his shame he hadn't seen Ben in order to avoid such a scene and he missed his little son. He wondered too about Gina, his awkward, prickly daughter who was so set on being different. Things can't have been easy for her, especially with Fiona as a mother.

The bombshell came the day after Greg had been to his solicitor to instruct him to begin divorce proceedings. It took not only a couple of salesmen by surprise but a few customers as well. Surprise was putting it mildly as all those in the showroom jumped out of their skin when the huge plate glass window shattered. It shattered because Fiona had driven her car into it. For a moment even she looked shocked, but not as shocked as those in close vicinity. While they rushed towards her thinking that she had had a terrible accident she was struggling to get out of the car.

'Where is he?' she screeched.

'Where's who?' asked the young salesman nervously.

'Greg bloody Clark, that's who,' snapped Fiona.

'He's not here. Are you OK? What happened? Did you hit the accelerator instead of the brake?' the young man asked anxiously. After ascertaining that Fiona was not injured she was taken home by a member of staff and it was arranged for the car to be checked over

When Greg arrived back from his meeting he was livid when he heard what had happened. Later that day, Charlotte persuaded him against going round to see Fiona, which was his first instinct, and to continue to contact her through his solicitor. He wasted no time in doing so. He told them that he wanted to arrange to see Ben; he had waited too long already. In fact, he wanted to spend Christmas Day with him. In the meantime, he demanded weekly access and arranged for it to start that Saturday.

Greg was nervous when he went to Chestnut Grove to collect Ben at the appointed time. He wasn't keen on coming across Matt or Ellie and he certainly wasn't looking forward to seeing Fiona. However, his solicitor had obviously spoken to her solicitor and she stuck to what had been agreed. Greg arrived promptly and parked outside the house, the door opened and he saw Fiona framed there, watching while Ben trotted down the drive.

'Daddy, Daddy, Daddy...'

Greg picked him up, nuzzling his face in his neck and breathing in his individual smell.

'Ben, mate. How's my boy?'

'Stop it Daddy, You're squeezing me too tight.' Ben wriggled.

Blinking rapidly, Greg strapped him in the car.

Greg and Charlie had discussed what they could do and they felt that it wouldn't be a good idea to take him to the flat on the first meeting. Father and son needed to spend the day together. Greg had never been the type of father to take his children for days out and he'd had to think long and hard about what to do with Ben. There was a zoo, of sorts, a few miles away and he'd decided on that. And so it was that, on a bright but cold autumn day, the two of them wandered around looking at some miserable animals pacing their enclosures. Ben held his hand tightly as they walked but said little. All the spark seemed to have gone out of him. He brightened up at the monkey house.

'Look Daddy, they're swinging... and look at that one jumping on top of the other one.' He drew in a sharp breath 'Ooooh! Look – that one's having a wee!'

Ben's surprised face made Greg laugh and they both chuckled.

During lunch Ben politely said please and thank you but he barely ate anything, just picked at his food. Although Greg wondered about Gina he was determined that he wouldn't question him about the situation at home and the boy volunteered little information.

'How's school going?

'OK. I'm good at sums and reading.'

He chattered on with Oscar and Hugo's names cropping up quite often. Greg was surprised that Fiona had maintained a connection with her neighbours. If he was honest, Greg was glad when it was time for Ben to go back to Fiona, but it was with a heavy heart that he watched his little boy trudging slowly up the drive to the front door which was quickly shut behind him.

Greg couldn't think of what to do on Ben's next visit.

'I don't want to be one of those fathers spending time with my child sitting in a fast food outlet trying in vain to make the meal a happy one. Do you think it's too soon to introduce him to you?' he asked Charlie.

'Maybe a bit. I'm not brilliant with children because I just don't know any and I don't want to make him feel uncomfortable. Why don't you bring him here and I'll go to work? Fantastic though my team is, there's always too much to do.'

This became the routine for the next few weeks. However, with Christmas looming Greg felt the time had come for Charlie and Ben to meet and so, the following Saturday,

Charlie was at the flat when they arrived. When they were introduced she shook his hand and he politely said 'How do you do' which amused both adults. She kept her distance allowing Ben to become accustomed to her. Over the next couple of weeks she took more of a part in his visits and Ben became less shy and, although still quiet, a little bit chattier.

Fiona was surprisingly compliant over Greg's request that Ben spend Christmas Day and Boxing Day with him and even went as far as suggesting that he had him for Christmas Eve as well.

Greg was delighted with the way Charlie had taken to Ben. A couple of weeks before Christmas the three of them went shopping. Ben's eyes lit up as they wandered around the toy store and Greg and Charlie tried to glean some clues as to what they could buy for his stocking. Ben soon became tired but before leaving the store they joined a queue to see Santa Claus.

On the way home, clutching his parcel close he said, 'That wasn't the real Santa you know, Dad, just a pretend one.'

'Really?' exclaimed Greg. 'How do you know?'

'He had trainers on his feet. The real Santa wears boots.'

Chuckling at this bit of wisdom they went back to the flat and Ben fell asleep in the car, still holding his unopened gift. Greg carried him inside and laid him on the sofa, still asleep.

'Is it normal for a six-year-old to be this tired, do you think?' he asked Charlie.

'I don't know. It's coming to the end of term and he's had a lot to cope with over the past few months. But then, I don't know anything about children so you're asking the wrong person.'

When Ben woke up, Charlie helped him to make some paper chains to decorate the flat and they put up a Christmas tree. She showed him the bedroom in which he would sleep on his visit the following week.

'Will I be sleeping in that big bed all on my own?' he asked in wonder when he saw the king sized bed.

'Well, not quite, you'll have to share it with Growler,' said Charlie, pointing out a soft toy dog which she'd thoughtfully bought and was perched on the pillow.

'I don't like dogs,' said Ben.

'This one is a special dog. I saw him in a shop all on his own and he said that he had no one to look after him. I told him that I knew a very nice little boy who would, and do you know what he said then?' Ben shook his head, his round, dark eyes moving from Charlie to the toy. 'If he looks after me then I'll look after him.' She put the dog in his arms and Ben stroked the fur.

'Okay,' he said, 'will he be all right until I come?'

'Oh yes, he'll be here waiting for you.

Chapter 13

Summer had now turned into winter and life had turned into a different kind of normality in the Harris household.

Ellie and Matt co-existed in their separate bubbles, as she thought of it, but put on a front of unity with their children. Ellie missed Tom desperately and wished that she could have talked more with him before he left and made some sort of peace with him. She couldn't wait for the Christmas holidays, which would soon be upon them, to see him again.

Despite being hurt that he didn't want her to go to Durham with him it had turned out well that Will had gone in her place. She didn't know if Tom had spoken to him, or if the return journey with just him and Matt had given them the opportunity to talk, but Will had come back a changed boy. He was no longer unpleasant with her and, even though he still stiffened when she gave him a hug, he did occasionally kiss her on the cheek.

He also seemed to be working hard at school. Ellie always felt a bit sorry for Will. Success came easily to Tom, academically and on the sports field, and he mixed well with everyone. Will found it more difficult. He had to work hard at his studies and he was more of a loner, content with his own company and enjoying his pastimes of climbing and bird-watching.

Since Tom left, Will had taken more notice of the twins and he often took them to the park to play football, which they loved. With the resilience of youth the little boys seemed to be coping well with the changes around them. For a few weeks, however, Oscar had reverted to sucking his thumb and Hugo had wet the bed several times but, much to Ellie's relief, this now seemed to be a thing of the past.

Little Ben from next door was still a frequent visitor. Ellie knew that Fiona was using her as a free babysitter but she didn't mind at all. They rarely spoke, except to make arrangements for Ben, but Ellie guessed how difficult it must be because Greg had yet to come back home. She was a little concerned about Ben and she mentioned it to Matt.

'I'm a bit worried about Ben. He's so pale and he's lost his baby plumpness. What do you think?'

'Yes, I suppose he has, just growing maybe. But he's had a lot to cope with these past months.'

Guiltily, Ellie bit her lip.

Gina still hadn't come home either to add to Ellie's guilt. Will had mentioned that some of her friends had asked him if he knew where she was.

'Don't you think it's odd that Aunty Fiona and Uncle Greg haven't tried to find Gina?' he had asked her one day.

'Maybe they have.'

'I asked Aunty Fiona a couple of weeks ago and she just said she'd come back when she ran out of money.'

'Poor Gina.'

'If I'd done what Gina did would you look for me?'

'Will,' Ellie turned and put her hands on his shoulders. 'You could never do anything so bad that I wouldn't be looking for you the minute I knew you'd disappeared,' she reassured him. She was rewarded with a smile and one of his rare kisses on the cheek. Ellie wondered if Greg was in touch with Gina. She hoped so. For all her bravado and attempts to be different by adopting the Goth style of dress and make-up, Ellie was convinced that Gina was just a young girl who was trying to get her parents' attention. Why couldn't they see that?

Ellie wondered where Greg was. Not that she ever wanted to see him again. The door was firmly shut on that part of her past and she regretted that she had ever opened it and let him in. What a price she'd paid for that one stupid act. She missed Matt so much, missed living in the security of his love, in the comfort of a life of sharing their days and laughing together.

Her parents still called frequently but it was obvious from her greeting where her mother's sympathies lay.

'Hi, Ellie,' she would breeze in, then 'Hi Matt, dear. How are you?' Her father's hug would last that little bit longer than usual as if compensating for her mother.

Later that evening, twins asleep and Will in his room with his homework, Matt walked into the lounge after answering the telephone in the hall. Ellie was watching the television and she turned down the volume looking expectantly at Matt.

'That was Tom,' he said.

'Oh! How is he? I can't wait to see him for Christmas.'

'Well... err... that's why he was phoning. He's not coming home. A group of his friends are going skiing and someone has dropped out so he's been asked to go.'

'Oh no!' Ellie's disappointment brought tears to her eyes.

'There's something else,' Matt continued, 'two guys have pulled out and he wondered if Will would like to go too.'

'Christmas without Tom *and* Will? Isn't Will too young? The others will all be older than him.'

'It would do him good to see that we trust him. And he would be with Tom.'

'Can we afford for him to go?'

'It's a lot of money I know, and if we pay for Will we'd have to pay for Tom too. It would be their Christmas presents with absolutely nothing else but yes, we could afford it.'

'I suppose we'd better ask him if he wants to go.'

Matt called Will downstairs from his bedroom and he walked into the lounge nervously. 'Have I done something wrong?'

'Tom's just been on the phone about this skiing trip. Do you know anything about it?'

'Well,' he hesitated, 'Tom did mention it to me.'

'Do you want to go?'

His face lit up but with some caution. 'Do I? You bet!'

'Your mother and I've had a chat and it's okay with us if you want to go and it can be your Christmas present from us.'

'Wow! Thanks.'

'But you've got to promise that you'll behave yourself. And you'll have to find your own pocket money,' Matt continued.

'Yeah, that's great. Oh! Thank you both so much.' He hugged Tom and went over to kiss his mother. 'I promise I'll be careful and you won't need to worry about me. Thank you, thank you. I'll ring Tom now.'

Will left the room and Matt looked at Ellie with a wry smile. 'Well, we've made someone happy, and that's Christmas sorted for two of our kids.'

'It's going to be a strange sort of Christmas isn't it?' Ellie said. She took a deep breath as if plucking up courage. 'Matt, what's going to happen to us. I've told you time and time again how sorry I am for what happened. I don't know what else to say or do. I dread to think what the effects of a broken marriage would have on the boys but I can't go on like this. Do you still want to be married to me or do you want to end things?'

Matt looked at her. 'What?! I don't want us to divorce and I don't want us to separate either but I don't know how to move on.' He ran his fingers through his hair and paced around the lounge.

'I can't take your coldness towards me any longer.'

'And I can't get the image of you and him out of my mind. It haunts me.'

'Well, if we're going to make a go of things, you're going to have to,' snapped Ellie. 'I'm fed up with feeling guilty all the time, of being the whipping boy. I'm human, I made a mistake like we all do, and my mistake is hard to forgive. I understand that, really I do, but I just can't take it any longer. I've had enough. I'm going to have to live with the guilt for the rest of my life, whether I live here with you or somewhere else without you. It's time for you to choose. If you don't want to live with me, say so, and once Christmas is over I'll find somewhere else for me and the boys to live. You can divorce me. I won't contest it.'

Chapter 14

Charlie walked into the flat, kicked off her ankle boots and draped her coat over the back of a chair. A few months ago she wouldn't have done that: she would have walked into her bedroom, placed the boots on the shoe rack and hung her coat in the wardrobe. Neatness had been ingrained into her from attending boarding school at a very young age. She went to the kitchen, brushed a few crumbs from the worktop, and flicked on the kettle to make a cup of coffee. Once she would have used the expensive coffee machine but over the past few months she had surprised herself by developing a taste for instant coffee. She snuggled into a chair. Unusually she was home before Greg and the flat was quiet. She savoured the silence briefly but it felt wrong, something was missing, Greg was missing.

Charlie's self-sufficiency and independence had become part of her personality which is why when Greg turned up all those months ago she was rather taken aback. She liked him well enough and had enjoyed his company on the few occasions when they'd met. He was an attractive man. He had made it clear that he had been in an unhappy marriage and it would have been surprising if a man of his mature age was not carrying some baggage. But when he knocked on her door on that summer evening she was surprised that there was no-one else he could have gone to. She wondered if she had led him on, that he had thought there was more to their relationship than there was. It took her some time, keeping him at arm's length, to realise that he was a very lonely man, very different from his public persona. Gradually she had come to know the real man, which is why she was sitting in her quiet flat waiting for him to come home. She couldn't pinpoint when her feelings had changed. But changed they had, and those feelings influenced everything inside her. When had she stopped minding about things being left lying around and work surfaces left unwiped? Her showroom of a flat was more like a home now, empty without the sound of someone else moving around, leaving his presence in the atmosphere and his unique man-smell in the bathroom and her bedroom which had now become theirs.

However, there was something more to cope with than a bit of untidiness. There was the matter of a small child. How did she feel about him? Well, he was an improvement on a baby. He was just a little person really and he was cute and interesting. She had surprised herself by becoming fond of him. She recalled her own distant childhood and felt sorry for little Ben. Not that she had ever felt sorry for herself, it just never occurred to her, but she empathised with the little boy in having such an upheaval in his short life. If she could help to make things more pleasant for him, she would endeavour to do so. She wasn't sure how she would cope with him taking a large space in her life, but at least he wouldn't be living with them full time. It wasn't as if her arrangement with Greg was a permanent one and she hadn't thought far enough ahead to wonder if she wanted that.

She stirred herself and looked at her watch, wondering where Greg was and, while not exactly being worried at his lateness, experienced the realisation that her concern was born out of caring. Charlie, not one of the world's greatest cooks, decided she would surprise him by cooking a meal herself for a change.

Chapter 15

For the past few months Matt had taken solace in his work. He was a partner in a busy accountancy firm. He put in many hours at the office but it was apparent to his colleagues that all was not well with him. One day, when he turned up for work looking dishevelled with a smell of alcohol on his breath the senior partner, Charles Mason, called him into his office.

'Matt, I hate having to talk to you like this but it's obvious that there's something wrong,' Charles spoke gently.

'What do you mean, why do you think there's something wrong? Everything's fine,'

'No. It's not,' insisted Charles quietly but firmly.

'I don't know why you think that.'

'I'll tell you then, shall I? You come into work looking a mess: your clothes are untidy and your hair needs cutting. While nobody says that you come in drunk, there is a smell of alcohol on your breath occasionally. You're impatient with the junior staff and snap at them for the least thing. You've lost weight. You can't seem to concentrate and you've made several mistakes which, but for the vigilance of the junior staff you've lost your temper with, would have had serious consequences. Furthermore, you are creating problems in our relationships with our customers – you don't call them back when you say you will and you're not meeting deadlines.' Charles paused. 'It isn't like you, Matt, so I know there must be some reason for this change in you.'

Matt sat there, shocked. 'Have I been that bad?' He thought he'd been able to put on a brave face.

'We've known each other for a long time, haven't we, Matt? Surely you know you can come to me if you have any problems, with work or with your personal life. Are the boys all right?'

'Yes, they're fine.'

'No health problems?'

'No, everybody's okay.'

'Is everything all right between you and Ellie?'

Matt sat up straight and fiddled with his tie. He had known the older man for many years and considered him a family friend. It was thanks to him that he was now a partner in the firm so he felt no annoyance at the question. He opened his mouth to speak but, to his dismay, no words came out and he broke down. Charles rose from his chair and came to sit on the desk in front of Matt.

'I see,' he said. 'So that's the problem. Do you want to talk about it?'

Taking a few minutes to compose himself, Matt said, 'I can't.'

'That's fine. You don't have to tell me anything.' Charles went to the door and opening it a little, he asked his secretary to bring them some coffee.

The two men sat in silence as Matt took a few deep breaths to calm down but it wasn't an uncomfortable silence. In a way he was relieved that Charles was aware of the situation and he knew he could depend on his support. When a quiet knock came at the door Matt got up and went to look out of the office window until the secretary had put down the tray and left.

'Do you need any time off?'

'No, really, I'd prefer to be at work. I'm sorry that I've let things get this bad. I just hadn't realised.' He sipped his coffee.

'Take the rest of today off anyway and remember, if there's anything I can do to help you, you must let me know. If the work load is too much we can do something about it, and if you need time off, that can be arranged. You have a lot of friends in this firm, remember that.'

'Thank you, Charles, I appreciate it.'

Charles shook his hand and patted him on the back. 'Off you go. It's Wednesday, don't come back until Monday. That's an order!'

Matt returned to his office, cleared his desk, picked up his coat and, as he passed through his assistant's office he called out to her 'I'll be out of the office until Monday, Amanda. See you then.' And he was gone before she had a chance to say anything.

It felt strange to be walking down the high street at this time of day with no appointment to attend. When he was young he'd once played truant from school. He had felt excited and scared at the same time and thought everyone was looking at him. He had that same feeling now. On the day he'd played truant he hadn't known what to do with himself so he'd sneaked back to school after missing only one lesson and no-one noticed that he'd been gone. He'd clearly never been a rebel! He didn't know what to do or where to go now.

He debated whether to go to a pub but, to be honest, he wasn't a big drinker even though he might have consumed more than his fair share over the past months. He had walked past a unisex hairdresser when he paused and retraced his steps, recalling Charles's comments about his appearance.

'Do I need an appointment?' he asked the receptionist.

'If you wait for about ten minutes we can attend to you shortly,' she smiled. He sat and flicked through some magazines until a young woman approached him. 'I'm Shelley, your stylist. Would you like to come this way please?'

Matt was starting to have doubts. Stylist? What was he doing with a stylist? Why hadn't he just gone to the barber as usual? Shelley? She didn't look more than about fourteen. What was he doing here?

Forty-five minutes later, after Shelley had washed and conditioned his hair, cut, layered and dried it, Matt looked at his reflection. What an improvement! He thanked her and smiled warmly and it was to his credit that his smile didn't slip when he learned the cost of his visit to the salon. He even added a generous tip.

Matt continued on his way, and turned into the shopping precinct and ambled around, pausing at his reflection in a shop window. Oh yes! It was him – the hair might be different but the suit was the same. Perhaps that was it. Ellie found him boring. He turned into the next shop selling men's clothes. He must have looked a bit lost, or maybe like a shoplifter, as he wandered up and down the aisles, because two young shop assistants approached him from opposite directions.

'Can I help you, sir?' asked one, smartly dressed in a crisp fitted shirt and narrow tie. He wore a gold earring and his hair was short.

'I'm not sure,' hesitated Matt.

'Are you looking for anything special?'

'Err... I'm not sure,' repeated Matt. Realising how stupid he must sound he quickly made up his mind and said more determinedly, 'What I mean is, I'm not sure what I want but I just want something a bit different, a bit more modern.'

The two young assistants exchanged glances and smiled with delight. 'My name is Jason and this is Kyle. Just leave everything to us.'

'I can't afford to spend a fortune,' Matt said. He was beginning to have cold feet.

'You don't need to spend a fortune to look good,' said Jason, or maybe it was Kyle, 'and it's quiet this morning, it's never busy on a Wednesday, so there's no rush.'

Before he realised what was happening a tape measure had been whipped out and Matt found himself in a large changing room with a cup of coffee. He wasn't sure if the conversation that went on around him involved him or not but Kyle and Jason seemed to decide between them what would suit him.

Matt stood in the changing room which had the Pet Shop Boys belting out their latest hit. It wasn't as good as the Elvis Presley version in Matt's opinion, and the irony of the words *Always on my Mind* weren't wasted on him. The two young men went tirelessly back and forth from the shop floor with things for Matt to try on. He, in turn, stood like a little boy while Kyle and Jason assessed him through narrowed eyes and pursed lips giving the occasional enthusiastic nod. They seemed to resent the intrusion of other customers who were served and sent on their way as quickly as possible.

Eventually Matt's changing room contained a selection of clothes which, according to the Kyle/Jason combo were a "definite yes". It was simply up to Matt to decide what to buy.

'I can't make my mind up,' Matt dithered as the lads looked on, arms folded. Suddenly he clapped his hands. 'I'll take the lot!'

'That's great. You can't go wrong with these clothes. You'll be ready for anything.'

They persuaded him to wear one of the outfits: casual trousers, a check shirt and a soft leather jacket and he left the shop with several bags and a credit card which had never seen as much use before in a men's outfitters. He had only walked a few paces when Kyle rushed after him with yet another bag.

'Something from Jason and me,' he grinned.

Matt smiled in surprise. 'Thank you so much, how very kind.'

'Thank you for trusting us. It was a pleasure to help you. It's only a tie and one of the free samples that come in. Come back to us any time.'

'I'll definitely do that. Thanks again.' He turned away and once again he caught sight of himself in a shop window and this time he stopped and studied the reflection. It was thinner than the old Matt, the hair and the clothes made him look vaguely, dare he say it, stylish. But there was another difference – a slight smile – something he hadn't worn for a while.

Matt wasn't stupid enough to believe that his life was going to go back to what it had been just by waving the magic wand that was his credit card, but he felt that in changing his appearance he had taken the first steps towards moving on. He had been bitterly hurt, there was no doubt about that. He was still bitter and hurt. The very foundations of his life had been shaken and, since that awful evening, almost four months ago, he had been in a kind of limbo. He'd plodded on each day as if he existed in a glass jar, watching his life going on but feeling disconnected from it somehow. It had taken Ellie's statement about leaving to force him to start thinking again.

As if from a distance, he had watched her change from his beautiful, loving wife to a shadow of her former self. Had he taken some perverse pleasure in seeing her shrinking into herself, losing her confidence and tiptoeing around him politely? Subconsciously, maybe so, but now it was obvious that things had to change and it was up to him. He took out his mobile phone.

Ellie put down the phone with a sinking sensation. This was it, the moment she had been dreading. The end of her marriage. Her stomach churned. Matt had asked her to meet him in town for lunch. He'd said they needed to talk. She supposed the kind of talk he needed would be easier in unfamiliar surroundings. Well dammit! If he was going to leave her she was bloody well going to show him what he was losing. She had less than an hour to get herself ready and meet him at the Phoenix – a surprising choice, well known as it was for smart and expensive dining. A suitable venue for a farewell lunch, she supposed, as they were unlikely to bump into anyone they knew.

The couple who had been married for nearly twenty years didn't recognise each other at first when the maître d' brought Ellie to Matt's table and he hastily got to his feet. Ellie took in his hair and his smart casual clothes. Her heart fluttered as she felt the old attraction to this handsome familiar stranger who was her husband. As they took stock of each other, the maître d' cleared his throat and pulled out a chair for Ellie.

Taking her seat opposite Matt, Ellie waited until they were alone before speaking. 'Okay, Matt, let's get this over with. You want a divorce, don't you? Fine. I won't contest it. But I just want to say, yet again, how sorry I am.'

Matt stared at her, a confused expression on his face.

'Is that what you really want – a divorce?'

'I think it's time you told me what *you* actually want,'

'I asked you to join me for lunch because I want us to make a new start.'

'A new start as in...?'

She watched Matt square his shoulders and take a deep breath. *Here it comes*, Ellie thought, *this is the end.*

'Ellie, I love you and I always have. You are part of me and I can't imagine not having you in my life. Yes, you've hurt me, and hurt me badly, and in some childish way I've wanted to hurt you back but I've hated the last few months. I want things to be like they were before. I know though that they never can be but maybe we can cobble some sort of a marriage even if only, and I hate saying it because it's like some sort of a cliché, for the sake of the children.'

Ellie sat there stunned; she hadn't been expecting this. 'Oh Matt!' She reached her hand across the table, tears in her eyes.

Matt took her hand in his. 'Well, what do you want to do?'

With a watery smile and a wobbly voice Ellie said, 'There is nothing in the world that I would like more than to spend the rest of my life with you. Every day I'll try and make up for hurting you.'

Taking both her hands in his and squeezing them gently Matt said, 'Hold on, there will have to be some ground rules. There is to be no "making up" as you call it. I know you're sorry for what happened. I'm sorry about whatever I did or didn't do to drive you away. Maybe I took you for granted?' Ellie tried to protest that he did nothing wrong but Matt shook his head and went on, 'It doesn't matter now. It's happened and we won't refer to it again but I'll never forget it, and I know you won't either. We'll just move on, being the wiser for what we could have lost. What we have lost in a way, because things can never be the same, we can't undo what's happened. Perhaps we'll find that we can't go on but I'm willing to try if you are.'

'Yes, I am,' she nodded, tears spilling down over smiling cheeks.

The waiter appeared at their table with the menu.

'May I see the wine list please?' asked Matt, but then changed his mind. 'No, just bring us a bottle of champagne.'

'Champagne at lunchtime. How decadent, Matt!'

'I think the occasion warrants it, don't you?'

Ellie and Matt chatted and laughed over their delicious lunch, giggling when Ellie hiccoughed over her champagne. It felt like ages since they had connected in such a way. Had it been because being parents had taken over from being friends and lovers? Ellie was surprised to see the time when she glanced at her watch and she got up from the table to phone her mother to ask her to collect the boys from school. She hoped this was the first layer to cover the huge chasm in their lives and she would do her best to ensure that there were many other layers to come until the huge crack in their lives was healed.

'Of course, that's no problem at all,' said Elizabeth. 'Is everything all right, Ellie?'

'Oh yes, Mum! Everything's very all right,' was the reply, and she smiled guessing that her mother would be both intrigued and puzzled.

Chapter 16

When Elizabeth received Ellie's phone call asking her to pick up Oscar and Hugo from school, she knew something must have happened but she hardly dared hope that Matt and Ellie were going to rekindle their marriage. Every day she dreaded hearing that they were going to separate. The cosy family suppers they had shared so happily in the past no longer happened and whenever she and Anthony called, there was an atmosphere of strain and false jollity.

Later when Ellie told her that they were going to make a go of things she had thanked God that her prayers had been answered. She still couldn't believe that Ellie could do such a stupid thing. She and Matt seemed to have been made for each other: a "golden couple". There were moments when her annoyance with Ellie at risking so much and hurting Matt so badly made her sharp with her. But she must get over it and, like them, put it in the past. If she was honest she knew that Ellie was closer to her father than to her and he had always indulged her. Maybe there was a tiny bit of jealousy on her part?

Elizabeth and Anthony were delighted when Ellie and Matt accepted the invitation to stay with them over Christmas. Although they didn't live far away it was a car journey, and having them sleep over would allow everyone to partake in a glass or two of wine without worrying about driving. Christmas would be different this year and not just because Tom and Will were away.

The only ones who weren't keen on the idea were Oscar and Hugo. They confided to their granddad that they were worried that Santa Claus wouldn't know where they were and they wouldn't get any presents. Anthony was quick to reassure them and showed them a letter he had written to Santa explaining that the boys would be staying with their grandparents. He gave the address and asked for the presents to be delivered there. The boys went with him to the post box and watched carefully as he popped it through the slot. They didn't see that he also posted another letter addressed to them from Santa himself. Now that problem had been sorted out the twins were much happier and looking forward to their Christmas.

For the past week Elizabeth had been rushed off her feet with all the preparations. Anthony had done his best to help and the house looked lovely with a huge Christmas tree in the hall and another smaller one in the lounge. It was now Christmas Eve and Matt had been over earlier in the day with the boys' gifts which were safely hidden in the garage. Everything was done and they were just waiting for the family to arrive. Despite her tiredness after being so busy, Elizabeth's eyes sparkled with anticipation.

'They won't be long now, dear. Come and sit down and have a sherry with me,' coaxed Anthony.

'That would be lovely.' Elizabeth turned down the volume of the Christmas carols on the music centre and sat down on the sofa with a tired sigh. They smiled as they gently clinked glasses.

'Happy Christmas, darling.'

'And to you, my love. Let's make it a good one for everybody.' Elizabeth took a sip. 'I've been so worried for the past few months.'

'I know you have. So have I. But it's behind us now.'

Their glasses had barely been emptied when the doorbell rang. Everyone outside was singing carols. Elizabeth scarcely had a chance to say hello when she opened the door before the boys dashed up to her, both talking at once.

'Grandma, we've got presents for you.'

'And for you, Grandad, and you mustn't open them until tomorrow.'

'If you don't like the colour of the scarf, Grandma, you can change it.'

Ellie rolled her eyes as they all laughed.

'Something smells good,' said Matt.

'It's just some soup and sandwiches. I thought we'd have a light supper before we stuff ourselves tomorrow.'

Supper was a jolly affair as Oscar and Hugo told their grandparents what they were hoping Santa would bring them. Matt and Ellie exchanged glances when they heard some of the items for the first time and shrugged with a smile as Santa definitely wouldn't be bringing everything!

After their bath two tired, excited little boys made their way to bed with their stockings.

'We had a letter from Santa,' said Oscar 'and he said he would leave our presents under the tree in the hall.'

'But he'll put one present in our stocking if we go to sleep like good boys,' added Hugo.

They were snuggled under the bed covers and Ellie and Matt were reading the poem *Twas the night before Christmas* when Ellie held up her finger.

'Shh! What was that?'

They heard the tinkling of a bell coming from outside. The boys shot out of bed and looked through the window at the night sky.

'I know what it was,' said Matt also peeping through the curtain. 'It was Santa's elves going round to check that all good children are in bed.'

That was enough for the boys to dash back under the covers and say goodnight. As they went downstairs Matt and Ellie saw Anthony coming through from the kitchen holding Elizabeth's little crystal glass bell which he replaced carefully on the shelf in the lounge.

'It's cold out there,' said Santa's little elf. 'Let's have a sherry.'

Christmas Day was a happy occasion. Santa had provided Oscar and Hugo with almost all they had asked for. They were reluctant to go to church but they went with the promise that there would be more gifts to open after lunch. Elizabeth and Ellie worked companionably in the kitchen to produce a delicious lunch, with all the trimmings, while the men amused themselves with the boys' racing car set, ignoring the protests of the boys impatiently awaiting their turn. Tom and Will telephoned to say they were having a wonderful time on the ski slopes and they had taken part in a torch-lit run which had been "dead good".

After lunch Ellie and Matt insisted on washing up while Anthony and Elizabeth put their feet up while the boys played happily with their new toys. After the queen's speech they were feeling so lethargic that everyone thought they would benefit from some fresh air. They enjoyed a short walk to the park and were amused by those children trying to master riding their new bicycles and scooters, before the chilly air and darkening clouds sent them back home.

After putting two very sleepy little boys to bed Ellie and Matt came downstairs to find that Anthony had prepared a tray of turkey sandwiches and opened a bottle of wine. Everyone protested that they were too full to eat but they enjoyed them all the same.

Elizabeth produced an envelope. 'We've one final present to give you,' she said handing it to Ellie and Matt. 'We know you've had difficulties over the past few months and we couldn't be more pleased that you're giving your marriage another chance. We hope this little treat will help.'

Matt and Ellie looked at each other in surprise as they opened the envelope. It contained a voucher to spend a weekend at a luxury hotel in Wales over the New Year.

'Mum... Dad. I don't know what to say.'

'How very generous of you. Thank you so much. I'd just like to say how grateful Ellie and I have been for your support and, most of all, for your non-interference in our recent... difficulties... which are well and truly behind us,' said Matt.

'Yes, thank you so much,' echoed Ellie, 'and thank you for a lovely day.'

As everyone prepared to turn in for the night, Elizabeth's eyes followed Ellie out of the room. She was looking much better these days. She had looked positively haggard a mere few weeks ago; adultery obviously hadn't suited her. Elizabeth sincerely hoped that it had been, as she said, a moment of madness that she regretted and not a love affair that would have been difficult to live with.

Chapter 17

When Greg collected Ben on Christmas Eve he walked up to the front door of his old home and rang the bell. Fiona opened it. It was the first time they had seen each other face to face since August. They stood in silence for a moment. Fiona was as glamorous as ever, well made-up and not a hair out of place. The tenseness showed on Greg's face, wondering if she would make a scene, but with Ben at her side looking anxiously between his parents she smiled down at him 'Have a nice time with Daddy. I hope he's got you lots of presents.'

Greg took Ben's rucksack from her and asked, 'How's Gina?'

'I've no idea,' she replied starting to close the door.

'What do you mean, you've no idea?' said Greg, putting out his hand to stop the door closing.

'Just exactly that. I don't know.'

'Why don't you know?'

'She left.' She put her finger to her cheek in a sarcastic gesture. 'Let me think, what could have happened last August to make her leave home?'

'You mean she's been gone since then and you didn't think to tell me?'

'And since last August you didn't think to ask after her? The only thing I know is that she must be in the Liverpool area because she sent Ben a present and that was the postmark on it.'

The door closed, leaving him standing there holding Ben's hand and his rucksack. His mind was on Gina as he strapped Ben into the car and drove off. A little voice from the back said quietly, 'I miss Gina. She sent me a present. Look, Dad, it's a racing car.'

Greg pulled himself together. 'I'm sure you do, mate, and it's a super car. But I bet she's having a great time somewhere just like we're going to have because...'

'IT'S CHRISTMAS!' the two of them chorused.

Charlie was waiting for them at the flat with hot chocolate. Ben was mesmerised by how the place had changed since his last visit. Decorations were everywhere and multi-coloured fairy lights glittered. The first thing he did was to open his rucksack and bring out two rolled up pieces of paper. He gave one to Charlie. It was a drawing of a robin and some holly. Charlie studied it seriously.

'Wow! This is brilliant. Who is the artist who drew this fantastic picture?'

'Me!' exclaimed Ben proudly, a huge grin on his face.

'You? Well you're a very clever young man. There's just one thing,' she added handing him a pen, 'artists usually sign their work.'

The artist in question took the pen and with the tip of his tongue sticking out, carefully wrote Benjamin James Clark on the bottom.

'This is for Growler.' He took the other piece of paper and dashed off to the bedroom. Climbing up on the bed he unrolled it in front of the toy. It was a picture of a bone. Charlie and Greg watched, smiling, from the doorway.

Later that day Charlie came into the lounge, having put Ben's drawing in a picture frame. She removed the print of the *Tree of Life* from above the fireplace and replaced it with Ben's drawing.

'Thank you, darling,' said Greg, touched at her thoughtfulness. 'I bet that's the first time Gustav Klimt has been upstaged by a six-year-old!'

That evening an exhausted Ben slept deeply, guarded by Growler who was tucked under his arm. Greg and Charlie sat on the sofa enjoying a glass of wine, her head on his shoulder.

'I'm so grateful to you Charlie for all you've done for Ben.' He kissed her head, rubbing his cheek on her soft blonde hair, inhaling the fresh scent of her shampoo.

'I didn't think I liked children, but he's adorable. I love having him here with us.'

'And we both love being here with you.'

Sometimes he looked in the mirror and wondered where the old Greg had gone. He cringed when he thought of how cocky he was when he first arrived at Charlie's, expecting her to welcome him with open arms. Over the months he had been there that he had learned humility and gratitude and it was all thanks to Charlie, and now he had never felt so content. He was amazed that this beautiful, clever young woman found him attractive and seemed to want to be with him. He kissed her long and deeply.

Gone was the casual, temporary feel to their relationship and in a very short time they had become so close. He just wanted to be with her all the time, to do things for her and to share things with her. He had never felt like this with anyone before. It struck him like a physical blow. He was in love with her. He realised he'd never loved anyone before. He sat up suddenly putting down his wine.

'What's the matter?' she asked, startled by the suddenness of his movement.

He turned and, taking her face in both hands, looked into her eyes. *I can't tell her*, he thought, *I'll only drive her away. What would she want with someone seventeen years older than her who was still married to someone else?* He kissed her again.

'I'm a bit worried about Gina,' he said, returning to the thought which had been niggling at him all day.

'Why? What has she done?'

'Fiona doesn't know where she is.'

Gradually, over the time they had been together Greg had gradually told Charlie the details of the break-up, difficult though it was. He knew how badly he had behaved and Charlie made no attempt to make him feel better as she made her feelings at his actions clear.

'She left home last August and hasn't been in touch since,' Greg admitted

'Maybe she's with a friend?'

'I was awful to her; a proper bastard. I thought that was the reason she hasn't been in touch with me. I hurt her badly with the terrible things I said.'

'Why don't you try calling some of her friends?'

He turned sadly to her, 'That's just it. She doesn't have many friends and I don't even know the ones she had. Some sort of father I am. Tom was the only one she was close to and I can hardly contact him. The only thing Fiona said was that she must be in the Liverpool area because she sent Ben a present from there.'

Putting her hand on his shoulder Charlie said, 'Well if she went in August a few more days won't make any difference. But it really is something you must follow up in the new year.'

The following morning Ben was still fast asleep. The huge bed, in which he looked so tiny, was covered in colourfully-wrapped parcels. Charlie kept peeping in to see if he was awake. When the phone rang she let it ring several times to see if it would wake him, but no. After her conversation with her parents who were ringing from their home in Barbados to wish her a happy Christmas, she and Greg again peeped in and Ben was starting to stir. He rubbed his eyes and looked around him, obviously wondering where he was. He smiled at Growler and kissed his nose before noticing first the parcels, and then Charlie and his dad in the doorway.

'Santa's been!' he exclaimed before throwing himself with excited enthusiasm into the task of opening everything.

That night, after he went round switching off the various lights, Greg peeped in on his sleeping son. Why had he never realised before how precious he was? It was as if Charlie had unlocked something deep inside him, made him able to feel properly for the first time ever. He bent down and kissed the little chap before joining Charlie in their bedroom. She, too, was fast asleep. It had been a wonderful day. OK, maybe the sprouts were a little burnt, the potatoes might have been a little hard but neither of them made any claim to being good cooks and if they did forget to serve the pigs in blankets, what did it matter? He had never enjoyed Christmas more and if he knew that Gina was safe and well it would be perfect.

Chapter 18

As I worked on Christmas morning my thoughts kept going back to my little brother. Hopefully Ben's present would have arrived safely and I hoped he liked it. With no more time to dwell on the past I knocked gently on the door of Henrietta's room. Of all the residents of Clover House, Henrietta was my favourite and such good company that I spent more time with her than any of the others. Apparently she had lived in a large house in Hoylake until ailing health meant she could no longer manage alone. Her husband had died some ten years ago, her son lived in America with his family and her daughter was currently in the Middle East where her husband worked.

'Merry Christmas, Henrietta,' I said quietly. 'Let's get you up and about.' My smile was returned warmly by the frail old lady. Despite her age and poor health Henrietta was very particular about the way she looked and I knew the routine well by now, finishing the washing and dressing process with a nice brooch on the scarf around her neck, a dab of perfume behind ears and on each wrist, a slick of lipstick and a dab of powder.

'Before you take me to the lounge would you just open the top drawer of the chest of drawers and look inside?' I complied, and saw a wrapped parcel with my name on it. 'Merry Christmas, my dear. It's just a little something to say thank you for your kindness.'

'Henrietta you really shouldn't have!'

'Nonsense. Go on, open it. I hope you like it.'

I opened the parcel carefully to discover a box containing a watch. 'Oh! It's beautiful.' Then I hesitated and bit my lip. 'But – '

Henrietta held up her hand. 'I know what you're going to say but it's all right. I asked my daughter to buy it when she was home a couple of weeks ago. We spoke to Mrs Fisher to tell her what I wanted to do so I've cleared it with her.'

The home had a strict rule about staff accepting gifts from the residents, apart from the odd box of chocolates, and I was touched, not only by the gift but by the fact that Henrietta had been so thoughtful.

'This is something just between the two of us so perhaps best not to tell the others, my dear. I've made a donation to be shared out among the rest of the staff.'

With tears in my eyes I kissed the soft, papery cheek. 'Thank you so much. It's lovely and I'll treasure it.'

Later that day I sat in the lounge with the residents and staff listening to the queen's speech. Not all the residents were paying attention, it must be said. The sherry, and a glass of wine with the excellent Christmas lunch, had made some of them drowsy and one or two were slouched in their chairs, eyes closed, Christmas hats askew. Those who were awake and listening carefully, nodded sagely from time to time.

I looked around at the old folk. In the short time I had been here I had become very fond of several of them especially Henrietta. None of them were here from choice I supposed. Who would want to give up their home and move into an old folks' home, excellent as this one was? I assumed they must all be wealthy or from wealthy families. It wasn't cheap to live in a private place like this. One or two of the girls on the staff had worked in other homes and shared their horror stories with me. The owners themselves visited frequently but they entrusted the day to day running to Mrs Fisher, the manageress, who ran the place with a rod of iron, ensuring that a high standard was maintained.

My shift over, I went to say goodbye to Henrietta whispering a quiet thank you again for my gift. Then I changed out of my uniform to meet Darren, Carla's boyfriend, who was picking me up from work as there were no buses running. I had volunteered to work today because I didn't want any of my friends to feel under any obligation to invite me to share their Christmas. However, it turned out I had made things even more inconvenient for Carla and her family as they were insistent that I join them with Mrs Mac and were waiting until I had finished work to have their late Christmas lunch.

I had been totally overwhelmed by the kindness I had been shown by almost everyone I had met since I had come to live in the north west of England. Why on earth had I got on that train for Liverpool? Was it some sort of karma or was someone up there looking out for me? Whatever it was, I was more grateful than I could say.

When I opened the door to Carol's house my nostrils were assailed with such delicious cooking aromas that my mouth watered. Then, when I heard Bill, Carla's father, say 'Here she is. Our Gina's arrived' I felt a tingle of belonging. This is where I wanted to be, this was where people wanted me to be – far away from those who were supposed to love me and where I had spent eighteen years of my life. This was what a real family was.

Cries of "Merry Christmas", "Sit here our kid", "Move up" and "Mind the hot dishes" filled the air as I manoeuvred my way to sit down. Apart from the Layton family, Darren, Mrs Mac and I sat down for the meal. Mrs Mac's kitchen table had been borrowed and put next to theirs; a single bed sheet was used as a tablecloth and all the spare chairs and stools had been called into service and squeezed around them. The tables looked lovely, if a bit haphazard, with crackers, holly and candles among the mismatched glasses and tableware. I sat next to Mrs Mac and squeezed her hand 'Are you okay?' I smiled, noting the older lady's flushed cheeks.

'Fine,' came the returning giggle. 'But the sherry I had earlier's gone to my head.'

'Never mind the Guinness before that,' laughed Bill.

'It's your fault. Plying me with drink on an empty stomach. No wonder I've gone all neak at the wees.' We all roared with laughter at Mrs Mac's spoonerism.

Eventually, laden plates sat in front of everyone but before anyone ate, Bill tapped his glass and declared that they should all say grace. 'Grace' came the immediate response from Mark and Mrs Mac who looked at each other and giggled.

'Dear Lord. Thank you for the food you have laid here before us and thank you for giving us family and friends to share it with. We remember in our prayers all those who lost their lives in the terrible plane disaster in Lockerbie. Have mercy on their souls.' Carol and Mrs Mac both crossed themselves while the others sat in silence for a moment thinking of the terrible events of a few days earlier when so many people had been killed. Bill continued 'For what we are about to receive, please make us truly thankful. Amen.'

Echoes of "Amen" were preceded by Carol's command 'Now eat up while it's hot.'

After the happiest Christmas that I could remember ever, I eventually went home with Mrs Mac, hooking my arm through the old lady's as she wobbled along.

'How many sherries have you had, Mrs Mac?' I teased.

'Maybe one or two,' she chuckled innocently.

'Let's get you home and tucked up with some hot cocoa.' But when I took the drink upstairs later Mrs Mac was fast asleep and snoring gently.

Not quite ready for bed I went downstairs and switched on the electric fire. Sipping the cocoa I once again reflected on the past few months. What were things like in Chestnut Grove? Had Mum and Dad split up? What about Uncle Matt and Aunty Ellie? Strangely enough it was them I felt most sorry for; unlike my parents, they always seemed a loving couple and were always kind to me, never commenting on even my most "way out" looks. And what about my Tom? My stomach lurched as I thought of him. My Tom, indeed. He could never be mine now. How was he getting on? I knew he would have passed his exams. I wonder how I did? My exam results, never collected, didn't matter any longer as, in my rebellious mood, I hadn't made any plans for the future. I wished I could say sorry to everyone for what I did. I bit my lip when I thought about Ben, missing cuddling him and answering his constant 'Why?' He was another who never judged my appearance. At my most garish and strange, when my parents mocked me, Ben would always say 'I think you are very pretty.' What had possessed me to go through such a silly phase? Did I really think I looked nice?

No-one would recognise me now, that was certain. Carla's sister, Karen, had worked wonders with my hair and took it as her personal mission to keep me looking groomed. She had cut it into a sleek bob, gradually colouring it by reducing it from the flat, stark black until it was back to my natural rich, shiny chestnut. I had also lost a lot of weight which, according to Karen, brought out my cheekbones in my heart-shaped face and showed my blue eyes. But I think she was just being nice because when I looked in a mirror I could just see ordinary old me.

I hadn't made many new friends but was still in touch with Elaine, Sarah and Nicola, the three nurses I had met on the train. Occasionally I saw Tracy who was busy with her student life but we tried to get together from time to time. Of the five girls I had so luckily met on that fateful day last August I was closest to Carla. Sensible, practical Carla had become such a good friend. And her wonderful family had absorbed me so smoothly and completely that I felt secure and wanted and, dare I say, loved, for the first time ever. I knew if I ever had any problems I could turn to them. They never intruded or enquired about my past. The only reference that was ever made was an observation by Carol not long after we had first met.

'I don't know what it was that made you leave home and I'm not asking. But, at your age, it's up to your parents to sort it out not drive you away. But sometimes, when you leave the past behind, you find yourself, or discover the you that was always there. If you ever want to talk about it, or want me to help in any way, just come to me.' These kind words were accompanied by a warm hug. It was no wonder that I felt I belonged, and in just a few short months.

Chapter 19

Ellie and Matt waved their goodbyes as they set off down Chestnut Grove. Impatient to get back to their toys, Oscar and Hugo had already gone indoors as Ellie's parents waved back. It had been easier for them to come and stay there so the boys could play with their Christmas presents rather than take the boys to them.

As they drove away Matt said, 'Wasn't that thoughtful of your parents to treat us to this mini-break?'

'Yes. Not sure about the timing though. Winter in Wales!'

'We've never been away for New Year before and it is a luxury hotel so I'm sure we'll make the most of it.' Matt patted Ellie's thigh. 'I'm quite excited.'

'So am I.' Ellie smiled, 'I'm looking forward to being just the two of us. And of course relaxing in the lap of luxury, as this hotel is supposed to be.'

Since their reconciliation their relationship was slowly becoming closer. There were days when both of them seemed to keep their distance, seemed to want their own space. If one or the other wondered what was going on, they never asked, just waited for the moment to pass, the chill to fade into warmth. It was starting to feel more like it had been when they first met: they treated each other with respect and the old affection and teasing was gradually replacing the coldness and hurt. In the process of reestablishing their friendship they were slowly rediscovering the deep love they'd shared for so many years.

After a brief stop for lunch in a small pub, which looked more inviting than it was, they continued on their journey. Thanks to Ellie's need to hold the map in the direction of travel, and confusion over the Welsh place-names, they made a few wrong turns. Although only mid-afternoon, it was already dark and gloomy as the clouds hung low in the sky, and it was with some relief that they saw the sign for Glanaber and drove into a small coastal village. Two police cars passed them going in the opposite direction.

'Two police cars in a small place like this! I hope that's not a bad sign and the place isn't full of criminals,' joked Matt.

They passed a pub, whose windows were lit invitingly, two chapels, a church and several houses. They had to pull to one side to allow a fire engine to pass, again going the opposite way.

'I hope the chef hasn't burnt tonight's meal,' remarked Matt.

Eventually they saw a sign for Ewyn Môr Hotel only to find a road closed sign across the entrance to the drive. There was a light in the lodge next to the gate and a woman came out and approached the car bringing with her the smell of smoke that told them that the problem was more than a burnt dish.

'Mr and Mrs Harris? 'I'm Anwen Thomas, the manageress. I'm so sorry but we've had a terrible fire and the hotel is almost gutted. Such a beautiful building and it's nearly in ruins. The fire's out now but there's still a fire engine on stand-by.' She pointed up the drive but the hotel was out of sight. We've been trying to contact the guests who were arriving today but we couldn't get hold of you.'

Ellie guessed that as her parents had made the booking the contact number would have been theirs, and they were in

Chestnut Grove. 'I'm so sorry. How awful for all of you. Was anyone hurt?'

'No, luckily, but thank you for your concern. Not everyone has been that pleasant when they learned we had to cancel their bookings. As if we had a choice!'

'Have you any suggestions as to where we could stay tonight? We've had a long drive and we don't know the area at all.'

'Don't worry. I've been in touch with Mair who runs the Tŷ Gwyn pub in the village and she has a room for you.'

'Thank you for going to so much trouble on our behalf when you've had such an awful day.'

'Yes, it's been terrible. Huw and Bethan, the owners, have put so much into making it a lovely place, never mind spending a fortune. They're devastated. Anyway, you just need to turn around and go back to the village and the Tŷ Gwyn is on your right. Mair is expecting you.'

The drove back a couple of miles the way they had just come. The glow from the pub's windows looked even more inviting as they parked and went inside, to an empty bar. Wooden settles and assorted chairs waited for customers and a fire flickered in a huge stone fireplace at one end of the stone-flagged room. Brasses gleamed as did the glasses behind the bar. A tortoiseshell cat sitting as close as she could to the log fire blinked at them and flicked her tail once before returning her gaze to the flames. Matt rang the bell on the bar and a plump, middle-aged woman bustled through a door at the back.

'Hello,' she smiled. 'You must be Mr and Mrs Harris.'

'Yes, how did you know?' asked Ellie.

'Well, you're not local or I'd know you and you're the only two others I'm expecting tonight so *Croeso*, that's Welcome in Welsh, by the way.'

'Thank you. It's very kind of you to put us up at such short notice.'

'Not much call for rooms in Glanaber at this time of year,' she smiled wryly. 'We can't pretend to offer you the luxury of the Ewyn Môr but we'll do our best to make you comfortable for tonight, and even longer if you feel you want to stay. Now let me show you up to your room. I've lit a fire so it should be nice and warm.'

'That sounds lovely Mrs...?'

'Oh, call me Mair – everyone else does.'

'And we are Ellie and Matt.'

They followed her up the narrow stairs to a cosy room lit by the glowing coals in a small fireplace and two bedside lamps.

'Oh, it's lovely,' exclaimed Ellie, taking in a room that was far more elegant than she was expecting with a double bed covered by a Welsh wool blanket in tones of rust and red. Heavy red curtains covered the window and there was a matching rug on the dark polished floorboards.

'I'll leave you to get settled. I'll make a meal for about seven o'clock if that's all right.'

After she left, Ellie bounced on the bed. 'This seems comfortable enough.' She felt a little self-conscious. Matt had only recently returned to their bedroom from the spare room.

'I'm sorry you're missing out on your spa treatment for tonight – a massage wasn't it?' asked Matt. Ellie was about to say "You can do it instead" but she bit her lip. They were still a little shy with each other physically. That side of their marriage had yet to return.

After unpacking and showering in the tiny *en suite* they went down to the bar to be greeted by Mair. 'It's a bit chilly in the dining room so I've put a table over there for you.' She pointed to a corner by the fireplace where a table was set for two, romantically lit by a flickering candle. 'It'll be quiet tonight. Not like tomorrow. New Year's Eve is always busy here, being the only pub in the village.'

A few customers came into the bar as they ate, all of whom nodded in their direction or called out a greeting. Everyone seemed to know each other, and in this rural part of Wales they chatted to each other in their own language. When Ellie and Matt moved to the bar they switched to English to include them in their conversation. The main topic was the fire at the Ewyn Môr Hotel.

'I feel very sorry for Huw and Bethan,' said Mair. 'They've worked so hard to build up that business.'

'Well I suppose they had to do something with the old family home. Everyone knows that farming doesn't pay,' said one of the regulars.

'It's certainly in the right place for a luxury hotel with those views from the headland. With what they've put into it I hope they've got good insurance,' remarked someone else.

At half past eight the following morning a knock on the door awakened Ellie and Matt. As Ellie yawned and stretched, Matt opened the door to find a tea tray on the landing. After pouring Ellie a cup of tea he opened the curtains. 'Wow! Ellie, come and look at this.' She joined him to see a beautiful day and a stunning view. Across a field lay a stretch of golden sand with the sea glittering beyond. 'What do you want to do today? Do you want to go back home or shall we stay and explore the area?'

'Let's stay. It looks like a lovely place and no-one is expecting us back for another couple of days anyway.'

When they went down for breakfast Mair apologised if she had woken them up. 'I wasn't sure if you had a long journey to get back home.'

'Actually, we would like to stay for a couple more nights if you can put us up.'

'Of course, I'd be delighted. But I must warn you it might get a bit noisy tonight with it being New Year.'

After a hearty breakfast Mair asked 'Can I get you another *panad*?' They looked at her blankly. 'Oh!' she laughed 'It's what we say for a cup of tea – *cwpaned o de*.'

'That's one I'll have to remember,' smiled Ellie who was very partial to her cup of tea.

'What are you going to do with yourselves today?' asked Mair.

'We thought we'd go for a walk.'

'Would you like me to make you a picnic?'

'After that breakfast I don't think I can eat anything else today.'

'Well I hope you will. I can't make a meal for you tonight because every New Year's Eve I make food here for everyone. I make a big pot of *lob scows* to start with, then I serve bacon rolls, sausage rolls and sandwiches throughout the evening to keep everybody going 'til midnight. It's a kind of thank you for supporting us throughout the year. You're welcome to join us.'

'That's very kind of you. Thank you, we will.'

As they were setting off for their walk Mair called after them, 'Here you are, something to keep you going' and handed them a bag.

The cold, crisp air bit into their lungs as they took the path along the side of the field behind the pub – a shortcut to the beach, according to Mair. Eventually they reached the expanse of sand, gleaming so brightly it was almost colourless. They stood there taking in the beauty of their surroundings. The sky had been scoured clean of the previous day's clouds leaving it a beautiful clear blue. The sea sparkled, too lazy to send waves breaking on the shore, lapping it gently instead. There wasn't a soul to be seen anywhere.

They walked along leaving their footprints in the sand. 'Look,' said Ellie, 'all this empty space and only us and our footprints.' Like children they raced each other until they were out of breath. Matt picked up a stick and wrote in the sand 'I love you' surrounded by a heart. Ellie kissed him. 'I love you more than you'll ever know, Matt.'

Arm in arm they walked and chatted, pausing now and then to watch the noisy oystercatchers skimming the waves and the dunlins turning over the seaweed in their search for food. Occasionally Ellie bent down to pick up a particularly pretty shell. Matt found her a heart-shaped stone which she stored safely in her pocket. They clambered over rocks to reach a beach on the opposite headland from where they could see what they assumed were the blackened walls of the Ewyn Môr Hotel. Half the roof seemed to have fallen in.

'What a shame,' remarked Matt. 'I think it would cost a fortune to rebuild that.'

'I hope they do. It's in a lovely location and such a loss to the village according to everyone we spoke to last night.'

They had walked for some time and a breeze had blown in from the sea. They sat in the shelter of a rock to investigate the bag Mair had given them and enjoyed the snacks she had provided, surprised that they could be hungry after such a large breakfast.

The winter sun was low in the sky when they turned to walk back and the tide was on the way in, creeping over the sand.

'Look,' pointed out Ellie sadly, 'it's washing away our heart.'

Matt turned her towards him. 'Nothing can wash away the way I feel about you.' As he said it she hoped he was telling the truth.

'Did you enjoy your walk?' Mair greeted them from the bar as they entered. She was folding napkins around the cutlery. She introduced them to her daughter, Eira, who had been called into service for the busy evening ahead. She was a pleasant young woman of about thirty who would one day look exactly like her mother. 'I've lit a fire in your room and Eira's made some scones so I'll bring you up a *panad* in a minute.'

After the refreshments Ellie yawned. 'The fresh air has made me sleepy.'

'Why don't we have a lie down? It will be a late night tonight.' Matt, too, gave a yawn.

Slipping off their shoes they lay on the bed with Ellie in the crook of Matt's arm. He turned and kissed her. 'You taste of salt from the sea and butter from the scones. It's rather nice.' He kissed her again and she returned his kiss, gently running her fingers through his hair as his kisses became more demanding. She was a willing partner to his lovemaking and allowed Matt to set the pace but this was their first attempt at intimacy since the summer. Suddenly Matt stopped and turned his back to her, sobbing quietly. 'I'm sorry. It's just the thought of him with you.'

Ellie put her arms around him, 'Shh, it doesn't matter,' she soothed quietly. 'I love you.'

As she lay beside him with her own tears leaking out of the corners of her eyes she thought to herself about how much it did matter. How deeply she had hurt him. Would they ever get over this? They were trying so hard but they didn't fit together the same way any more. Their marriage felt like wearing shoes on the wrong feet.

When they went downstairs later that evening the bar was beginning to fill up. Mair had changed into a sparkling black top and presided over the bar offering glasses of mulled wine and the barman, busy pulling pints.

Matt and Ellie found an empty table and sat, gazing at each other. They each seemed so sad. Occasionally Matt stroked Ellie's arm and she squeezed his hand. Was this not only the end of 1987 but the end of the road for them?

Mair came over to speak to them. 'You look as if the sea air has done you the world of good.'

If only you knew, thought Ellie as she smiled back. 'We've had a wonderful day. This is such a lovely place and you've spoilt us too.'

The evening flew by. One or two people who had been in the bar the previous evening came over to chat. Mair served everyone her *lob scows* which was a tasty stew with meat and vegetables. Before they knew it Mair rang the large bell above the bar to call for silence and count in the midnight hour and to welcome in 1988. Cries of '*Blwyddyn Newydd Dda*' rang out which Ellie and Mair tried their best to reciprocate in the hope that they weren't murdering the Welsh language with their pronunciation. Kisses and handshakes were exchanged all round. A hush fell as one man started to sing and then others joined in, harmonising with each other. Even more joined in the chorus. They segued from one song to another. Although they couldn't understand the words Ellie was moved to by the beautiful singing and the very air seemed to vibrate with music.

They paused to fill their glasses after one lively song to which people clapped. Ellie asked Idris, to whom she had chatted during the evening, 'That was the most lovely sound I've ever heard but what were they singing?'

'A lot of the lads belong to the local male voice choir and they've won prizes in *eisteddfodau*. There was a bit of everything there but mostly hymns. Apart from that last one.'

'Yes, that seemed quite catchy. What was it about?'

'*Bys Meri Ann*? I don't know how to begin to translate it for you. It's a nonsense song, very popular in rugby matches and the like, about Meri Ann hurting her finger and... I give up!'

Moving to Matt, who was at the bar, Ellie watched Mair pull yet another pint.

'That's one thing I've never done,' she said. 'Is it as easy as it looks?'

'Come round and have a go.'

'Look everybody,' called out Idris. 'Ellie's pulling her first pint.'

Ellie felt her face flush as heads turned to watch. Holding the glass at completely the wrong angle she ended up with half a glass of beer and half a glass of froth.

'You've got a lot to learn, girl,' laughed Idris.

'Yes, I'll just stick to making a *panad*,' said Ellie with a grin, flaunting the one Welsh word she remembered and making him roar with laughter.

'*Duw, Duw*! I'm pleased to hear you've started learning the language of heaven,' he said.

When the party started to break up Ellie and Matt could barely keep their eyes open, they said goodbye to those who had made the evening so enjoyable and thanked them for including them in their festivities. 'Come back soon,' many of them said, and they hoped they would.

Despite the late night the couple woke early having slept well.

'Shall we go for an early morning walk?' asked Matt.

There was no sound as they went downstairs. Peeping into the bar they could see it was in chaos after the previous evening.

'Poor Mair must have been too tired to clear up. Shall we make a start? We can go for a walk later,' Ellie said.

After an hour, much of the shambles had been cleared. Mair rushed into the kitchen as Ellie was running another sinkful of hot water.

'Oh! I'm so sorry, I slept late. And you waiting for your breakfast.' She looked around and glanced into the bar. 'What have you been up to? You shouldn't have, you're guests here. I don't know what came over me. I'm usually up before seven and now it's nearly nine o'clock! Oh dear me!'

'We're happy to help. We had a lovely evening last night. No wonder you slept late, you were busy all day and on your feet for hours.'

'Well thank you very much. You've been life savers. I'll take over now and then I can start preparing our New Year lunch. Luckily Eira and I prepared all the veg last night and I'll get the turkey in the oven now. I've already cooked the ham.'

'Is there anything else we can do? We really are willing to help,' Matt assured her.

'If you don't mind then, I thought we'd put the tables together in the dining room for lunch. Can you do that and set the table for nine, that's Eira and Gareth and their three children, you two, Idris and me. By the time you've done that I'll have some tea and toast ready for you.' Mair turned back to the kitchen muttering 'Nine o'clock and no shape on me.'

Tasks completed and breakfast eaten, Ellie and Matt set off for a walk. The weather wasn't as good as it had been yesterday and the keen wind carried some rain. It stung their faces so they ended up just taking a brisk walk round the village. They passed one or two people who called out a greeting and Idris, walking on the opposite side of the road, called out laughingly, 'I'll have a pint Ellie.'

Returning to the Tŷ Gwyn, Mair insisted there was nothing they could do so they went up to their room. Ellie intended to read or watch television. She looked at Matt with a tinge of sorrow, knowing that at one time things would have been different when he turned the key in the lock.

Lunch was served mid-afternoon and it was a jolly affair with far too much to eat, crackers and games. Idris, a long-standing family friend, joined them as he did every year. Eira's husband, Gareth, was a pleasant but quiet man and their children were delightful. Matt and Ellie soon realised how much they were missing their boys.

After breakfast the following morning, with their bags packed and loaded into the boot, Ellie and Matt went to settle the bill and thank Mair for the warm welcome they'd been given.

'There isn't anything to pay,' she assured them. The Ewyn Môr told me to send them the bill.'

'But we've had so much more from you. There was the food on New Year's Eve and yesterday's lunch,' insisted Matt.

'You were here as our friends for that, not paying guests.'

Overwhelmed Ellie gave Mair a hug, mentally noting that she would send her a huge bouquet when she got home. 'I don't know how to thank you. We've had a wonderful time.'

'*Croeso*,' she replied. 'Just promise me one thing. You'll come again and bring those boys of yours.'

As they drove off waving to Mair, Ellie turned to Matt. 'Hasn't it been wonderful? Is all Wales like this or did we just find the friendliest, most magical part?'

Her heart lifted when Matt said, 'An ideal place to mark a new beginning.'

When she turned and smiled at him Matt felt awful. It was a silly thing to have said as he wasn't sure he meant it. He wanted to mean it and he had tried his best all weekend. Goodness knows, he had tried but he felt that he had been putting on an act because it was the right thing to do. Ellie had been considerate, loving and anxious to please but, deep down, the bitterness still filled his inside like bile burning his gut. He was fed up with feeling like this and often thought that it would have been better if they had separated immediately. Other people did and the world still turned, children adapted and life went on.

He had been telling the truth when he told Ellie that he had never slept with anyone but her but lately he had been thinking of it. His assistant, Amanda, had been openly flirting with him. He supposed she always had but he was more aware of it now. Why not take it further? What harm would it do? Ellie would know how it felt for a start. Would it make him feel any better if she felt as hurt and betrayed as he did? It would serve her right but she had tried so hard this weekend and, he had to admit, there had been flashes of how their life used to be and it had felt good. Was it enough for them to have a future together? If only she could tell him why she had done it. He sighed deeply.

'Are you okay?' Ellie asked putting her hand on his knee.

'Yes, just concentrating on my driving,' he replied abruptly.

He felt bad when she snatched her hand back and wondered if the magic of the weekend was wearing off already?

Chapter 20

Fiona was surprised to receive a phone call from Greg asking to see her. She assumed it was something to do with the divorce and arranged to meet him at an hotel in town, not wanting him in what she now thought of as her house.

She knew that Greg was puzzled at her agreement to a speedy divorce but it suited her. She wasn't about to tell him but she had met someone else. Greg might have thought she'd be broken-hearted when he left, but she was more angry at the humiliation than anything else. He had been no more than a means to an end, a change of lifestyle with a veneer of respectability and, of course, the money. He had done rather well for himself over the years. She had never loved him, not really, he had just been a way of escaping from fear. Their family image was based on nothing more than habit and convenience, more convenient that he knew.

She didn't love Alistair, her new man, either. But he would suit her and suit her nicely. He had been staying at the hotel where an event she had organised was taking place last autumn. At sixty he was older than her but she didn't care. He was a tall, good-looking man who carried his years well. She thought back to that evening with a smile.

'Would you do me the honour of having a drink with me,' he had asked?

He had seemed a little bit lost and hadn't mixed much with the others at the conference.

'I'd be delighted.'

She wouldn't be any good at her job if she didn't know that he was the owner of Peak's Engineering. After the initial niceties the conversation fell into a lull.

'Tell me about yourself.'

Alistair didn't need much encouragement. 'I lost my wife a year and a half ago and life just hasn't been the same since. She enjoyed this sort of function and she was good at mixing with people. Me – not so much.'

'Life's been difficult then.'

'Oh yes. I'd all but retired from the company and we hoped to have many happy years to enjoy ourselves but it wasn't to be.'

'Do you have any children?'

'No, we were never blessed with children, which was a source of pain for both of us but, as the years passed with no sign of babies, we got used to it to such an extent that we never did anything about finding out why. We'd bought a large house, hoping to provide a home for the family we wanted. It kept Margaret busy though.'

Fiona said nothing, allowing him to continue.

'My nephew, Andrew, runs the company now but he persuaded me to return to work in an advisory capacity to help me occupy my time.'

'I'm sure there's more to it than that. I would say that he values having you back at work.'

'You are kind. And so easy to talk to. I haven't spoken to anyone like this before.'

Fiona had taken his hand in both of hers. 'I'm honoured that you've shared your sadness with me. I know it isn't the same but since my husband left me, I've been so lonely too.'

The following morning there had been a note at reception from Alistair asking her to telephone him if she wanted to meet up again. Before agreeing she had made it her business to find out more about him and his company – and he was wealthy. If she'd thought Greg was doing all right then Alistair left him in the shade.

With Fiona's subtle encouragement their relationship had developed quickly. She could see that Alistair was close to his nieces and nephew. He told her that the girls, Audrey and Jane, did their best to look after him and were frequent visitors to his house. She was sure that none of his family expected that he would meet someone else, and certainly not as soon. Alistair told her hesitantly that they were all very concerned that, after knowing Fiona for barely a couple of months, he was spending so much time with her so he had insisted on taking them all out for a meal in order to introduce her. Fiona saw how the family felt about her as they had made it patently obvious but she totally ignored their thinly-veiled hostility and was charm itself.

She wanted the divorce from Greg to go through as quickly and as smoothly as possible so that she could be sure of hooking Alistair while he still found her so adorable. Fiona had introduced him to Ben and he seemed to be fond of him, if at a loss as to how to talk to a six-year-old child. He said the idea of becoming a stepfather appealed to him. Rather than tempt fate she had felt it better to keep them apart at this early stage of their relationship. It was for this reason that she had been happy to oblige Greg with as much access to Ben as he wanted, leaving her free to spend time with Alistair so that he would become more dependent on her.

Fiona arrived at the hotel a few minutes before Greg and was sitting in the lounge bar waiting for him. She watched as he walked across the room. He was still very handsome in his middle years. Meeting Alistair had swept away any bitterness she felt towards Greg; in fact by now, she felt he had done her a favour by leaving. Not that she was going to make things easy for him, she was determined not to be short-changed in the divorce.

He bent and kissed her cheek before sitting down and ordering them both a drink.

'What did you want to see me about? And I'm warning you that anything to do with the divorce is going through my solicitor.' Fiona laid her cards on the table straight away.

'No. It's nothing to do with the divorce. I'm happy to leave it in the hands of our solicitors and I'll be reasonable with you if you'll be reasonable with me. Let's face it, our marriage has been on its last legs for years so there's no need for any bitterness.'

'That's fine then. The sooner the better as far as I'm concerned. I'm so over you, Greg, you wouldn't believe. I couldn't be happier that you're with Charlie. Ben adores her which makes her all right by me and he loves spending time with you both.' She thought if she put it like that it would leave her more time to spend with Alistair. 'So, are you going to tell me why you wanted to meet up?'

'Actually it's Ben I'm worried about. You must have noticed that he's not looking well and he always seems so tired. I think he's even lost weight. I know he's growing but he looks quite skinny now. Do you think you should take him to the doctor?'

'Yes, I did think he wasn't looking well but I put it down to the divorce. He does know that we're divorcing but do you think there's more to it?'

'There could be, I don't know, but I don't think it's normal for a little boy to be as tired as he is. He always seems to have bruises on him.'

'What are you trying to say, that I'm doing something to hurt him?' She started to get to her feet.

'No, of course not, don't be ridiculous. Neither of us is that sort of parent.'

'He's a little boy, they play rough so they get bruises, I suppose, I haven't really noticed.'

'Yes, but Ben isn't really a rough and tumble kind of boy, is he?'

Fiona thought for a moment. 'Okay, I'll take him then but there's nothing stopping you doing it, you know. You are his father.'

'I don't mind at all. I just thought that you, as his mother, would prefer to take him.'

'All right. It's probably nothing, so I'll take him,' Fiona agreed, not wanting to appear uncaring.

They sat and finished their drinks agreeing that they would do their best to be civil in the divorce and to ensure that Ben would be their priority. Before leaving, Greg asked, 'You've still not heard anything from Gina then?'

'No, nothing. Not a word after she just upped and left. She merely sent that parcel to Ben at Christmas.' Fiona was dismissive.

'Aren't you worried about her?'

'Aren't you?'

'Well, yes, I am. I've asked the school if anyone there knows anything and they don't. I even asked an acquaintance of mine in the police and he said that, as she's over eighteen and seems to have left home willingly, there isn't a lot they can do. I even went to Liverpool one day. Silly really. It's a big city, I just wandered around the city centre as if I would bump into her.' He shrugged, 'Told you it was silly.'

'Gina's a survivor,' said Fiona. 'She'll be back when she's ready. I've always thought that.'

'I must say, I'm astounded at your complete lack of interest in her.'

'Are you really, have you ever wondered why?'

'What do you mean?'

Greg waited but Fiona bit her lip as if she regretted her comment – she clearly wasn't going to go any further.

'I admit I haven't been much better, you will let me know if she gets in touch?'

Chapter 21

Ben's health didn't improve over the next couple of days. In fact one of his teachers approached Charlie on one of the days that she picked him up to express her concern.

'He seems very tired, and some days he's a bit weepy. Of course, we make allowances because we know there are problems at home.'

'Thank you, we are aware of the situation and everyone's doing their best,' said Charlie, holding the little boy close. On the days that he was too tired to go to school, no-one insisted. The inevitable delays between seeing one doctor and being referred to another frustrated them all. Throughout everything Ben remained placid and uncomplaining, even laughing when his school trousers became so loose that they nearly fell off.

'Ooh!' said Charlie. 'I'm going to have to make another hole in your belt or everyone will see your dinosaur pants!' She hugged him close and despite the laughter of all three of them she exchanged an anguished look with Greg.

Whenever Fiona took him to one of his appointments she never seemed able to absorb any information she was given or ask questions. As a result it was usually Charlie or Greg who took him and they always tried to make it an event. Sometimes he would have a toy or at other times they would take him out to eat, although he was usually more interested in the complementary toy than the food.

It seemed that there was an appointment every week for a test of some kind or another. It saddened Charlie that Ben knew his way around the hospital, and the way he accepted that he was to have another blood test despite the fact that it hurt almost broke her heart.

A few weeks later, Greg and Fiona sat with the consultant who seemed to be too young to have so many letters after his name. He shook hands with them, shuffled his papers and cleared his throat. What was he about to say? That Ben was just a bit anaemic surely. They'd give him a better diet, and some vitamin supplements. There were some days when he was absolutely fine. All these things Greg wanted to say but the words seemed to have become stuck somewhere around his Adam's apple, making it difficult to swallow and impossible to speak.

What Mr Markham said about the outcome of the tests shocked them both. He told them that Ben was a very sick little boy. He used some long, unfamiliar words but the word leukaemia stood out. He told them about the various methods of treatment that were available among which was bone marrow donation. They sat, stunned, trying to absorb what had been said, shock turning into disbelief.

Fiona spoke first, 'But you can make him better, can't you?'

The consultant cleared his throat again and talked about the treatment that was available, the steps that needed to be taken and gave them statistics that they didn't understand. They might have heard the words but it was questionable as to what they had digested.

'Yes, but he will be all right, won't he?' Fiona insisted. Greg held her hand firmly.

Eventually, the consultant stood up. 'It has been a difficult morning for you both and I'm sure it hasn't been easy to take in everything I've said. I've made an appointment with the specialist nurse for you and she can go through it all again. She'll try and answer any questions you may have but if there's anything you want to talk to me about, give my secretary a ring and I'll see you as soon as I can.' He shook hands with them both.

After Greg and Fiona left his office and walked to the playroom where Charlie had taken Ben while they saw the consultant, they stood for a moment and watched through the window as he played with some cars. Fiona turned to Greg and wept. 'Precious little Ben, poor little baby,' she cried. 'Oh! Greg. What are we going to do? I can't cope.'

Greg gripped her shoulders and looked at her seriously. 'Fiona, you're going to have to. *We're* going to have to. I hated hearing what that doctor said as much as you did. I just wanted to punch him for saying those things about my little boy. We've got to do our best for him. It might be a long road to recovery but we'll be with him all the way. Charlie adores him and we'll both take care of him whenever you let us have him. At a time like this I don't think it matters about equal access.'

'You're right. And Charlie is fantastic with him. I know he likes coming to you and to his dog Growler. When Charlie took you on she didn't expect this, though.'

'I know she'll be terribly upset. Do you want us to take him home with us to give you some time to yourself?'

'Thanks,' she replied, thinking it would give her an opportunity to see Alistair as he would have to know.

Chapter 22

It was patently obvious to Charlie that the news Greg and Fiona had received from the consultant wasn't good. They both seemed to be in a trance and she could see that Fiona had been crying.

'Shall we go for a cup of tea?' she asked, but they both declined.

'Let's just go home, shall we?' said Greg putting on an artificially jolly voice as he bent down to Ben. 'Would you like to come back with us? Growler is waiting for you.'

Ben looked at them. 'Have you got a headache Mummy?' he asked

'Yes, a bit,' she replied.

'Maybe I'd better come home with you and look after you. Growler won't mind.'

She bent down and hugged him close, biting her lip but failing to stop the tears filling her eyes. 'No, it's okay. I'll have a glass of milk like you brought me the last time I had a headache and it made me better. You go with Dad and Charlie and I'll see you soon.'

Greg picked Ben up but he looked anxiously over his shoulder at his mother who was speaking to Charlie.

'Will you be all right?' Charlie asked.

'Yes. Thanks for taking him.'

'I do love having him with us, you know.'

The two women had a surprisingly cordial relationship. There was no competition between them for Greg's affections.

When they reached the car Charlie sat in the back with Ben. Greg's eyes caught hers in the rear view mirror and she knew what he had to tell her wasn't good, but there was time enough for that later. She was so glad that she had persuaded Greg to speak to Fiona about Ben's health. It had been apparent for some time that something was wrong. It was too convenient putting it down to the stress of the separation.

'Right, home, James,' she said

'... And don't spare the horses,' finished Ben with a giggle.

Back at the flat Ben was allowed to choose what he wanted to do and that was to watch his favourite video of *Jungle Book*, which was also a favourite of Charlie's, so they both sat cuddled together with a bag of sweets.

'But it's not Saturday!' said Ben referring to his weekly treat.

'Let's pretend it is, shall we?' smiled Charlie. 'Then I can have some too!'

They covered themselves with a fleece blanket with a pattern of paw prints about which Charlie had made up a story, saying that Growler must have got into a pot of paint when they were out and walked all over it.

'He wouldn't do that,' Ben giggled, knowing a fairy story when he heard one but still wanting to defend his Growler.

'Are you going to watch it with us?' Charlie asked Greg.

'I... er...' he drew his hands through his hair. 'Do you mind if I don't? I need to pop out for a while. I won't be long.'

At bedtime Ben jumped up and reached for his toy. 'Growler,' he said fondly. 'I've missed you. Have you been having lots of sleeps?' Growler had become a firm favourite and although Charlie had said he could take him back to Chestnut Grove he firmly refused, saying 'This is where Growler lives and he likes to wait for me to come here. He looks after me when I sleep so he sleeps when I'm not here.' And with that logic he tucked him under his arm and snuggled down into bed. Greg sat by the bed reading him a story, watching the little boy as his eyes flickered and he went to sleep.

Charlie sat by the fire and waited for Greg, sipping at her wine, reflecting on how her life had changed over the past months, since Greg had turned up on her doorstep on that August day.

Charlie had poured a glass of wine for Greg ready for when the bedtime story had put Ben to sleep. When he told her what had transpired at the hospital she put her arms around him.

'Oh! My darling, I'm so sorry. I've come to love Ben and I'll do whatever I can to help. I love you so much.' They looked at each other for a moment, stunned. It was the first time the love word had been mentioned in their relationship.

'Oh, Charlie. I love you too. I've known for a while but I've been afraid of saying anything in case I frightened you away but I've been close to saying it so many times.'

'So have I, but after Fiona, I thought you wouldn't want any commitment for a while.'

'Charlie, my darling. My lovely, lovely Charlie. I don't know what to say to you.'

'What do you mean?' she looked at him nervously.

'I'm afraid that everything that comes out of my mouth will sound corny. But I've never felt like this before. I'm a different person when I'm with you.'

'I know. I feel the same. I just want to be with you all the time.'

'I look at you and I wonder what a beautiful young woman like you sees in me.'

Charlie took hold of his hand and said, 'I just see a wonderful man whom I've fallen in love with. I didn't mean it to happen, it just sneaked up on me.'

'I'm not that wonderful you know. I've done things in the past that I'm not proud of, things I've never told anyone. But I just don't want you to have any illusions about me.'

'It sounds as if you've killed someone!' Charlie exclaimed.

'Good grief, no! I'm not that bad. Just business deals really when I haven't played fair. A few tax fiddles. I wasn't honest with Fiona about my finances. That sort of thing.'

He stood up and paced around the room, gulping his wine from time to time. Charlie watched him with a slight frown of anxiety. 'Where do we go from here Charlie? Is this too much and is it too soon?'

'Where do you want to go? We need to be completely straight with each other.'

He didn't re-join her on the sofa but sat on a chair. 'Okay,' he drew a deep breath and went on. 'I love you, Charlie. It's true what I said. I've never felt like this before. There have been other women, plenty of them, most of them while I've been married to Fiona – that should tell you a lot about me. In loving you as I do, there isn't another woman in the world I'd look at twice. I want to be near you all the time. Ideally I would like to marry you but I can't ask that of you. I'm too old for you and I have a son who is sick and a daughter I neglected and have hurt so badly that she's run away and cut off all contact. It's no more than I deserve. You're young and beautiful, inside as well as out. You deserve better, and more, than I can offer. There's a young man out there who can give you so much but he'll never love you more than I do.'

As he spoke Greg kept his eyes downcast, focussed on the empty wineglass. When he eventually finished speaking he looked at Charlie. She saw in his eyes such love, sadness and vulnerability that she was moved to tears. She knelt before him.

'Greg, lots of people have done things in their past that they're not proud of and the best thing you can do is to make things right wherever you can. You'll do the best you can for Ben. And as for Gina, we'll just have to hope that she'll get in touch soon and you can try to make amends. As for being too old for me, that's ridiculous. Yes, you are older but you're not geriatric for goodness' sake. And,' she continued with a coquettish smile, 'if you were to ask me to marry you, the answer might, just might, be a positive one. But if you don't ask you'll never know will you?'

'Do you mean it? Charlie I want to be your husband and I want you to be my wife. Please, please will you marry me?'

'Yes, my darling, I will. But I think we've got things a bit wrong somehow."

He was about to kiss her but he hesitated. 'Why?'

'Isn't it supposed to be you that gets down on one knee, not me down here on both!' Laughing he bent to kiss her.

'What will your parents say?' he asked her later.

'They'll be happy if I'm happy. And I am.'

'You know what people will say, don't you. They'll say you were looking for a father figure.' There was a hint of a question in his statement.

'I promise you, Greg,' she smiled at him, 'the last way in which I think of you is as a father.'

They spent the evening discussing plans for the future but the main decision that they'd made was that the champagne would be on hold for a while and no engagement announcement was to be made for the moment. Ben was their first priority for the coming months. It had been a day of the most amazing highs and the most heartbreaking lows.

Chapter 23

When Fiona rang Alistair she sounded so upset that he insisted that she went over to his house. Her distress was genuine as she told him of the conversation with the consultant and she was soothed by his strong arms around her.

'Tell me, what can I do? We can get a second and even a third opinion if you want. Money's no object.'

'I don't think there's any point. The consultant we saw is supposed to be ahead of the field according to our doctor. But thank you.'

'Why don't we get married then, as soon as possible, and you can both move in here? There's plenty of room for us to be able to hire a live-in nurse.'

'Oh! Alistair, that's so kind of you.'

'It's not the way I would have chosen to propose to you, my dear, but I've had it in mind for a while.'

'Nothing would make me happier. I'd be delighted to marry you,' smiled Fiona graciously. Despite her sadness about Ben there was a part of her that was saying "Yesss!"'

'I'm honoured. At least by blurting it out like that I've been spared the indignity of going down on one knee.'

'You do know that my divorce isn't final until the end of the month?'

'Shall we arrange things for as soon as we can after that? Will you have enough time to organise things? Get yourself a dress and all that?'

'Alistair, my job is to organise things! But I don't want a fancy wedding with lots of guests. Why don't we do it quietly, just the two of us?'

There was a slight hesitation before his reply. 'I would like to ask Audrey, Jane and Andrew and their families, they're all I have.'

'I don't have any family except Gina and Ben. It would make me feel awkward to have them there.' Fiona was thinking that she might as well start as she meant to go on and have as little as possible to do with his family. She had given him a heavily edited version of Gina leaving home, painting herself as the anxious, caring mother of an ungrateful, hippy child.

Alistair patted her hand, 'I know it's a great source of distress to you that your daughter ran away as she did and now you have this terrible burden of Ben's illness. So if it's a quiet wedding you want, that is what you shall have. We can always arrange a celebration dinner with the family afterwards.'

Fiona looked at him with apparent sincerity. 'Thank you Alistair. I know I'll never be able to fill Margaret's shoes and I wouldn't dream of trying, but I'll do my best to be a good wife to you.'

'And I'll endeavour to be a better husband than the rascal you had.' He kissed her cheek gently.

Fiona gave a deep sigh. Relief? Satisfaction? There was no way she was going to be the type of sainted wife Alistair had had previously. She knew that his nieces and nephew had their suspicions about her. There was a gap of over twenty years between them and they thought she was just after his money. They were right, thought Fiona. Tough. What could they do about it? The new Mrs Peak would do all she could to distance herself and her husband from them.

'Do you think we'll be able to fit in a few days for a nice honeymoon?'

'That would be lovely, Alistair. I'm sure we can. Greg and Charlie are more than willing to look after Ben any time.'

'I thought somewhere like Brixham would be nice. It's quite nice in late spring and it wouldn't take us long to get home if there was an emergency.'

'Oh...' Fiona was taken aback. Other places starting with B had been in her mind: Bermuda or Barbados. She didn't push it though, thinking it wiser to proceed with caution at this stage. 'You're so thoughtful, Alistair,' was all she said. For the moment.

Chapter 24

The shock of Ben's illness had a profound effect on everyone. It made everything else less important somehow. At least for some.

When Ellie answered her front door and saw Fiona standing there she was surprised, and then astonished, to hear her ask, 'May I come in?' Wordlessly she stood aside and Fiona stepped past her and headed for the kitchen as she used to do when they were friends about to have a gossip over a cup of tea. She stood there looking around the kitchen, which had once been so familiar to her, as if she had never seen it before. Ellie approached her tentatively.

'Fiona, is everything all right?'

To Ellie's amazement Fiona threw herself into her arms. 'Oh Ellie, it's so awful,' and burst into such sobs that her body shook. Ellie held her tightly, as she would if it was one of her children, and allowed her to cry. When the worst seemed to pass she ushered her into a chair at the table and, still saying nothing, handed her some kitchen paper towel and went to put the kettle on.

Pouring out two cups of tea, Fiona's black and weak with half a teaspoon of sugar, she went and sat at the table and waited for Fiona to speak.

'You remembered,' said Fiona, indicating her mug.

'Of course I remembered. The one with the lemon has always been yours and mine's the strawberry one.' Fiona had bought the two fruit decorated mugs years ago after dropping a tray and breaking some others. Ellie waited, both of them sipping their tea, Fiona shredding the paper towel.

'It's Ben,' she said eventually. 'He's got leukaemia.'

'Oh no!' Ellie's hand flew to her mouth and tears filled her eyes. 'I'm so sorry.' They sat in silence for a moment, Ellie thinking of Oscar and Hugo and imagining how she would feel if it was one of them. 'How bad is it?'

'To be honest, I'm still trying to take it in. But there's a good success rate with leukaemia in children, and we'll do everything to make sure he gets through it. They're looking at bone marrow donation among other things, and Greg and I are both going to be tested He's got such a lot ahead of him, poor baby. He has to have lots of tests over the next couple of weeks and he's staying with Greg. I'm no good with hospitals.'

'Poor little Ben. Is there anything we can do?'

'No, I don't think so. I... I just wanted to tell you.'

'Thank you. I'm glad you did. I appreciate it. I've known him since the day he was born.' Ellie reached over and squeezed Fiona's hand and Fiona held on to it. They sat there for a moment before Ellie said, 'Fiona, I'm really sorry... you know... about everything.'

'It doesn't matter. It isn't important now is it?'

'Not in the face of what you've just told me.'

'It's none of my business, I know, but what about you and Matt?'

Ellie smiled, 'We're getting there. At least I hope we are. I'm not sure sometimes. It hasn't been easy. He didn't deserve what I did to him – neither did you,' she hastened to add.

'It wasn't all your fault. Greg has always had a way with him. He could charm the birds from the trees. I was surprised because I thought you and Matt were rock solid.'

'So am I really. I had everything: a happy home and a husband who loved me and I love him. I'll never understand why I did what I did, and it was just the once, you know.'

'Yes, well, it's happened, it's in the past and we've all moved on.'

'There's no chance that you and Greg would get back together?' Ellie asked tentatively.

'No, none whatsoever. There wasn't much between us for years if I'm honest.' Fiona swirled the dregs of cold tea in the bottom of her mug. 'You know you were only one of many women, don't you?' Ellie flinched at the dig. 'You did me a favour in the end. We're having a quick divorce, it will be through any day now.'

Ellie sat there in silence. What could she say? She watched as Fiona fiddled with her mug. She started to say something else, took a deep breath, then hesitated as if she had changed her mind. Instead, she put her cup down firmly.

'I must go,' she said but remained seated for a moment, as if still within two minds whether to tell Ellie something.

Ellie waited for a while and then asked, 'How's Gina?' This broke the spell and Fiona immediately rose to her feet.

'She's in Liverpool and she's fine,' she replied brusquely.

'Perhaps you could let me have her address. Tom's always asking after her and I think he'd like to get in touch. He's always had a soft spot for her.'

They walked across the hall and Ellie opened the front door. The two erstwhile friends stood and looked at each other for a moment.

'Don't forget, if there's anything we can do to help with Ben, you know where we are.'

This brought tears to Fiona's eyes again. 'By the way,' she said. 'I'm selling the house and moving away.'

In a way Ellie was relieved but didn't allow her feelings to show. Her guilt made her wary of bumping into Greg when he came to collect Ben and seeing Fiona, even occasionally, always made her feel uncomfortable.

'Where are you moving to?'

'Not too far away.'

'You must let me have your new address.'

'Yes, of course. I'll send it to you,' replied Fiona as she turned to leave. She walked down the drive without looking back.

Ellie closed the door quietly behind her and knowing that she never would.

Chapter 25

A fortnight or so passed during which Ben underwent a battery of tests, none of which had been pleasant. Both Greg and Charlie had been with him every step of the way, and if Ben noticed that his mother wasn't there, he said nothing. The process was helped by the fact that he had made friends with a nurse who singled him out for special attention. Her name was Daisy, and Ben now spent his time drawing pictures of the flower which he proudly presented to her.

The day of the appointment with Mr Markham, the consultant, was one which they all anticipated with hope and fear. Fiona waited outside his office and when he opened the door to usher her inside she hesitated, 'There's no sign of Ben's father yet. He'll be here soon, I'm sure.'

'I'm sure he will, but do please come in. It will give us a moment for a little chat. As you know we have been looking for a bone marrow match for Ben.'

At the hospital, Greg was driving around the car park in frustration. There wasn't a single parking space to be found. He banged the steering wheel in annoyance when he saw one car so badly parked that it had taken up two spaces. Up and down the rows he went and when a car got to the only empty space before him he jumped out to plead with the driver to let him have it.

'Sorry, mate,' said the young man, helping a very pregnant woman out of the car. We think the baby might be coming. It's our first one so we're a bit nervous.'

'Good luck,' he replied and returned to the car to continue his search.

Eventually, later than the appointed time Greg arrived outside Mr Markham's office, hot, sticky and out of breath after having jogged from the furthest point of the car park.

'I'm so sorry I'm late. I just couldn't find anywhere to park,' he told the nurse.

'I'll take you along now,' she smiled. 'Your wife is already there.'

He once again started to apologise for his lateness but the consultant brushing them off. He sensed the tension in the room. Fiona stood with her back to him looking out of the window. Reading her body language Greg knew straight away that something was wrong.

'What is it?'

'We haven't discussed anything in depth at the moment, just in general terms.' Mr Markham glanced at Fiona as he spoke. 'I'm afraid Mrs Clark wasn't a match for Ben.'

'What about my test? Am I a match for him?' asked Greg anxiously.

Mr Markham seemed to fidget uncomfortably. 'I'm afraid not,' he said quietly.

Fiona still hadn't turned away from the window.

'But why?' Greg searched his mind for valid reasons for the doctor's obvious discomfort. 'Is there something wrong with me? Surely one of us must be suitable.'

There was silence for a moment and then, 'Oh, for Pete's sake, you might as well tell him.'

Greg was bewildered. 'Tell me what? Why can't you use my bone marrow? I am his father after all.'

At last Fiona turned to face him. 'That's just it. You're not!'

'What?' Greg sat there in shock. 'What are you talking about? Of course I'm his father!'

'Well it seems you aren't.'

Greg stared at her trying to swallow but his tongue seemed to have stuck to the roof of his mouth. Mr Markham poured him a glass of water and addressed both of them.

'I'll leave you for a while to give you some privacy to talk. I'll be back in ten minutes.'

Greg sat looking at Fiona who was leaning against the windowsill with her arms folded. The silence in the room made the noises from the corridor seem loud: footsteps going past, voices exchanging greetings and the distant ringing of a telephone.

'I'm not Ben's father?' Greg whispered eventually.

'Apparently not.'

'Have you always known?'

'It's come as much of a surprise to me as it has to you.'

'I can scarcely believe that. You're the one who was sleeping around.'

'Well how about that, Greg! What's sauce for the goose is sauce for the gander. Just think about it. How am I so different from you? I just got pregnant, that's all.'

'That's all? That's all! I can't believe you've just said that. All these years and you've let me think that he's my little boy. Who is the father?' Fiona hesitated and that was enough for Greg. 'You don't know do you?'

Her protestations were weak. 'Of course I know, but we're not in touch.'

At the time of his conception, she had organised a successful conference at a large hotel for a group of salesmen. The managing director had been grateful and insisted on buying her a drink that evening. Several drinks later she had ended up in bed with him before he left to return home to his wife and family the following day. Fiona had some loose ends to tidy up so it was much later in the afternoon before she was ready to leave. Unfortunately her car wouldn't start so she had to spend another night in the hotel. During the evening she was sitting in the bar when she met another man and spent the night with him. All these years later she couldn't remember their faces, let alone their names.

Greg put his face in his hands and then suddenly got to his feet. He walked up to Fiona, his fists clenched at his sides. Fiona tried to recoil but he stood right in front of her, his face close to hers. 'Ben IS my little boy and he always will be my little boy and if you ever, EVER, say anything different I'll sue you for any money you've got and I'll make sure everyone knows what a slut you are.'

Mr Markham entered the room and cleared his throat. Greg turned and went back to sit in his chair and said, 'I know that you are bound by patient confidentiality and I'm sure that extends to the family of patients. What has been said in this room is to remain in this room and no-one else is to know about it – ever. I am Ben's father and I always will be. It is my name that is on his birth certificate and my partner and I intend to be his primary carers. I doubt if my ex-wife will have any objections.' He turned to Fiona with a raised eyebrow.

'No, none at all. I'm quite happy for Greg and Charlie to look after Ben as long as I have as much access to him as I want.'

Mr Markham nodded and opened the file in front of him, going on to detail the steps that were to be taken to treat Ben. Eventually he stood up and said, 'Don't forget, you know where to find me if you have any further questions.'

He shook hands with them both, 'Good afternoon, Mr Clark, Mrs Clark.'

'It isn't Mrs Clark,' smiled Fiona smugly. 'It's Mrs Peak.' Then she turned and stalked out of the room.

Chapter 26

Greg went down to the children's ward after seeing Mr Markham. Ben was lying in bed with Charlie sitting by his side.

'Greg, are you ok?'

He reached over and cupped her cheek briefly while gazing at Ben.

'Hello, son,' he said gently bending down to hug him. He held him for so long that Ben began to struggle.

'Daddy, you're squashing me.'

'I'm sorry.' Greg ran his hands over Ben's face and the hair that was becoming thinner due to the treatment. He took in his soft brown eyes, the dimple on his chin, his little round nose, none of these features reflected in his own he thought sadly.

'Are you tired, Ben?' he asked.

'Yes. Charlie was reading me a sleepy time story and you came and made me awake.'

'Okay. I'm sorry about that. I'll tell you what I'm going to do. I think Charlie needs a bath because she's a bit smelly, isn't she?' Ben laughed at Charlie's shocked expression. 'So,' Greg went on, 'I'm going to take her home so she can have a nice bath and change her clothes and we'll come back later. You can have a little sleep while we're gone. I'll ask Daisy to keep an eye on you. Is that okay with you?'

'Yes.' When Charlie gave him a kiss he whispered in her ear, 'You're not really smelly.'

Greg didn't say a word as they walked out of the hospital and when they reached her car she could see how distressed he was and insisted that he leave his car until later.

'Yes, let's just go home,' he said.

The flat smelt stuffy so Greg opened a window while Charlie sat on the sofa and waited. Eventually he spoke the last words that Charlie expected to hear. 'Ben isn't my son.' He went on to relate all that had happened earlier that afternoon. Charlie took him in her arms and held him.

'It doesn't matter that he's not yours. He isn't mine either and I've known him less than a year but I love him so very much.'

'I know you do. As far as I'm concerned he is mine, my precious little boy and I've made that clear to Fiona and the consultant. No-one else need ever know.'

'Oh, Greg, my love. I'm sorry this has happened on top of everything else. I don't know what to say to you.'

'You don't need to say anything. You're a better mother to Ben than Fiona could ever be. You really are the best thing that's ever happened to me.'

She kissed him. 'You look tired. Why don't you go and have a lie down while I go and make myself less smelly in the bath,' she smiled.

Later, wrapped up in a towel, she went to the bedroom to find Greg fast asleep. She slid onto the bed quietly trying not to disturb him but he sensed her presence and turned towards her, stroking her soft, sweetly-scented skin, seeking solace in her comfort.

After they had made love Charlie whispered to him, 'One day, darling, I'll give you a son... or a daughter... or both. I can't wait for us to have a baby of our own.'

Greg held her at arm's length and studied her face. 'Do you mean that? I thought you were an out and out career girl?'

'So did I until you came into my life. You and dear little Ben. You've turned me into a maternal time bomb. I keep looking at little babies and smiling and I used to think they were smelly, noisy things.'

'I think you'll find that they do have those characteristics.'

'Even at work, there's nothing I like better when a customer comes in wanting us to design a nursery. I snatch that kind of work out from under the other designers. I can't get over myself!'

'You don't think I'm too old to be a father?'

'Not at all, silly. My father was older than you when I was born but he was born old in his ways. You'll be a fantastic father.'

'I haven't got a great track record though, have I?' he said, thinking of Gina.

'Well, I'll be here this time and we'll help each other to be the best parents a child could have. Neither of us has been shown the best examples of good parenting have we?'

'It will be lovely for Ben to have a little brother or sister. We'll be such a happy family. As soon as Ben is on the mend I want us to get married. I want to be able to call you my wife and I want to be your husband. I want us to belong together for ever.' Charlie squirmed with pleasure at the thought. 'By the way, I forgot to tell you, Fiona landed me with another bombshell this afternoon. She certainly doesn't do things by halves. Apparently she's got married.'

'Married?' Charlie sat up in bed and leaned over to look at his face. 'That was quick. Who's the lucky man?' she asked with irony.

'Somebody called Mr Peak, it seems. I don't know any more than that.' Greg's hand was drawn to Charlie's pert breast which was inches from his face. She slapped it away reluctantly.

'Darling, much as I'd love to, we must go back to the hospital. I'll take a rain check as the Americans say.'

'You're right. Ben could end up having another sibling sooner than we thought!'

Chapter 27

Fiona wasn't concentrating on her driving and she caught the wing of her car at the hospital exit resulting in a nasty scrape. 'Damn,' she muttered and then brightened at the thought that Alistair might buy her a new car. He hadn't been over-generous so far but it was early days. They'd only been married for a fortnight or so, after all.

The wedding had been a quiet affair as they'd agreed, albeit reluctantly on Alistair's part. He had insisted on taking his nephew and nieces and their families out for a meal the day after. When he announced that he had married Fiona their faces were a picture. Fiona smiled at the thought. Poor Alistair had looked round them, smiling nervously, as he took in the stunned silence that took the place of congratulations. Fiona sat at his side and tried not to look like the cat who had the cream and, as she looked at them in turn and they looked back at her, they all knew that things were about to change.

It had taken a few moments for Andrew, his nephew, to recover from the shock but he had, with a thin veneer of graciousness, stood to make a toast.

'Uncle Alistair, you are a man of surprises and you've certainly surprised us today. On behalf of us all may I welcome Fiona to the family. Fiona, I hope you will make our much-loved uncle as happy as he deserves to be. To the bride and groom.'

As a welcoming speech it left a lot to be desired but Fiona didn't care. Everyone raised their glasses and if the echoing 'To the bride and groom' appeared half-hearted it was enough for Alistair and he rubbed his hands with delight. Andrew's sisters, Audrey and Jane, exchanged glances with each other and looked at Fiona with stiff smiles on their faces. Fiona smiled back at them, their smiles speaking a language that only women understood.

After that, Alistair had whisked her away for a honeymoon. They had both had their wish of a destination beginning with the letter 'B' even if it wasn't the one either of them wanted. Brighton had been pleasant enough and they had enjoyed the luxury of a suite at the Grand Hotel. The physical side had been better than Fiona expected, even though Alistair was apologetic about his efforts. He was an enthusiastic lover and she would soon teach him how to please her. The week had flown by as they spent time wandering the Lanes, walking along the promenade and pier as they got to know each other better. After all, they had been strangers five months ago.

As she drove home Fiona's thoughts returned to Mr Markham's office. If Greg had washed his hands of Ben she didn't know how she would have coped. She was no good with illness. When she had uttered the words 'in sickness and in health' during her wedding vows her fingers had been crossed. If Greg and Charlie were happy to take responsibility for Ben, she was content to let them. Obviously she would visit as often as she could. She loved her son, she really did. But maybe she loved herself more.

Fiona turned into the gateway of her new home. 'Home', she gave a contented sigh. Would she ever get used to this tree-lined drive which turned at the last minute to reveal the beautiful house that stood before her. She frowned when she saw Audrey's car parked at the side. This was something she was going to have to sort out soon. These visits. Couldn't they see that Alistair didn't need them calling all the time now that he had her. Fiona had wandered in after a stroll round the grounds with Alistair the other day to find Audrey in the kitchen boiling the kettle. She'd brought them a cake and had let herself in.

Alistair and Audrey were chatting in the sitting room when Fiona entered. He got up and asked anxiously, 'How did you get on?'

She smiled but her voice wobbled with genuine emotion as she told him what was ahead of Ben.

'I bet he was pleased to see you?' he asked.

'To be perfectly honest I didn't go down to the ward. I was so upset and I didn't want him to see me like that. Charlie was with him anyway. I suppose it's easier for her because she isn't his mother. I'll go tomorrow. By then I'll have had time to clear my head.'

It was obvious from her smeared make-up that she had been crying and Audrey seemed to make an effort to be more friendly. After all, they were married now. She, too, got to her feet and went over to Fiona. Holding Fiona's hand in both of hers she said, 'I'm so sorry about your little boy's illness. I don't know how I'd cope if it was one of my children. They can do so much these days though, can't they. I'm sure he'll pull through in the end. I'm looking forward to meeting Ben. You will let us know when you bring him home won't you, so that we can come and see him?'

'Thank you. That's really kind of you. Alistair has been so kind as well.'

'Well, he's my stepson isn't he?' said Alistair. 'I'm looking forward to getting to know him properly. I might even have to start practising some of my football moves. As you know Margaret and I couldn't have children but I've always wanted a son and now I have one.'

The devil must have been sitting on Fiona's shoulder because she couldn't resist saying, 'There's nothing stopping us having a son if you would like us to try for a child.' The shocked look of horror on Audrey's face was something that would bring a smile to Fiona's face for many a day.

'Well that's a thought isn't it.' Fiona felt a bit guilty at Alistair's obvious delight at the idea. The chances of her having any more children were non-existent, she'd make sure of that. Still smiling Alistair said, 'I'll come with you tomorrow to see Ben. We can stop off on the way and buy him a super present.'

As Audrey took her leave Fiona walked with her to the car on the pretext that she had left something in her own car. When Alistair had turned to go back inside Fiona asked Audrey, 'I wonder if you would mind giving me your key. I've lost mine.'

'I'm sure Alistair will cut you another one,' replied Audrey.

'Yes, but I'm afraid I've been a bit silly. It was in a little leather key holder and the address was inside so I'm going to have to get the lock changed in case anyone breaks in. At my cost of course. I don't want Alistair to know until it's all done because I don't want him to think he's married someone so careless.

'Oh. Of course,' Audrey hesitated and removed the key from her key ring. 'If you wouldn't mind, I'd be grateful if you could let us have a new key. It's handy to be able to drop in on Uncle Alistair and he never hears the bell in this great big house.'

Fiona smiled and Audrey reached over to give her a hug. 'Remember what I said about meeting Ben. Good luck with his treatment.'

Fiona held herself stiffly and patted Audrey's back. 'Thank you.'

She stood on the drive, watching her drive away, a half smile on her face, hoping that Audrey hadn't noticed the leather key holder on the hall table.

Chapter 28

Ellie lay in bed pretending to be asleep and preparing herself for the surprised expression she would need when Matt and the boys came in. It would be any minute now, judging from the loud stage whispers and rattle of crockery on the landing.

'Wake up. Happy birthday.'

'Mummy. Come on, we've made breakfast for you.'

The surprised look must have been convincing because Hugo remarked, 'You are a sleepyhead. We've been up for ages.'

'I went to the garden to pick a rose to put on your tray but it stung me and there was blood,' Oscar complained dramatically thrusting his finger in Ellie's face.

'Yes, he's right,' said Matt. 'We almost needed a magnifying glass to see it.'

'Let me kiss it better,' she grinned, searching in vain for any visible sign of injury. 'This is a lovely surprise,' she went on, looking at the tray set nicely with fruit juice, tea, a mountain of toast and the offending rosebud in its little vase. 'I'm never going to be able to eat all this toast though.'

'It's all right. We'll help you,' assured Oscar.

Matt gave her a wink and she recalled the last time they had brought her breakfast in bed with two slices of toast: the twins had eaten one each.

'We've got presents for you,' Oscar said handing over a parcel. He was as useless as ever at keeping a secret and as Ellie was opening it he said, 'It's bubble bath.'

'Oscar, you aren't supposed to say what it is. It's a surprise,' Hugo told him crossly.

'Thank you very much. It's my favourite.'

Hugo then handed over his gift. 'This is from me and I helped Daddy choose it.' Before Ellie had a chance to open it, he whispered, 'It's soap,' making both his parents laugh.

'Thank you, boys. You are very kind. I'm looking forward to having a lovely soak in the bath with these thoughtful presents.'

The boys had lost interest by now, seemingly mystified as to why someone would enjoy having a bath; something to be endured, and quite unnecessary most of the time, as far as they were concerned. They sat on the bed and tucked into the toast waiting to see their dad's present.

Ellie opened her cards first. 'I could do without the number being displayed so prominently,' she grimaced.

'Don't worry, you don't look it and you know what they say. Life begins and all that.'

Matt handed over his beautifully-wrapped gift, 'Happy birthday.'

'Ooh, this looks interesting,' she smiled. 'Jewellery perhaps?' When she opened it, the box contained a lovely little golden Welsh dragon on a chain.

'Oh darling, this is beautiful. Thank you so much.'

'I believe it's made with a touch of Welsh gold.' Matt bent to kiss her and handed her an envelope. 'That's not all.'

She squealed with delight when she opened it. Matt had booked for the family to stay at the Tŷ Gwyn, Glanaber for five nights, leaving the following week which was half term. 'How wonderful. Oh, I can't believe it. Guess what, boys, we're going to have such a good time. Is Will coming too?'

'Yes. We're only going for five days because his exams aren't quite over yet and he needs to revise.'

As if on cue Will came in, yawning and hair on end. 'Do birthdays need to start this early? Happy birthday, Mum,' he said bending to kiss her cheek as he handed over his present.

'Thank you, sweetheart.' Upon opening it she found a box of her favourite truffle chocolates. 'Ooh, yummy. I love these.'

'You could open them now if you wanted,' said Oscar hopefully.

'No, indeed I'm not, they're mine.'

'Yes, but it's nice to share.' He echoed the words she had said to him so many times when he was reluctant to give his twin his fair share of sweets.

'Touché son, touché,' she muttered quietly.

It was a beautiful day when they drove into Glanaber village. The sky was even bluer than on their previous visit six months ago and, obviously, it was much warmer as was the atmosphere between Ellie and Matt. It was ten months since that awful August day last year and they were slowly crawling their way back to a partnership of sorts. It would never be the same; they would never be the same. They were different people now. More tolerant, more forgiving, able to put petty problems into perspective now that they had faced the ultimate test.

'I just wish Tom could have been with us too,' sighed Ellie. 'He would love it here.'

The pub looked lovely; white walls dazzled in the sunshine, hanging baskets and tubs of flowers stood either side of the heavy oak front door which stood open in welcome. As soon as the car stopped Mair came out to greet them.

'*Croeso*. How nice to see you again.' She gave Ellie and Matt a hug. 'And who are these young men?' She shook hands with the boys. 'Goodness me, you don't look old enough to have big boys like this.' She looked up at Will who was taller than her. 'Come on in. I've got a *panad* waiting for you.'

Will raised a quizzical eyebrow at his mother who patted his arm. 'Don't worry. You'll learn.'

Later, they were about to unpack but the boys couldn't wait to go down to the sea.

'You go with them, Matt. I'll do the unpacking and follow you.' It felt odd to be sharing a room with Matt again. Neither of them had made any comment when they were given the same room as they had over the New Year. When they returned home Ellie expected and hoped that Matt would move back into their room from the spare room but he didn't. She was disappointed as a double bed for one was the loneliest place in the world. In the ten months since that awful night they had built up their friendship but they had yet to sleep together as man and wife. She wasn't sure how Matt felt about her and she often thought that he was simply marking time in their marriage, waiting for the children to grow, waiting for something better to come along or waiting to see if she was serious about wanting to make a go of things. Whatever the reason, she would wait. She'd wait for the rest of her life hoping that Matt would love her again. He still had periods where he tortured himself by asking her again and again why she did what she did. When she had said simply 'lust, I suppose' he became angry. He seemed to want a deeper reason. During one argument she had snapped back at him

'Because I was bored, I suppose. Bored with being Mrs Perfect living the perfect life, looking after you and the boys. We married young and I never had the chance to be me. To find out who I really am. To know what it's like to have sex with other people.'

'Well I'm very sorry that, in my attempts to be a good husband and provide you with a happy family life, that it wasn't enough for you,' he said sadly.

Her answer seemed to satisfy him. It gave him a reason. She wasn't even aware of having felt like that, wasn't even sure if it was true. But it seemed to have helped Matt come to terms with it and things had improved between them. She was astonished that he had arranged this holiday and she was determined to make it the happiest that she could.

As she passed through the bar on her way out Ellie called over to Mair, 'How's Idris? Is he around?'

'Erm, no. He's gone to fetch a parcel from town,' she replied turning away.

A couple of hours later they returned to the Tŷ Gwyn, bright-eyed and rosy-cheeked after the fresh sea air. The twins had managed to get sand everywhere and the bottoms of their jeans were wet after they had insisted on going for a paddle. Ellie was taking them straight upstairs when Mair called from the bar.

'Can you spare a minute, Ellie?'

She stepped inside and gasped with surprise, 'Tom!'

'Hello, Mum. A belated happy birthday!'

She ran over to him and he hugged her and swung her around. 'Oh! This makes everything just perfect.'

Amid the greetings Matt went over to Idris and shook his hand. 'Thanks, Idris, I appreciate your help.'

'You mean Tom is the parcel you had to pick up from town? What a lovely birthday this is.'

'Many happy returns,' said Idris. 'You're looking good for fifty, girl!'

'You cheeky thing, I'm only forty,' she laughed.

'It's forty you are, is it? Mair wouldn't tell me. I know now though. You've given the game away,' he said chuckling into his pint.

The days they spent in Glanaber were idyllic, with exceptionally warm weather for early June and blue skies every day. Mair supplied all the paraphernalia for long days on the beach and they set off each morning with chairs, windbreaks, buckets, spades and, most important of all, a picnic. Each one a feast; Mair didn't consider a pack of sandwiches as good enough so, in addition, there were pies and pasties, sometimes a flask of soup, as well as cakes, biscuits and juicy, crunchy apples. When they set off every morning Matt complained about the weight of all he had to carry and swore they would never eat much after their huge breakfast but, when they trudged back at the end of each day, the picnic bag was always empty.

The boys swam in the sea, Tom and Will taking great care of the twins. They played cricket and made sandcastles, some of which were quite spectacular when Oscar and Hugo were able to persuade Tom and Will to help. They studied the wonders of the rock pools, watched the sea anemones open and close their fronds and found crabs under seaweed. They ran races across the hard sand but, strangely enough, it was always Oscar and Hugo who won, the others mysteriously running out of puff before the finishing line! Idris had arranged for Tom and Will to have a wind-surfing lesson and they were soon able to get their balance and make hesitant progress across the waves. They walked along the coast and were pleased to see that the Ewyn Môr was being rebuilt bringing employment to the locality. Will spent a lot of his time snapping away with the new camera he had received on his recent seventeenth birthday. As they returned to the Tŷ Gwyn at the end of the afternoon Oscar and Hugo were worn out and Tom and Will gave each a piggy-back.

Ellie bathed the twins' sand-dusted little bodies while Mair made an early meal for them. Worn out by fresh sea air, sunshine and constant activity, they were ready for bed by about seven o'clock. This meant that Ellie and Matt could enjoy their evening meal in the company of their two older boys. In an atmosphere of comfortable relaxation the boys opened up to each other and their parents about what was going on in their lives, and even shared some of their hopes and dreams. It was clear that there was a strong bond between the brothers as Ellie and Matt listened to them chatting.

'I'm really enjoying the course and I'm so pleased I chose Durham. I love it there. I wouldn't mind settling down in that area one day. What about you Will, are you any nearer in deciding what you want to do?'

'I want to study Geography. I know I've got another year at school, but I'm not sure if I'll go to uni straight away or take a gap year first.'

This came as a surprise to Ellie and Matt as he had never mentioned it before. Her stomach flipped at the thought of her little boy, now a young man, going off on his own but she smiled and covered his hand with hers.

'That sounds so exciting,' she said.

Ellie couldn't believe the change in Matt; he seemed to want to be with her and he gave her little hugs and pecks on the cheek. When they were walking he sought her hand. She wondered at first if it was for Tom's sake but didn't think so. At one point on the beach he kissed her long and deeply until she felt weak and breathless. Taking his hands she looked into his eyes and convinced herself that she saw love. Tom broke the moment by taking Hugo's little bucket and, much to the delight of the little ones, threw water over them warning them laughingly, 'Not in front of your four children!'

All too soon the holiday was over and as they lay in bed on the last night Ellie reached over and kissed Matt gently. He held her in the crook of his arm.

'Thank you for this birthday present. It's the best I've ever had. Being here with you and the children has been wonderful.'

'It has, hasn't it, I'm glad it made you happy.'

'Are you? Happy I mean.'

'Yes, I am, I really am.'

He kissed her forehead, before kissing the rest of her face until he reached her lips. The soft, sweet kiss soon turned deeper and more passionate. His hands moved over her body which willingly responded to him. Feelings which were familiar, and yet new, swept through her. How could she feel this nervous with her husband of almost twenty years but she was afraid of going too far in view of what happened last time, in this very bed. But when she felt him tug at her nightdress, she took it off in seconds. She felt as if her body was on fire as his lips roamed all over it. Their lovemaking made her feel lighter and joyous, as if it had washed away the pain of the past several months. She dared to hope that there was a better future for them. That night they slept wrapped in each other's arms and when Ellie stirred the next morning she found him leaning on one elbow watching her struggle from sleep to snuggle closer to him. The knowledge that they had to get up in order to go back home didn't prevent them from making love again, giggling as they ignored calls of 'Get up, you sleepyheads!'

Glanaber had cast its magic again and it was a happy, united family that said their goodbyes to Mair. Will asked Idris if he would take a photo of them all outside the Tŷ Gwyn. After much ceremony, rearranging positions and ensuring everyone was in the frame, Idris announced that he was ready to take the photo – and pushed the wrong button. Amid the ensuing laughter he found the right one resulting in a natural happy photo and Will promised that he'd send them a copy. Tom stood with Mair and Idris to wave everyone off because Idris was taking him to catch a train later.

Ellie turned back to wave once again, a smile on her face. She knew she would come back again to this wonderful place.

Chapter 29

Charlie had put her work on hold for the moment. She wanted to concentrate on being available for Ben. That wasn't to say that she was abandoning the studio completely. She had worked too hard to get where she was today to let things slide. She entrusted the day to day running of the business to her staff. As well as being colleagues they had become friends and the company was as important to them as it was to her.

Charlie also wanted to be available for Greg. He wasn't coping well with Ben's illness and he was torn between wanting to be with him and hating having to watch him suffer. He was often reduced to tears when Ben complained of pain and when he was sick. They went constantly to and from the hospital and, during the periods when Ben was an in-patient, Charlie chased Greg to the garage, where his mind could be occupied with other things.

'Are you sure it's OK for me to go to the garage for a while? I'm not as lucky as you are with being able to leave things to the staff, even though they're quite good.'

'Of course it is. I'm here, aren't I, and I'll call you immediately if I think it's necessary.'

'I wish I didn't have to go to Germany for that meeting. I might put that off.'

Fiona continued to play a part in Ben's care, even if it was a small one, but it suited them all. Charlie felt sorry for her in a way, as she was obviously an inadequate mother, despite her love for Ben. She didn't seem to know how to behave with a sick child and vacillated between impatience with his illness and overbearing kindness.

By now Charlie and Greg had met Fiona's new husband, Alistair. He seemed pleasant enough and they could see how besotted he was with Fiona. It was clear that he was completely unused to children by the way he treated Ben with a false heartiness. Whenever he and Fiona came to the hospital they brought expensive toys in which Ben showed little interest. In the end, there were so many that Charlie asked if they could be donated to the ward where all the children could play with them.

Greg tried to avoid visiting at the same time as Fiona. Although they were civil with each other his resentment of her ran deep. If she was at the hospital when Fiona arrived Charlie normally left to give mother and son time together. She was acutely aware that she was not Ben's mother even though she was devoted to him. Some of the hospital staff had made that mistake more than once and, to make things easier for everyone, both Fiona and Greg had informed them that she, too, was to be given all information relevant to Ben.

Charlie was reading a story when Fiona arrived one day. She closed the book and got up to leave. Ben had turned to her, 'Don't go.' Charlie glanced at Fiona.

'Please don't leave on my account.' She went on to tell Ben about his new home, describing the house she now shared with Alistair. She told him of the room that had been prepared for him and decorated with a Tarzan theme. It was all due to be finished by the time Ben's current cycle of treatment was over and he would then go and spend some time with Fiona and Alistair. Fiona seemed to be looking forward to having her son with her for a while. She said she had missed him while he had been with Charlie and Greg and she had been busy with her wedding and her move from Chestnut Grove to The Grange, now her home.

Although she would miss him, Ben's stay with Fiona and Alistair suited Charlie as her parents were flying in at the end of the week to visit her father's elderly twin aunts, Dotty and Dissy, for their birthday. It was a visit they made every year, as well as one at Christmas. Charlie's father was their only nephew and he tried to keep an eye on them despite living abroad. He was extremely fond of them and despaired of their eccentric ways, knowing that he could never change them, and in a way he didn't want to. They had charmed him and made him laugh since he was a boy. They never had children and they doted on him and also on Charlie when she came along. Sometimes, during her holidays from boarding school, Charlie went to stay with them, but who looked after whom was questionable.

Charlie had told her parents that she was in a relationship but hadn't said much about Greg. Arrangements were being made for them to meet at the weekend before Greg flew to Germany.

On the night in question Greg was a bag of nerves.

'For goodness' sake, Greg, you're only meeting my parents, not receiving a knighthood. You're fine as you are,' laughed Charlie coming into the bedroom strewn with Greg's clothes. 'They'll be looking at the man you are, not at what you're wearing.'

'I want them to think I'm worthy of their beautiful daughter even if I am old enough to be her father.'

'You're just being ridiculous now. To be absolutely accurate there are sixteen years and nine months between us. You're talking as if it's forty years.' She came and put her arms around him. 'You are a man in his prime and I love you; now stop fretting.' She turned to put on her jewellery.

'But look at you, you're gorgeous.'

'You do say the right things,' she smiled giving him a twirl. She was wearing a teal-coloured dress which hugged her slender body. Her blonde hair hung down to her shoulders in loose curls and she wore a pair of diamond stud earrings and a simple gold bangle. She exuded grace and elegance. Picking up a soft cashmere pashmina she said, 'Let's go, they'll be waiting for us.'

Greg threw back his shoulders and took a deep breath as he and Charlie entered the foyer of the hotel where Philip and Susan Taylor sat waiting for them. Even though they hadn't seen their daughter for several months their greeting was formal and undemonstrative. Philip got to his feet and kissed Charlie on the cheek.

'How are you, my darling?' he asked rhetorically, eyeing Greg as she bent down to kiss her mother.

'How lovely to see you both,' she smiled, 'especially as I have someone important who I would like you to meet. This is Greg, Greg Clark.'

Philip, a tall distinguished-looking man, stepped up to Greg and, shaking his hand, said formally, 'How do you do.'

Then Greg bent down and shook hands with the seated Susan. 'I'm so pleased to meet you. I can see where Charlie gets her looks from.' Susan's reply was a cool smile.

'Would you like a drink before we go through to the restaurant?' Philip asked cordially.

'Can we go straight in? I'm jolly hungry,' said Charlie.

Philip and Susan chatted with Charlie in their reserved manner, telling of their recent travels. Susan glanced at Greg. Once the conversation about health, their travels, Charlie's business and the food had tailed off it was inevitable that it would turn to Greg.

'How did you two meet?'

'Initially at a charity function.'

'When we were chatting I told Greg that I was looking for larger premises for the business and he told me about a garage in town that was about to become vacant, and with parking, it's ideal for us. It's been amazing. The shop floor has been divided into rooms to display our goods and I have a separate design studio. I'll take you there before you go back.'

Greg smiled at her enthusiasm. Then he decided to broach the subject they seemed to be avoiding, rather than skirt around it.

'I'm sure you must be wondering what your beautiful, successful daughter sees in me. That is something I ask myself every day so I understand your reservations. I'm older than her, divorced and have two children. I'm estranged from one and the other is very ill. The last thing I was looking for was love – until I met Charlie that is. I love her with all my heart and I want to marry her. I would be honoured if you would give us your blessing. I intend to spend the rest of my life making her happy and supporting her in anything she wants to do.' He slumped back in his seat and looked at Charlie. She reached over to hold his hand, tears in her eyes.

'There you are, Father, Mother,' she said turning from one to the other. 'He loves me and I love him. We want to be married as soon as we can.'

Philip Taylor, never one to be hurried, sipped his wine slowly and appeared to consider all that had been said before speaking. 'You are certainly a forthright man, and, as you say, you are a lot older than Charlotte.'

'If I was twenty... thirty years younger I still wouldn't live long enough to show Charlie how much I love her. One of my life's biggest regrets is that I didn't meet her sooner.'

'How long have you and Charlotte known each other?' The question made them both fidget uncomfortably.

'About two years. And, before you ask, yes I was married at the time. My marriage had been one of convenience for many years. When it eventually broke down I turned to Charlie... Charlotte. I knew very quickly that I had fallen in love with her but I wasn't sure how she felt about me. And then, when she told me she loved me...' He paused. 'Would you excuse me for a moment,' he said and left the room. It diffused some of the tension that had come to the table and gave Charlie and her parents the opportunity of to speak freely without him there. The three of them watched as he walked from the dining room.

'Charlotte, my dear, I think we all know how he feels about you. Are you sure you reciprocate those feelings?'

'I certainly do, Father. He's the man I'm going to spend the rest of my life with. With your blessing, I hope, but without if necessary.'

'But you've had so many boyfriends over the years, lots of them from some lovely families and a lot nearer your own age. Are you really sure?'

'Mother! You make me sound like some sort of tramp. I haven't had lots of boyfriends really, maybe a couple of relationships and a few casual boyfriends but I've been too busy putting an awful lot of time into making the business a success to be chasing men!'

'Yes, and we're very proud of you,' reassured her mother. 'Only the other day I was talking to someone whose daughter had part of her new home made over by Charlie Taylor Design. She didn't believe me when I said my daughter owned the company – she thought it was a man! I really don't know why you call yourself Charlie.'

Charlie was only half listening to her mother as her eyes sought the door waiting for Greg's return. Her father observed the light in her eyes and the flicker of a smile as he came back.

'I'm sorry about that,' he said as he sat down.

'Don't apologise. It's quite humbling to see what an effect our daughter has on you, and you on her, apparently.' Philip called over a waiter. 'I think some champagne is in order. It seems we have a wedding to arrange.'

'Does that mean you're happy for us?' Greg asked.

'Charlotte has always known her own mind and if you're the man who is going to make her happy then we're certainly not going to stand in her way. Congratulations.' He reached over and shook Greg's hand.

Susan clapped her hands. 'When can we go shopping for wedding dresses?'

Charlie held up her hand to stop her mother. 'Hold on, things aren't that simple.' She explained about Ben's illness, the reason why they didn't want to set a date at the moment. She explained that, in any event, she didn't want a large wedding, just something small and intimate, preferably just the two of them. 'I'm sorry if that disappoints you, Mother, but I really don't want a big wedding and all that goes with it.'

'Of course not, dear,' she replied, although Charlie guessed she was actually quite disappointed. 'You must have what you want. Perhaps you could come out to us in Barbados and get married there? Lots of people have weddings on the beach.'

'Maybe. We've other things to think about for now though.'

The evening drew to a close on a high note. The younger couple said their goodbyes without waiting for coffee and brandy as Greg was leaving for Germany the following morning.

It was 2 a.m. two days later when Charlie was awoken from a deep sleep by the ringing of the telephone. It was Fiona.

'It's Ben, he's not well. I'm taking him to the hospital.'

'I'll meet you there.'

Charlie was immediately awake and ready to leave in a matter of minutes. She arrived at the hospital a few minutes before Fiona and Alistair, who was carrying Ben wrapped up in a duvet. As soon as he saw her he reached out his arms.

'Charlie,' he said, starting to cry.

Sitting him on her lap Charlie soothed him gently until a nurse came to them. Fiona told them what had happened. It seemed that Ben had woken up screaming, perhaps from a nightmare, and became distressed at being in unfamiliar surroundings. He had then been sick causing Fiona to panic and phone the hospital who had told her to bring him in.

It didn't take long to ascertain that Ben was all right. His treatment meant that he often felt nauseous and was sick but, as he hadn't spent much time with Fiona she wasn't as used to it as Greg and Charlie. The kindly nurse had changed his pyjamas and said he could be taken home. Fiona wrapped him in the duvet again.

'Want to go home with Charlie,' he said.

Charlie looked at Fiona questioningly. She nodded and bit her lip and bent to kiss him.

'I'll take good care of him.'

'I know you will. Thank you.'

Turning to Ben she said, 'You be a good boy for Charlie, then. She'll look after you.'

'And Growler will too.'

He seemed unconcerned as his mother and Alistair left and snuggled in Charlie's arms as she carried him to the car. He was asleep when they arrived back in the flat.

The sun was shining when the telephone woke Charlie, Ben and Growler by her side. It was Greg and when she told him of the night's events he wanted to catch the next plane home. She insisted that there was no need and he was reassured after talking to Ben who had also been woken by the phone.

Over a leisurely breakfast Charlie listened as the little boy chatted away. He seemed to be cross with his mother. When she had said she was taking him home he thought he would be going back to Chestnut Grove and he had been looking forward to seeing his friends from next door. He hadn't realised, until then, that he would never go back there again. Charlie had often heard him mention Oscar and Hugo. She wondered if she would be able to arrange for them to come to the flat to play with him. Upon reflection she thought that, in view of what had happened in the past with Greg and their mother, it wasn't one of her best ideas, even if the intention was well-meant.

Charlie had just finished bathing Ben and was still in her dressing gown, when the flat's buzzer rang. It was her mother

'I'm so sorry, Mother. I completely forgot that we'd arranged to go shopping and have lunch,' she said before going on to explain about her eventful night. She introduced her to Ben who was sitting on the sofa, looking on with interest.

'Why don't you go and have a shower while Ben and I have a chat,' Susan suggested.

After Charlie left the room Susan, unused to small children, or children of any sort for that matter, struggled to find something to say and came up with the question that all adults ask children.

'How old are you?'

'Seven.'

A pause while she tried to think of something else but Ben, who was looking closely at her said, 'You are Charlie's Mummy?'

'That's right.'

'You look like her – a bit.'

'Do I?'

'Yes, but she's more pretty.'

'Do you like Charlie?'

'Yes,' he was enthusiastic in his reply. 'We love her. Daddy and I are Charlie's men – Daddy's her big man and I'm her little man.'

Susan smiled down at him. 'Would you like me to read you a story?'

'No, thank you,' Ben replied politely. 'But you could tell me a home-made one.'

'What do you mean?'

'I like it when Charlie tells me a home-made story. You know... one from her head, not from a book.'

'Oh! I see.'

'When she was a little girl, did you used to tell her home-made stories?'

'No, I don't think I did.'

'Not even when she used to come into your bed in the mornings?' Ben seemed surprised.

Susan looked down at him and smoothed her fingers over his hair which was becoming thinner by the day. She couldn't ever remember her daughter coming to their bed in the mornings. It would seem that Charlie had been more of a mother to this little boy, in a few months, than she had ever been. How many memories of shared happiness did Charlie have to remember? Was she making up for what she had missed by sharing what she would have liked, with this dear little boy?

'Let me see,' said Susan. 'I'll try and tell you a home-made story like Charlie.'

Ben snuggled into her side as she told him a story based on the warm seas and sunshine of Barbados. By the time Charlie came back, freshly showered and dressed, Ben was fast asleep and Susan was in awe of her kind and loving daughter, and acutely aware of her own shortcomings as a mother.

Chapter 30

Ellie was wandering round her garden half-heartedly dead-heading the roses. Her parents had taken Oscar and Hugo out for the day and she should really be tackling the weeds in the flower beds which is what she had intended to do, but it was hot for September and she didn't feel too well. She found the scent of the roses too cloying so, using that as an excuse to herself, she decided to make the most of the peace and quiet without the twins by relaxing in the sun.

Fetching a magazine and a cold drink she made herself comfortable on a sun lounger beneath a parasol. It really was a lovely day and just perfect for the barbeque they were to have that evening. She looked around the garden, it was bright with flowers, unco-ordinating colours tumbling from tubs and calling attention to the flower beds edging the lawn. It was the lawn that appeared to be suffering from the unusual heat for the time of the year, with the odd brown patch here and there. Oscar and Hugo's games didn't help either, but they needed somewhere to play.

Like a cloud passing over the sun, the events of last year flitted through her mind, banished and not to be dwelt on. It had been the worst year of her life, made all the worse because it was all her fault. She reflected upon how happy she was now. She felt as if she had come out of a dark tunnel. What a difference that holiday in Wales had made. She and Matt had become close again. Tom and Will were both enjoying life and were busy with their holiday jobs. Tom had decided to take work in Durham as he was renting a house with some friends up there. She wished he was closer but they went up to see him from time to time. Will was also working away, as an Assistant Park Ranger, where he was enjoying the outdoor life. She couldn't imagine him ever working in an office environment. He was a self-sufficient young man, content with his own company and always looking for mountains to climb and new places to explore. When he came home to visit it was mainly to eat and sleep. The twins, at eight, were growing fast and kept her on her toes with their never-ending questions and all the activities in which they were involved. She was lucky. All her boys were fit and healthy. She wondered about Ben. How was he? She really did miss him. He used to spend so much time with Oscar and Hugo that she had sometimes thought she'd had triplets. They often asked after him, and Ellie wondered where he lived now. The new neighbours might have the new address but she didn't like to ask. If Fiona had wanted to keep in touch she would have given it to her. Her thoughts drifting to the tune of buzzing bees and chirping birds, Ellie was soon fast asleep.

She awoke with a start to feel someone gently rubbing her cheek.

'Hello, my dear,' said her mother, standing there with a cup of tea for her.

Ellie rubbed her eyes. 'Mmm, I was in a deep sleep.'

'I know you were. We couldn't understand where you were with the house being unlocked, and when you didn't wake up when I called we went and made ourselves a cup of tea. Dad said he was going to pinch the family silver but the boys assured him that you didn't have any. They're watching television now.'

Ellie drained her cup of tea. 'Thanks, that was very welcome. Matt will be home soon. I'll just go and have a quick shower and change.'

She popped her head into the lounge on the way past to say hello but the boys held their fingers to their lips and pointed to their grandfather who was asleep on the sofa, but she rather thought that they didn't want their television programme interrupted.

Ellie allowed Matt to think the success of the barbeque that evening was all down to him as he stood there in front of the embers, with her passing him the meat as if he were a surgeon at work. The accompanying salads and buttered new potatoes, not prepared by him, were also part of that success!

Ellie had a pounding headache and went off to bed as soon as her parents left, vowing never to fall asleep in the sun again. She woke up in the night feeling feverish and was sick. She assured a concerned Matt that he had not poisoned her with undercooked meat as she hadn't eaten very much at all. She refused his offer to stay home from work but when she tried to get out of bed after he left her head was spinning so badly that she rang the surgery and, despite telling them it wasn't urgent, she was given an appointment later that day.

When Matt arrived home that evening the house was quiet; the boys were watching their favourite tea-time programme and barely acknowledged him.

'Where's Mummy?'

'Upstairs,' said Hugo

'Yes, and she's jolly cross and we haven't even been naughty, have we Hugo?' Oscar was very miffed.

When Matt entered the bedroom Ellie was lying on the bed, eyes open staring at the ceiling. 'Hey, sweetheart, are you no better? You should have phoned me to come home.' At his gentle, softly-spoken words Ellie burst into tears.

'Come here,' he said putting his arms around her. 'Tell me what's wrong.' She was crying so much that she could barely speak. 'You're worrying me now. Please tell me what the matter is.'

'I went to the doctor.'

'Yes. And ...'

More tears brought even further concern to Matt. 'And ...' he said again.

'I'm pregnant.'

'What?'

They looked at each other in shock. Eventually Ellie spoke. 'Say something.'

'Thank God,' he replied, holding her close. 'I thought you were ill or something awful had happened.'

'But Matt, another baby! I'm forty!'

'I know it's a shock, a hell of a shock, but it's not a bad thing is it?' he asked quietly.

'But five boys! What if it's twins again? I couldn't cope.' The thought brought a fresh bout of tears. Matt rocked her in his arms.

'Hang on, let's not get ahead of ourselves here. It's not necessarily going to be twins, or another boy. It might be a girl.'

'Oh, Matt. What are we going to do?'

'What do you mean?' he asked looking into her face.

'How are we going to manage with another baby?'

He kissed her gently. 'We'll manage, my darling. It's a surprise, I know, but a lovely one.'

'You don't mind?'

'Mind? It's not something you've done on your own is it. I rather think I played a part, an enjoyable one too.' He kissed her nose. 'I think I'm rather pleased. What about you?'

'I think I am too. It's just such a shock.' She fidgeted in his arms. 'There's something else. I'm not telling Tom and Will. You can do that.'

'Why?'

'I'm embarrassed.'

'There's nothing to be embarrassed about, you daft thing.'

'Children of that age don't like to think of their parents having sex, never mind having another baby. There will be such a huge gap between them.'

'I'll tell them. They'll probably think their dad is a bit of a superman!'

'Not just yet, though. Shall we wait another month or so, just to make sure that everything is going to be all right?'

'OK.' Matt patted her tummy. 'Our little secret.'

The bedroom door started to open, 'Mummy...'

'Not now!' Ellie and Matt said in unison.

'Yes. She's still cross,' Oscar informed Hugo in a huffy voice.

Chapter 31

Greg and Charlie felt their lives had been suspended and they were living in some kind of parallel universe. They spent a lot of time with Ben, either at home or in the hospital. They were afraid he would catch some sort of infection, so his days out were limited as they tried to avoid crowds.

As his absences from work increased, Greg had eventually confided in his colleagues at the garage about Ben's illness. To his surprise, he received their wholehearted support. In a business which thrived on a competitive edge where increasing sales figures were the goal, he learned, with some humility, that his staff consisted of caring people. To his shame he had never thought of them as individuals; to him they had been the sales team, the office staff, the lads in the workshop. Of course, he knew them by name, some of them at least, but he didn't remember that Paul, his head of sales, had lost a child a few years ago to meningitis; or that Simon, another of the team had nursed his wife through cancer before her death last year. Certainly he had added his name to the sympathy cards and contributed to a delivery of flowers for them but he hadn't considered or shared their anguish. And yet, these were the very same people who popped their heads into his office and asked if there was anything they could do.

Greg had told them that Ben needed a bone marrow transplant and they were looking for donors. Greg couldn't show his gratitude enough to those who had volunteered for the painful process but, as yet, there was still no match.

Once a week Jane, from the office, baked cakes and biscuits and brought them in to work to sell to the staff at their tea breaks. Another member of staff organised a monthly raffle for customers who willingly purchased tickets. A couple of lads in the workshop took part in a fun run. All the money raised was donated to the children's ward where Ben was receiving treatment.

All this kindness made him feel so humble. He didn't deserve it. He cringed when he looked back at the man he used to be. It would be easy to blame it on his childhood but it wasn't until he had known love that he had been able to show love and consideration to others. How arrogant he had been, delighting in the realisation that people were afraid of him, relishing his sense of power. How different things would be when Ben was well again and living with him and Charlie. They'd buy a house in the country with a garden where he could play football with him. He would show his staff how grateful he was for everything.

If any good had come from Ben's illness it was that Greg had come to know his son in a way that he would never have done otherwise. He hadn't realised how much he loved him until his illness threatened to take him away from them. He was a clever, funny and brave little boy. He never complained and when Greg displayed any anxiety around him he would pat his hand and say, 'Don't worry, Daddy, I'm okay.' It seemed as if illness had brought him wisdom way beyond his years.

One day each week, Charlie went to work to ensure that all was well with Charlie Taylor Designs, and Greg and Ben enjoyed their 'man days' as they called them. They usually prepared a meal for when Charlie came home and when the three of them sat around the table chatting about their day, Greg knew what real happiness was.

Charlie arrived home from work one day to find the table set and a delicious aroma of cooking coming from the kitchen. Greg and Ben seemed to be in high spirits.

'What have you two been up to?' she asked.

'Nothing,' they replied in unison.

'Well, you've been busy doing something because I can smell something nice coming from the kitchen.'

'Oh! Yes. We've been cooking,' said Greg while Ben giggled.

'Did you go out anywhere?' she asked, slipping off her shoes and accepting a glass of wine from Greg.

'No.'

'Yes.'

'Hmm. Why am I thinking that you've been up to something? Greg, you haven't been out but Ben has. Has he been trying to sneak out to buy sweets, I wonder?' She looked at them both in mock seriousness, noting that Ben held his hand in front of his face to hide a smile. He was looking at his dad with a twinkle in his eye.

'Er... we did pop out but only to the shop for a minute for some ingredients to go with the meal. Now come on, let's eat. I'm sure you're starving. We are, aren't we Ben?'

'Oh yes,' he replied, although he ate very little these days.

Greg served the meal with great aplomb.

'This is delicious,' remarked Charlie and, from the way Ben laughed, she knew something was up. She played along. 'In fact, this is so nice that you can show me how you made it.'

When they had finished eating, Charlie insisted on clearing up and sent the men into the lounge. Then they heard her stern voice. 'Greg, Ben, come here.'

They looked at each other and both said 'Oh! Oh!' Sheepishly they went to the kitchen to find Charlie holding up a ready meal box.

'Guess what I found in the bin,' she said.

'We've been rumbled, son.'

'You're a couple of rotters – making me think you were fantastic chefs.'

She chased them back to the lounge where they all collapsed on the sofa, laughing. 'We did cook something, honestly! But we burned it so we had to throw it away and go to the shop. Daddy said you'd never guess!'

The following day was a hospital day and, as they wrapped Ben up warmly, Charlie reflected upon how quickly the past few weeks had gone by. Was it because time was more precious now? Greg was desperately searching for ways to find a suitable bone marrow donor. He had given talks at various groups and Ben's story had even been featured on the local news which had brought forth a flurry of volunteers but no match. This even brought a contact from Greg's past, a second cousin whom he hadn't seen since childhood with an offer to get tested because he was a blood relative. Even though Greg knew that this wasn't the case, he was deeply touched, and agreed for him to go ahead in the hope that if he couldn't help Ben, there may be someone else on the register that could benefit.

Their best chance was a match with Gina and Greg put an advert in the *Liverpool Echo* in the desperate hope that, somehow, Gina would see it. It was a shot in the dark – maybe she wouldn't be a match or maybe she wasn't still in the area, if she ever had been in the first place. The only thing he had to go on was the postmark on Ben's Christmas present last year. He had even hired a private detective to try and find her but he had come up with nothing. He didn't allow himself to wonder if his search for Gina was motivated more by his concern for Ben than worry over her. Whichever it was, he lived constantly with a feeling of guilt. Guilt at losing his daughter and guilt at not being able to help his son.

Ben's nurse, Daisy, took him to visit Jessica, a fellow patient with whom Ben had become friendly, leaving Greg and Charlie with Mr Markham, the consultant. His care of Ben couldn't be faulted and he was charming and funny with his little patients, but Greg had taken an unreasonable dislike to the man. This was the man who had told him that his son was very ill, this was the man who arranged treatment that caused him pain and discomfort, and this was the man who was failing to make him better. This was the man who had found out that Ben wasn't his biological son. Whether it was a reflection of Greg's attitude, or whether he couldn't relate to adults in the same way as to children, the consultant treated Greg and Charlie with reserve and distance.

Mr Markham said that, because of the poor state of Ben's immune system, he was prone to infection and, as his temperature was slightly elevated, he felt he should stay in hospital for a few days. Here they could keep an eye on him and treat him accordingly.

With a heavy heart they went to find him and tell him, but he didn't seem to mind very much.

'That's okay,' he said. 'My friend Jessica is here. She's a bit poorly at the moment so I can keep her company.'

'Do you want us to bring Growler in to stay with you?'

'No. I told you. Growler looks after me when I'm at home. And...' he went on, pointing a stern finger at Charlie, 'he doesn't need a wash.'

'I have promised,' said Charlie solemnly.

'Don't forget. I don't want to come home to find him upset.' He turned away and went back to play with Jessica, quite unconcerned at being left there.

Ben was referring to the day Charlie noticed that Growler had become rather grubby and suggested to Ben that he be given a wash. He was distracted with another toy at the time and when he went to the kitchen a few minutes later he saw Charlie reading the washing instructions on Growler's label and preparing the washing machine.

'What are you doing?' he had asked.

'I'm just going to pop Growler in the washing machine to make him clean again.'

Ben shrieked and snatched him out of her hand. 'No,' he shouted. 'You're not. No. No. No. He will be sick going round and round in that.' He stomped out of the kitchen giving Charlie such a dirty look that she was speechless. She and Ben had never had so much as a cross word before. She waited a few moments and then peeped around Ben's bedroom door. Ben was on the bed reassuring Growler that he didn't really need a wash and if he did he would do it himself. He wouldn't let that nasty Charlie touch him.

'Ben,' Charlie said quietly. 'Please may I come in?' He didn't reply, merely turned his back on her huffily. 'Please. I just want to say sorry.' Still no reply. 'I want to say sorry to Growler.'

Ben looked into Growler's face as if to gain his permission. 'All right then.'

Charlie sat on the bed and spoke to Growler in all seriousness. 'I'm really sorry, Growler. I just didn't think. Of course I should know that dogs don't get washed in washing machines. I'm really silly.'

She then turned to Ben. 'Do you think Growler is friends with me again now?'

'Yes. I think so aren't you, boy?' He put his arms out to Charlie for a hug.

Both Greg and Charlie loved the way Ben thought of being with them as 'home'. He hadn't been to stay with Fiona and Alistair since that night he had woken up and found himself in a strange place. Charlie, who was very much aware of her tenuous position in Ben's life, did all she could to make things as good as they could be. As they were trying to keep Ben away from situations where he could catch an infection she invited Fiona to the flat to see him. Greg usually went out when she came, and Charlie went to another room to work on some projects so that Fiona could have some quality time with her son. She knew that Fiona scrutinised the flat whenever she came, her eyes roamed over everything, taking in the décor and the furniture and no doubt finding them wanting now that she was mistress of what sounded like a stately home. Charlie, who had always been house-proud and had "a place for everything and everything in its place" rule for herself, knew that the flat could do with a bit of a spring clean, but time with Ben was the most important thing in their lives at the moment. She could also do with a bit of a makeover herself, her hair needed cutting and her highlights were growing out but that would take too much time in the salon. How unimportant everything was, except for Ben.

Although she came regularly, Fiona's visits were becoming shorter and shorter. Alistair had accompanied her once or twice but he didn't really know Ben, and conversation with him was stilted. Indeed, by now, it was a relief when each visit came to an end. Ben seemed strangely unaffected by not seeing much of his mother but Charlie mentioned her regularly in conversation as she didn't want him to feel torn between both his parents.

The next few days were spent going to and from the hospital. Ben seemed happy enough. He often went to see

Jessica in her room or played with the other children but he tired easily. It was clear that he wasn't well. Greg and Charlie knew that Mr Markham's frequent visits to see him weren't a good sign. He was often very sleepy. One day he opened his eyes and asked where Jessica was.

'I think she's gone home,' said Greg, hating lying to him.

'She told me she was going to die,' said Ben, in a matter-of-fact voice.

'Did she?' Greg was shocked at the thought of a child so young having to contemplate death.

'Yes. Am I going to die too?' Ben asked, his chocolate brown eyes huge in the small face as he searched deep in his father's eyes.

'Not if I can help it, son.' Charlie bit her lip as she watched Greg bury his face in his son's chest to hide the tears that filled his eyes. What a question for a seven-year-old boy to ask. His future should be inevitable and not finely-balanced like this.

The days passed without a sense of time. When the postman brought a report from the private detective, Greg's hands trembled when he read the letter from the private detective saying that he had been unable to find any leads.

He handed it to Charlie, muttering, 'Oh, Gina, Gina. Where are you? Are you OK and if so, are you happy?'

He constantly searched the faces of the medical team in case they were about to tell them they had found a donor. He'd given up asking if there was any news as he hated to see the shake of their heads as they said, 'Not yet.'

Strangely, the children's ward was a happy place, despite the desperate situation of the occupants. The positivity and good humour of the staff created an atmosphere of calm. There was no restriction on visiting and usually both Greg and Charlie were at Ben's bedside, but occasionally they took turns to use the family room allocated to them, allowing them to shower and have some welcome uninterrupted sleep. Inevitably they would awake with a start, feeling guilty at time spent apart from Ben. Fiona visited often too but never stayed the night. However, she told them not to hesitate to call her at any time if necessary. She was always smartly dressed and immaculately made-up whenever she came as she always had been during the years she and Greg had been married.

With a kind of desperate enthusiasm Greg told Ben about all the things they would do when he was better, all the places they would go and the fun they would have as soon as he was well.

'The first place we'll go is Disneyland'

'Yes, that would be good,' was Ben's quiet reply.

Charlie sat, watching her two men, feeling helpless at how she could help either. She looked across to Fiona who appeared to look as helpless as she did.

Ben slept more and more. The three of them sat watching him. Sometimes he opened his eyes and smiled at them. They had all become temporary Christians. Praying to a God they didn't believe existed, just in case He did. Making promises and bargains which they would never keep if Ben pulled through and, if he didn't, telling themselves they were right after all.

One night Ben seemed particularly restless. Charlie held his hand and whispered soothingly while Greg paced the small room.

'Don't leave him. I won't be long.' He turned on his heel and went out. Ben tossed and fidgeted and Daisy, his nurse, came in frequently to monitor him and moisten his lips. She spoke to him as if he could hear every word as she smoothed back his wispy hair. Eventually Greg rushed back into the room carrying something. He tucked it under Ben's arm. Ben stirred and opened his eyes.

'Growler,' he smiled, going back to sleep.

Fiona had left the room and Greg's head had fallen forward as exhaustion claimed him briefly. Charlie was holding Ben's little hand, stroking it with her thumb. She could feel every bone. Did she feel a tiny, almost imperceptible little squeeze?

Then, Growler fell gently to the floor, brushing Greg's foot and startling him into wakefulness.

And then Benjamin James Clark died.

Chapter 32

'I've passed! I've passed!' I almost frightened the life out of Mrs Mac who was sitting in the late autumn sunshine in her small patch of back garden. She jumped out of her chair and gave me a hug.

'Well done. I've been sitting here on pins, waiting for you to get back.'

'Ooh! You fibber! You were fast asleep.'

'I was resting my eyes, that's all,' laughed the older woman.

'I can't wait to get a car now. I hope I find one soon. You're going to be my first passenger. I'm going to take you for a ride out somewhere and I'll buy you lunch.' She had been saving her money for several months and hoped she had enough to put down a deposit on a second-hand car

Mrs Mac patted her arm. 'You're a good girl, Gina. You really are. I'll look forward to that.'

'I'm going over to Clover House now. I promised Henrietta I'd call to tell her how I got on.'

Even though it was my day off, I was looking forward to seeing Henrietta. There wasn't much time to chat during the working day, and some days I was so busy that I didn't get to see her at all. On my way to Henrietta's room, I popped my head into the kitchen to see Carol. I arranged my face in a solemn expression and hid something behind my back.

'Oh, Gina, you've failed. Never mind sweetheart. You'll pass next time.'

I couldn't keep a straight face though, and produced the torn L-plates from behind my back.

'Ooh! You little minx! Congratulations.'

As it was a beautiful day I persuaded Henrietta to allow me to take her out in the wheelchair.

'Shall we go as far as the Parade and see the sea?'

It took a few minutes to get Henrietta ready and, wearing a straw hat, lacy gloves, lipstick, her handbag and a light blanket over her knees despite the warm day, off we went. We paused every now and then to look at the gardens of the houses we passed. When a wheel caught in a hole on the pavement I said, 'Oops! Sorry Henrietta. I think I'd better stick those L-plates back together and put them on this chair!'

When we reached the seafront we both took deep breaths, filling our lungs with the fresh, tangy air.

'Are you warm enough?' I asked.

'Yes, isn't it a lovely day? It's so nice to be out and about on a day like this.'

I stopped the chair by the side of a bench, not far from an ice-cream van. 'Shall we?' I asked.

'Yes, let's,' replied Henrietta, grinning like a little girl and opening her handbag.

'You can put that away. It's my treat.' I returned with two cones, a chocolate flake in each.

'How lovely. I haven't had a 99 for years. Congratulations on passing your test, my dear.'

We touched our cones gently as if we were clinking crystal glasses with the finest champagne. The ice cream melted faster than we could eat it but, luckily, Henrietta's capacious bag held some tissues for us to mop ourselves. 'What are you going to do with your life, Gina? Surely you want more than working in a care home looking after people like me. I've sensed a restlessness in you over the past couple of months.'

'You know me too well!' I exclaimed. 'I love working in Clover House. I just wish everyone there was like you. I quite understand that social and physical problems can affect people and I wish I could do more to help them.'

'And...'

'I've been thinking I would like to take up nursing.'

'You'd make an excellent nurse. Apart from being intelligent, you are kind and caring.'

'I'm not really, you know. I've hurt a lot of people in the past.' I couldn't stop my eyes filling with tears.

'Tell me,' commanded Henrietta, looking out to sea. And so, on that sunny day, sitting on a bench on the sea front, gazing in the same direction as my friend, I recounted the events of over a year ago for the first time. It felt good to be able to unburden myself without interruption. When I had finished, the tissues came out of the handbag again and I knew that I had been right to trust this lovely woman. I felt relieved that I had been able to talk to her.

'You poor child. You poor, foolish child.' I looked at her in surprise. 'You've carried this needless guilt with you for a year. About something that wasn't your fault. Your parents must be worried sick about you.'

'No.' A rueful shrug. 'They won't be. We were never close. I was never what they wanted me to be. Looking back I can see that now. I was quite clever in school but they aren't academic people themselves so they were never proud of me. They are both good-looking and I wasn't pretty, so I guess I adopted a silly Goth look to antagonise them.'

'Not pretty? No, you're not pretty. You're beautiful.'

I gave a start of surprise. 'I wasn't happy as a child. In fact, I've never been as happy as I have since I left home.'

'Even more shame on them then. Parenthood is such a huge responsibility. Some take that responsibility seriously, some don't know how to and some don't bother. You've just been unlucky. Tell me about your childhood.'

'There's nothing much to tell really, typical middle class upbringing, I suppose.

'Go back to the beginning. Tell me what you remember.'

'I've never talked about my childhood before because I always thought it would sound ungrateful because I never wanted for anything; anything material that is.'

She nodded and, hesitant to begin with, I recalled things as I spoke. I told her about how I remembered sitting in my bedroom as a little girl, swinging my feet against the divan base. I had spent many hours in that room; its décor changing with the child that I was as the years passed.

At first it was my nursery. Pink, pretty, with no expense spared in the furniture and furnishings. And with a lock on the door. Once I had outgrown my "cuteness" I suppose, and changed into a tantrum-controlled toddler I had been thrust there and the key turned in the lock. I could remember kicking the door until I was tired, hurting my bare feet while the door remained unmarked.

Then it became the room of a "lucky" little girl, with more toys than a child could play with, and some I wasn't allowed to touch. These were the porcelain dolls my mother thought I should enjoy collecting. I was presented with one every Christmas and birthday and they all had names, perfect hair, pretty smiles and eyes that watched me. I hated these representations of everything that I was not and told my mother so. That earned me the label of "ungrateful" to be added to all the other words that described what I was: awkward, plain, attention-seeking. And more.

It was the word "lucky" I hated more than anything. The *au pair* used it when she locked in the little girl 'who was lucky to have such a lovely bedroom'. I was always let out an hour or so before my mother came home. Relishing the attention I was given by the *au pair* for the short time it took to impress my mother, I never said anything about my confinement.

As I became older, my room became my haven. The key was lost by now, lost in a slit in the lining of the bed's base. The porcelain dolls were long gone too. Smashed in a deliberate massacre which resulted in another label: "wicked". That had earned me a vicious spanking from my mother. At least the message had eventually got through. I'd never been given another doll.

The room then held a desk, bookshelves and a television set with no trace of pink. The grey walls were decorated with posters of heavy metal bands and young men wearing more make-up than my mother. Being sent to bed was no punishment for me. This was where I loved to be; reading, learning, dreaming. I did my homework at my desk every night and my teachers were pleased with my progress. They said I was clever.

When I was small I won a prize, a book token, for the pupil with the highest exam marks in the year. I rushed out of school to tell my mother, 'Look, look what I've won,' I panted, out of breath in my rush to show the evidence of my worth.

'Can't you see that I'm talking to someone. Now stop being rude and wait until we've finished speaking,' said Mum, in place of the expected praise.

I never did tell her. Nor my father. He never seemed to be there, and when he was, he was busy, too busy for me anyway. So "clever" wasn't added to the ever-growing list of words that were used to describe me, scattered like seeds over the years: lucky, ungrateful, awkward, plain, attention-seeking, wicked, rude. Lots more were attributed to me as I to grew up – most of them true and deserved, I suppose.

'So,' I said, 'in a way, I can never believe that people like me, and I feel that I don't deserve to be happy, especially after I hurt so many people.'

I hadn't realised that my cheeks were wet until Henrietta thrust some tissues into my hands for the third time. She squeezed my arm and I saw that she, too, had tears in her eyes.

'I would have been proud to have a daughter like you,' she said.

For the first time in many months, I felt a lightness of spirit as we exchanged watery smiles.

'And now, my dear, the rest of your life is in your hands, it will be what you make of it, despite your parents, not because of them. It's up to you to make the best of it.'

'Yes, it is isn't it? This is how it is now. The first thing I'm going to do is to speak to my nursing friends to see how to start training as a nurse.'

'Good for you, I'm proud of you.'

I smiled at her shyly. 'Thank you.'

When we arrived back at Clover House, Henrietta thanked me. 'I've had a wonderful afternoon, it was so good to be out in the fresh air. I'm very grateful to you, my dear, kind friend. Thank you, too, for confiding in me.'

'And I'm grateful to you too. I feel great now and ready for the future. I promise I'll still come and see you, even when I'm an important matron!' I bent and kissed the soft cheek, 'I'm on earlies tomorrow, so it'll be me bringing your breakfast.'

'See you in the morning.'

But I didn't.

I was humming quietly to myself as I carried Henrietta's tray along the corridor. I had pinched a sprig of honeysuckle overhanging from one of the gardens on my way from the bus and had put it on the tray. Knocking gently and opening the door I thought at first that Henrietta was asleep and put the tray on the table. Then I knew. A surge of sadness filled my body as I went down on my knees by the bed. I held Henrietta's hand which was still warm and kissed it. Laying my head on the bed I grieved at the loss of a friend of only a few months who, although over sixty years older than me, had meant so much to me. I knew I had to call somebody but I wanted a few minutes on my own with her so that I could thank her for all she had been to me and to say my final goodbye.

The manager of Clover House insisted that I should go home. Everyone knew how attached I was to Henrietta and they thought it best if I wasn't around for the rest of the day. She even suggested that Carol should take me home but I insisted that I would take the bus. But first, I retraced our steps from yesterday, returning to sit on the bench. Our conversation echoed in my head and I knew that what Henrietta had said was true. My life was in my hands and it was up to me to make the best of it. And I would.

Chapter 33

Later that day Carol was in her kitchen peeling potatoes over an old newspaper for the family's evening meal. She was about to roll it up when something caught her eye. It was the name in capital letters that drew her attention. There was a photo beneath it. It didn't look like anyone she knew and the paper was a bit wet and soggy, but she tore it out anyway and put it on the windowsill. She put the peelings in the bin but her eyes flicked back to the newspaper cutting. She went to her handbag, took out her glasses and read the words carefully. She bit her lip as she wondered what to do. Decision made, she took off her apron, changed her slippers and popped down to Mrs Mac's.

'Hello, love. Come in.'

'Is Gina in?'

'Yes, but I made her go for a lie down. She was very upset. She thinks it's her fault that this lady died you know.'

'Good grief! That's ridiculous! Why would she think that?'

'Because she took her out yesterday and it might have been too much for her.'

'Oh, the silly girl! Of course it wasn't her fault. Henrietta was an old lady and not in the best of health. She'd had a lovely time according to the girls at work.'

'What have you got there?' asked Mrs Mac, noticing that Carol was fidgeting with the newspaper cutting.

'Just something from *The Echo* that I wanted Gina to see.'

When she came downstairs in response to Mrs Mac's call Carol looked at her and remembered that when she first arrived her hair had been dyed black.

'Is your name Georgina?' she asked.

Chapter 34

When I came downstairs I was surprised to see her and Carol sitting there with serious expressions on their faces.

'Yes, my name is Georgina, but I've always been known as Gina.'

Carol handed me a newspaper cutting. It was an announcement asking Georgina Clark to get in touch with her father as soon as possible because her brother was ill.

'I just saw it in *The Echo* when I was peeling potatoes. It's a couple of weeks old. I save them to light a fire with but we haven't had a fire over the summer so they've been piling up. I don't know why we didn't notice it before. It is you, isn't it Gina?'

'Yes. Oh! No. Poor Ben. I must phone.' My hands shook as I read it again. The number given in the paper was smudged and illegible and Mrs Mac and Carol watched as I dialled the number of the house I had left over a year ago. They looked so worried for me.

'It's discontinued.' I turned to them. 'He's only seven. He must be really ill if Dad's trying to find me. What should I do?'

Directory enquiries were unable to come up with a telephone number for the names of either of my parents and the garage was closed for the evening. I didn't dare phone Aunty Ellie.

'There's nothing you can do tonight and that paper is a fortnight old anyway so one more night won't make much difference. Leave it until the morning and you can ring the garage and speak to your dad,' was Carol's suggestion.

I was awake early the following morning after a restless night. As soon as the garage opened I telephoned, only to be told that Mr Greg Clark was on a leave of absence. The only thing to do, I decided, was to go back and try and find out how Ben was. Carol offered to go but I refused, promising to let her know what was happening as soon as I knew.

The journey seemed endless until, eventually, I pulled up in a taxi in front of my old home. Unsure of my reception, I asked the taxi driver to wait while I walked, with some trepidation, up to the door and knocked. I was surprised to see a middle-aged woman opening the door.

'Oh! Er... I was expecting to see a Mrs Fiona Clark,' I stammered.

'I'm sorry but she moved out months ago and I'm afraid we don't have a forwarding address. It's a shame they didn't leave one with us because we've had several envelopes and parcels for the family and we've just had to give them to the postman marked "Gone Away".'

'Thank you anyway.'

I was shocked and my guilt surfaced again. This was all my fault. Jumping into the taxi I asked the driver to take me to the garage and again, to wait for me. Marching up to the reception desk I asked for Mr Greg Clark.

'He's on a leave of absence at the moment. Can anyone else help you?'

'I'm his daughter. I need to see him. Where can I find him?' I was becoming upset and frustrated.

'One moment please.' The receptionist dialled Paul, the head of sales, and asked him to come through. He ushered me to his office introducing himself on the way.

'You say your father is looking for you?' he asked, unaware of the situation between Dad and I.

'Yes,' I replied, realising that I would need to explain things more fully to this man to get any information. I told him the minimum, explained about the newspaper advertisement, and waited for his reply. He sat there twiddling with his pen uncomfortably.

'There's no easy way to say this. I'm terribly sorry to have to tell you, but your little brother died. Ben is being buried today.' He looked at me with great compassion.

I felt my inside turn to liquid as I looked at him in horror. I was so shocked I could neither speak nor cry.

'Let me get you a drink.'

He picked up the phone and before I knew it a young lady was placing a cup of tea in front of me. My hand was shaking so much that I could barely hold my cup. As I sipped it a knock came on the door.

'Excuse me, there's a taxi driver here who says he is waiting for a young lady.'

'Oh! Gosh, that's me,' I said and turning back to Paul, 'what time and where is the funeral?'

With the information he gave me, I jumped back into the taxi realising that I would be late but at least I would get there. I allowed my tears to flow freely causing the taxi driver to look in the mirror and ask, 'You all right, love?' although it was obvious that I wasn't. When we got to the church I asked how much I owed and thrust some money at him.

'Do you want me to wait again?'

'I don't know what's happening so no, you'd better go.'

I ran to the church just as a small white coffin was being carried out of the door. Nobody as small as Ben should be in a coffin. It was covered in white and yellow flowers. I gasped and reached out my hand to touch it. My mother, dressed in black and on the arm of a strange man, followed the coffin. Behind her came my father with a woman on his arm.

'Mum!' I called out through my tears reaching out my arms.

Fiona stopped in shock. She didn't seem to recognise me.

'You!' she hissed, talking a step towards me. 'Typical! You're no use here now. You're too late. You could have saved him.' She drew back her hand and slapped me so hard across the face that my head bounced against the church door's frame with a resounding crack. Time appeared to be suspended for a moment as everyone stood still, in shock. Then everything seemed to happen at once.

All eyes turned to Mum as the man next to her took hold of her. The vicar moved towards me. Dad called out to me but before anyone reached me I turned and ran out of the churchyard. The taxi driver who had been having difficulty manoeuvring around the parked cars had just turned his taxi around and was about to set off again when I jumped in.

'Take me back to the station. Quickly please.'

Chapter 35

Inside the church Alistair looked at Fiona in amazement until she turned and buried her face in his shoulder. 'She could have saved him,' she sobbed.

He patted her gently on her back, excusing her reaction as being due to grief but, not for the first time, he quashed a feeling of unease about his wife. Behind them, Greg was fumbling in his pocket for his car keys. He thrust them into Charlie's hands. 'Find her. Please find her.'

As Charlie rushed away and those behind them in the church started to mutter, the vicar took charge of the situation and led the way to an open grave.

Fiona's sobs shook her entire body as her husband held on to her tightly. Greg stood there with his head bowed. Neither was aware of individual faces in the crowd around them, amongst whom were Ellie and Matt. She held one hand protectively over her stomach and Matt held the other tightly.

Eventually people drifted away until only Greg remained. He stood there, a gentle breeze ruffling his hair. It was a beautiful day, not the sort of day for a funeral, especially one of a little boy who should have been playing and running in the sunshine. Was he though? Was he now fit and well and playing in eternal sunshine? Gradually Greg became aware of distant sounds: car engines, voices, children playing, dogs barking. He noticed two men standing discretely some distance away and, with a deep shuddering sob, he left to allow them to fill in Ben and Growler's grave.

Charlie cursed as she tried to manoeuvre out of the parking space outside the church. She took her foot off the clutch too quickly at one point, causing the car to jerk and nudge the car in front of her. By the time she managed to get out and turn around, the taxi was long gone. Where would Gina go, she wondered?

'Think, think,' she told herself speaking out loud, banging the steering wheel in frustration. 'What would you do?'

She decided to head for the station. If she had been living away, that would be the sensible option. There wasn't a parking space anywhere but Charlie parked across a couple of cars and dashed inside. A few people turned and looked at her, wondering at her haste, as there wasn't a train for another fifteen minutes. Charlie looked around her. She didn't know Gina and had only caught a glimpse of her at the church but none of the people nearby remotely fitted the bill. Again she asked herself what she would do. If she was upset she would go somewhere where no one would see her tears, she decided, and walked to the furthest point of the station. There, on a bench, she found a young girl, crying as if her heart was broken. Charlie sat beside her and put her arm around her shoulders. Gina started.

'It's all right. I loved Ben too,' said Charlie.

She held Gina until the tears subsided. A train came and went and still they sat there, in silence apart from Gina's ragged breathing. Eventually Charlie spoke.

'Your father sent me to find you.'

Gina pulled away from her and turned to look at her face. 'Who are you?'

'My name is Charlie. You dad is desperate to see you.'

'Is he?' she asked with irony. 'Just like my mum?'

Another train came into the station, hissing to a stop. Gina made to rise.

'Please don't go. There's so much to tell you. Please come back with me.' Gina hesitated for a moment. 'For Ben's sake.' Charlie knew it was thinly-veiled blackmail but it seemed to work. With a slight nod of her head Gina followed her out of the station.

Chapter 36

Charlie entered the flat with me trailing in her wake. I heard Dad call as he walked into the hall. 'Did you find...' He paused for a moment, seeing me behind her. I stood there. I didn't know how to act, what to say. He quickly brushed past Charlie and took me in his arms. It felt strange, alien, out of character. I stood there as he kissed the top of my head.

'I'm so very sorry. I'm sorry. I'm sorry,' he repeated over and over holding me tightly. Eventually my body relaxed into his and my arms crept around him of their own volition. I had learned the value of a hug and a squeeze of the hand when Carol and Bill had absorbed me into their family.

'Daddy. I'm sorry too.'

'You've nothing to be sorry for, my darling girl. Let me look at you.' He gripped my shoulders and looked down into my face, as tear-stained as his.

'I think you two have got a lot of catching up to do,' said Charlie. 'I'll leave you to it.'

'No, please don't go,' said Dad.

'Yes. You need some time to yourselves. I'll be back soon. Please don't leave before I get back, Gina. I want to get to know you.'

Holding me by the hand as if I would take flight and disappear out of his life again, he took me through to the lounge. Conversation started slowly, stilted and painful as we sat there, telling each other what had happened throughout the past year. The heartbreak of Ben's illness and death overwhelmed us. The afternoon slid into evening without us realising when we heard the front door open and Charlie came back.

'I'll make us a bite to eat,' she said, standing uncertainly in the lounge doorway.

'It seems odd to be doing normal things, like eating,' Greg shrugged. 'Are you hungry, Gina?'

'I suppose I must be.' I realised that I hadn't eaten all day.

'Has he told you about me?' Charlie asked warily over a plate of sandwiches.

'Yes. He's told me everything. At least I think he has.'

'How do you feel about me being on the scene?'

'It's none of my business,' I shrugged. 'If you want to be together, that's up to you. Mum has remarried anyway, according to Dad.' I sighed deeply, 'What did I do to make her hate me so much?' I asked turning to my father.

'You didn't do anything, my love. She's the type of woman who should never have become a mother. She does love you in her own way and she loved Ben.'

'She's got a funny way of showing it.'

'I know, my darling. She's a very selfish woman, and not a very nice person, who will regret her actions one day. Don't think about her and get yourself upset about it.' Dad got up and kissed me.

Charlie changed the subject by saying, 'I'd like to get to know you. How long can you stay with us? You will stay with us won't you?'

'Gosh! I never thought about staying. I never thought about going back either. I promised to phone home but I forgot. Can I do that?' I felt guilty. 'They will be so worried about me.'

'Of course you can. But you can't go back tonight. Please stay.'

Both Carol and Mrs Mac were relieved to hear from me. Mrs Mac assured me that she would mention Ben in her prayers. Carol kept asking if I was all right and did I want her to come down and fetch me. They both said that they were longing for me to come home.

'Will you be okay sleeping in Ben's room? His things are still there,' Charlie asked gently. 'We can't bear to part with anything at the moment.'

'Of course. I can pretend he isn't far away.'

'He isn't really, you know. He's in your heart,' she reassured me quietly.

When I went to bed, I spent a lot of time prowling around the bedroom, touching the toys Ben had played with, looking through his drawings. I opened a drawer and found it full of his clothes. I picked up a T-shirt, burying my face in it, imagining that it smelled of him. I wrapped my arms around it and took it to bed with me. It comforted me. As I lay down, the exhaustion of the day took over and sleep claimed me in minutes. As I drifted off to sleep I thought of Tom. Had he been in the church at Ben's funeral? How close had I been to seeing him again? He would be in his second year at university by now. I'd love to know how he was. Were Uncle Matt and Aunty Ellie there? Were they still together? I could hardly ask Dad about them.

When I woke up the following day, I was surprised I had slept at all. My throat hurt from the tears I had wept. I lay there for a while putting my world into perspective. I was sad, very sad. I had lost two people who were very dear to me in one day. I knew Henrietta was an old lady whose life had run its course but it still pained me to think I wouldn't see her gracious smile every day. But Ben. Ben's death just wasn't fair. Why should he have suffered and died? Ben, with his quick smile and affectionate nature. The thought that he would never snuggle up to me again, and that I would never tickle his smelly feet until he squealed with laughter, made me ache.

Dad was waiting for me when I got up. 'I was hoping that finding you wasn't just a dream. Are you all right?'

'No. I'm not. I keep thinking that if I'd kept in touch I might have been able to help Ben in some way, and I feel guilty that I didn't. He must have wondered where I was. Did he ask about me?'

'Yes, he did. I told him you were working away.'

'I should have come back to see him.' By now, I was openly crying. 'It was selfish of me not to come back and see him even if I didn't want to see you and Mum.'

Dad flinched. 'Don't think like that, my love. We treated you so badly. I don't blame you for not wanting to come back. Can you stay for a while? I don't want you coping with the loss of Ben on your own. We've known for a while that his illness was serious but, for you, it's been a huge shock.'

I found his concern for me strange and difficult to take. It was so unlike him and too overpowering. Without a doubt I knew the past had damaged and hurt me. I'd learned this by being with loving friends. It would take more than my sudden reconciliation with my father to heal that pain.

'No sorry, I can't. Anyway, I won't be on my own, I have friends who are like family to me.' I was adamant. 'I want to go and put some flowers on Ben's grave and then I'm going back.home.'

Dad winced at my words. 'I find it difficult to accept that a place far away, that I've barely heard of, with people I don't know, is home to you.'

'It can't be that difficult surely.' I knew I sounded bitter. 'A very dear friend of mine died before I came here and I don't know when her funeral is but I would like to be there.'

'Oh my darling girl. You've been through so much.' Dad put his arms around me. I couldn't stop my shoulders from stiffening.

'I know bereavement is a sad and unhappy time but I didn't expect grief to hurt as much as it does.'

'I know. It's like a physical pain inside, isn't it? But it will get better. At least so people tell me. But I wonder how many of them have lost a child. The clichés that people use are based on truth, they say, and time will heal.' It was unclear whether he was reassuring himself or me. 'I wish you could stay with us, though, to help each other come to terms with things.'

He wiped my tears with his thumbs as he held my swollen face. 'I feel as if I don't want to let you out of my sight. I've lost one child and I feel if you go I'll lose you again.'

'That's up to you, isn't it. You know where I'm living now.' I didn't know what more to say, what more he expected of me and what I expected for myself.

Charlie came up to me and gave me a hug. 'I'm so glad to have met you at last and that your dad has been able to tell you how sorry he is for all that happened. He really is, you know. Promise me that you'll come and see us again soon. There's so much we need to learn about each other. You do know that we want to get married, don't you?'

'No, I didn't get round to hearing about that!' I turned to Dad with a raised eyebrow.

'There was so much to say and now didn't seem like the right time.'

'Oops, so I've put my foot in it.' Charlie looked uncertain.

'I don't think the way I feel about you is any secret. Gina's not stupid, I'm sure she's guessed. Come back soon, eh, Gina? Promise me. We need to grieve for Ben together.'

I picked up my rucksack and thought of something that had been at the back of my mind. 'There's just one thing,

Dad. When Mum said "You could have saved him?" what did she mean?'

Dad seemed uncomfortable. 'Ben needed a bone marrow transplant and she thought you might have been a match for him.'

I could feel the air leaving my lungs like a slowly deflating balloon. 'So *that* is why you wanted to find me. That's the reason for the advert in *The Echo*. You didn't want a daughter, you wanted a bone marrow donor.' I felt myself shrink back into the nobody I had always been. It hurt more than I thought it could because for a moment, just a brief moment, I had thought I was loved for being me.

I turned and rushed out of the door aware of the protests behind me and hearing my name called but I didn't look back. Why had I thought he had changed? Why had I allowed a slight feeling of warmth to fill my body at the thought that he wanted to have me in his life? Why couldn't I just feel angry, and not so very, very hurt?

Mrs Mac seemed delighted to see me back home. 'My poor love,' she said enveloping me in a welcome hug. I absorbed the comforting smell of my friend and landlady: Palmolive soap, Avon perfume, Johnson's baby powder and a hint of onion which was also borne on the delicious aroma of cooking coming from the kitchen. 'How are you? Are you tired? Would you like a cup of tea? How about a nice hot bath or do you want a little lie down?'

'I don't know which question to answer first,' I laughed. 'I think I'll start with a cup of tea.'

'Kettle's just boiled.' Mrs Mac turned for the kitchen. 'Carol's off today and I said I'd let her know the minute you got back so I'll just give her two tinks if that's okay?' She was referring to their custom of telephoning but letting the phone ring only twice which meant that they not have to pay for a telephone call, and that she was to come round.

I knew that Mrs Mac had asked all the questions except the ones she really wanted to. In the time I had lived there she had respected my privacy and had never asked any intrusive questions. Neither had Carol, who came rushing in to clutch me to her bosom.

Over a cup of tea I said, 'Neither of you has asked any questions about my past. Why? You must have guessed something wasn't right.'

The two women looked at each other but it was Carol who spoke. 'We knew you were running away from something that had upset you badly. You were very introverted and you looked haunted. It took you a long time to show us the girl inside. We didn't want to intrude and for you to shut yourself from us. If you had wanted us to know you would have told us, and in your own good time.'

'But why were you so kind to me?

'You are about our Carla's age and if anything had ever happened to drive Carla away I hope someone would be good to her. And... I don't know, there was something about you – you looked so forlorn and lost.'

The time to tell them had now come and, over a cup of tea, I told them everything. Carol reached out and held my hand and allowed me to cry from time to time, knowing that tears can heal pain as well as be caused by it.

'I'd like a few words with that mother of yours,' she said when I had explained everything. 'I'm sorry she's lost her son, desperately sorry, but she doesn't deserve a daughter like you.'

'I wouldn't mind a few words with that father of yours too,' added Mrs Mac. They both looked at me protectively. 'What are you going to do now? Are you going to stay up here?'

'Yes, I'd like to, if you'll still have me,' I smiled. I then went on to explain about my intention of looking into a nursing career.

'Ooh! Our Gina, a nurse. You'll make a smashing nurse, love, won't she, Carol?'

'The best,' her friend replied confidently getting up to leave. 'I must dash now and get tea on for my lot.'

No sooner had she left than the phone rang and I picked it up to hear Dad's voice.

'I don't think we have any more to say to each other. Shall we agree to stay out of each other's lives? After all, I don't have anything you need now, do I? It's all too late.'

The phone rang so often that I unplugged it in the end. I didn't want to speak to him, not tonight, not ever. I didn't need to be part of his family, I had one up here.

I was glad to be busy at work. It stopped me thinking. Even so, I was acutely aware that Henrietta was no longer with us. How I wished I could talk to the gentle old lady again and benefit from her wisdom. I had so much I wanted to tell her. In just over a week I had lost a dear friend and a sweet little brother, had found my mother and been rejected by her again, and had found my father who had reaffirmed my worthlessness. It was no wonder my mind and my emotions were all over the place. I was often so tired that I couldn't concentrate and my eyes flooded with tears for no apparent reason.

The night times were the worst, when I pulled the bedcovers high and buried my head into my pillow and sobbed until my ribs hurt. The brief euphoria at having connected with my father again had long gone. I had always thought of him as a distant figure with the title of father and I'd managed without him for over a year. Perhaps I was foolish to have thought we could have built bridges, or was I wishing that I could have a family like Carla had?

The next thing I had to face was Henrietta's funeral. It was a dull, drizzly day, conducive to my mood. As I stepped into the church I caught my breath and was drawn to a halt when I saw the coffin covered in yellow and white flowers. Tears blurred my vision and what my mind saw fluctuated between a small white coffin with yellow and white carnations and a polished oak one with yellow and white chrysanthemums. One of my colleagues from the care home entered the church behind me, took my arm, leading me to a pew. I listened to the words of the vicar as he assured the congregation that Henrietta was living in eternal joy in the kingdom of heaven. I joined in the hymn singing, the words of 'Amazing Grace' and 'Abide With Me' moving me, once again, to tears.

Later, as everyone moved from the graveside Henrietta's daughter, Annabel, came up to me.

'I want to thank you for all you did for my mother. You were extremely kind to her and she appreciated it very much.'

'She was a special person. I thought the world of her and I'm going to miss her so much. You're lucky to have had a mother like her. She was kind to me, too. Look, I'm wearing the watch she gave me.'

Annabel smiled, handing me an envelope. 'Mum kept a diary, you know, and I've made a copy of the last entry because it mentions you. I've also put in a brooch as a small memento for you.' She pressed an envelope into my hand. 'I must go, please excuse me, there are people I want to speak to before they leave.' She shook my hand. 'I'll always be grateful to you, Gina, for all you did for her.'

The group of mourners was breaking up but I turned back towards the church. The organist was packing up his music and the church warden was putting away the hymn books. I slid silently into a pew and absorbed the atmosphere. Then I opened the envelope and read the last words Henrietta had written and knew I would treasure them forever. Blinded by tears and lost in my own sphere of grief I didn't hear the approaching footsteps of the vicar who had removed his vestments by now.

'Are you all right, my dear?' he asked quietly.

I bit my lip. 'Do you think it's true?'

'What?'

'That Henrietta and my brother Ben are living in eternal joy and have been reunited with their loved ones?'

'I know it's true. It's true for Henrietta and, if Ben has passed from this world, then it's true for him as well.'

'But there is no-one there for him. We're all still here.' I searched his face craving assurance from him.

After asking a few more gently probing questions the vicar told me, with absolute confidence and certainty, that Ben was safe in the arms of his loving, heavenly father. Comforted by his words, I realised as I got up to leave, that I felt better than I had in ages.

'Maybe Henrietta will look out for him,' I smiled at him.

'I'm sure she will.' The vicar took my hand and patted it gently. 'If you ever want to come to me for a chat, you know where to find me.'

The following day the postman delivered a letter. I didn't recognise the writing as it came from Charlie. Written across the top were the words 'Please read this'. Perhaps she had guessed that if Dad had written I would have torn the letter up. It was a long letter explaining that Dad had, in fact, tried to find me. How he had been furious at Mum's lack of interest in my disappearance; that he had spoken to the police who had been unable or unwilling to help because I was eighteen and had left home voluntarily. He had also written to the Salvation Army to see if they could help trace me. She said that he had even come up to Liverpool and wandered around the city in the vague hope that he would see me. She wrote of his deep regret about being such a poor father and how very much he wanted me back in his life. She said he would phone the following evening and would I please speak to him. I couldn't suppress the flicker of something inside me. He did try and find me. How hard had he tried though? Should I speak to him? I folded the letter and put it back in the envelope. To me, that was a sign. If I didn't want to speak to him I would have torn it up. So yes, I would accept his call.

When he rang Mrs Mac answered and called out to me saying "That Man" was on the phone, putting capital letters and quotation marks with her voice to show that, although she had never met him, she hadn't forgiven him for his treatment of me.

He was very hesitant and apologetic on the phone and the conversation was rather stilted. He reassured me that he loved me and wanted to see more of me. It was probably because he had said the words I wanted to hear that I agreed to regular telephone calls from him.

A couple of weeks later, after the latest conversation I turned to Mrs Mac and said, 'They're coming up to see me on Saturday. Dad and Charlie. They want us to meet somewhere.'

'And what's wrong with bringing them here? It is your home after all. Tell them to come here for their tea.'

'Are you sure? I'd love them to meet you.' I kissed Mrs Mac's cheek, I think I felt a bit excited.

By the time Saturday came Mrs Mac had worked herself into a proper state and was cursing her rashness at such a ready invitation. She'd soaked her best lace tablecloth in Glo-White, washed her best china and had all but spring cleaned the whole house. She'd dug out her recipe books and had made a fruit cake, a bun loaf, some fairy cakes and some scones. I laughed at her and told her not to go to such trouble, but she was determined to show them that nothing was too good for me. She looked at the neatly set table, there wasn't enough room for everything so she'd had to put up a card table to hold the jam and cream which she'd decanted into her crystal bowls. The sandwiches, with their crusts neatly cut off, sat under a layer of foil and the napkins were starched and ironed. Carol and Bill called carrying plates of the chocolate eclairs she'd promised to make

Carol remarked to Mrs Mac, 'My, you don't half look posh. And you've had your hair done.'

'Yes, your Karen's place couldn't fit me in this morning so I went to a multi-sex place on the high street.'

'Good grief! Where did you go, Mrs Mac?' said Bill almost choking on the éclair that he'd pinched off the plate.

'She means the unisex hairdresser,' said Carol laughing.

'Thank goodness for that,' said Bill turning away as he laughed silently.

'I'll give you two tinks when they arrive so you can meet them too.'

'Okay, I'll just pop my head in for five minutes and then I've got to go down to the shops so I won't stay.'

The visit was a resounding success. When Dad arrived he hugged me as if he wasn't going to let me go, leaving Charlie, who was hidden by the most enormous bouquet of flowers, to introduce herself. When I eventually extricated myself I introduced Dad to Mrs Mac who had been determined to be as frosty as she could to show her disapproval. It lasted for as long as the introduction as Dad took both her hands in his and kissed her on each cheek.

'I'll never, as long as I live, be able to thank you for looking after my Gina. So much could have gone wrong and she ended up in your home. You took her in when she was in dire need and I'll be forever in your debt.'

Mrs Mac, who hadn't expected such humility, fluttered nervously and patted her hair.

Charlie handed over the flowers and looked around. 'What a lovely home you have. It's so warm and welcoming.'

Almost half an hour had gone by with everyone chatting comfortably when Mrs Mac exclaimed, 'I've forgotten the two tinks!'

Greg and Charlie looked puzzled until I explained. 'It's the local semaphore. My friend Carol is going to call in and meet you too.'

Again, they were delighted to meet my friend. 'I believe I have you to thank for helping Gina find work as well as a home. I'll never be able to tell you how grateful I am.'

The afternoon had turned into evening before Greg and Charlie made a reluctant move to leave. Although they had tried their best and eaten their fill there was still a lot of food left over and Mrs Mac insisted on packing some up for them to take with them 'in case they felt peckish on the way home'. Charlie said she had never had such delicious home-cooked food before which made her Mrs Mac's friend for life.

'When will we see you again?' Dad asked.

'You'll be able to drive down when you get your new car,' said Mrs Mac.

'What new car? What are you having?' I explained that I was looking for one.

'You can leave that up to me – I am in the car business after all! Have you any preferences? I think the brand I sell might be too expensive for you insurance wise. The best-selling diesel this year is the Peugeot 205 or the Ford Fiesta is a good option.'

'Clearly we're on your specialist subject now Dad. I don't care what sort of a car I get. A smallish one would be best I think but I insist on paying for it.'

He smiled as he squeezed my hand.

Chapter 37

Later that evening, when Gina had gone out with friends, Carol called round to see how everything had gone.

'It looks like an undertaker's parlour in here!' she joked taking in the several vases filled with flowers.

'I know. I've used up all my vases and I've put those there for you.' Mrs Mac nodded towards a plastic bucket containing yet more flowers. And there's some food in foil there for you too. I know your Mark's a growing lad so I'm sure he'll polish it off.

'So, I gather you've given them your seal of approval, then.'

'Well,' Mrs Mac said slowly. 'He seems like a nice man and genuinely sorry for what happened. That mother of hers sounds awful though. But that Charlie's lovely. Bit young for him I think. She insisted on doing the washing up and wouldn't take no for an answer. I think things will start looking up for Gina now.'

'Let's hope so. Mind you, you know what they say, a leopard doesn't change its spots. And remember, Gina didn't stay down there with them – she came back to us.

Chapter 38

Mrs Mac sat in her chair in front of the fire. The house was quiet apart from the crackle and hiss from the coals. She would put the television on in a minute. *Blankety Blank* would be on soon and she did like that Les Dawson, he made her laugh with those faces he pulled and his quick wit. Just for now, though, she'd enjoy the peace and quiet before the youngsters came back, and she sip at her Mackeson, enjoying the rich, bitter taste.

She'd been a widow since 1969, thirty years, long years, and she still missed her Paddy, taken from her too young. It was his chest in the end. It was always weak, ever since he was a child brought up in poverty in Ireland, as was she, although she had no memory of it as she was very young when her parents left the old country. Paddy and Kathleen's marriage had been a very happy one. Even after all this time she still talked to him, in her head that was. Sometimes she thought that he answered her but she told herself not to be silly, and yet...

Mrs Mac missed their son, Peter, too. Sad that he had decided to go to Australia to work, she thought he would be back after seeing a bit of the world. He'd been home just once and he'd been so full of what a wonderful place Australia was. He lived in Sydney and Mrs Mac knew he'd never come back home. She had been lonely, so very lonely but she'd just got on with things - you had to, didn't you?

She'd had her job as a cleaner, her church, and she had been persuaded to go to the bingo once or twice with some friends. It wasn't really for her though. She wasn't quick enough to mark down all the numbers and too shy to shout out when she'd won in case she'd got it wrong. Afterwards, the others wanted to go to the pub but she wasn't a drinker. She took another sip of her stout, smiling ironically at her thoughts.

Mrs Mac felt blessed to have her son but she would have liked a daughter as well. One just like Carol from down the road. How lucky she was that they had come to live a few doors away. They were her family now. And that family was still growing. It wasn't that long ago that she had the house to herself and now she had two lodgers, not that she thought of them as such, just more family. First Gina had come into her life and what a blessing that had been, for both of them she supposed. And now look at how she was turning out. She was in college and was going to be a nurse. Then there was Darren. He lived here now too. Mrs Mac remembered the day that Carol had come round and told her that his landlord was selling up and he had nowhere to go. He'd been in care since he was a child and had lost track of his family. What could she do? As a good Christian woman with an empty bedroom her heart had operated her mouth before her brain had time to think, and she said he could come and stay with her. Her kindness had been repaid tenfold. He'd turned out to be a smashing lad. It wasn't his fault that his eyes were too close together, no, he couldn't help that at all. There was no task that he wasn't willing to take on. Her windows were cleaned more often than any of her neighbours', she never had to carry a coal bucket and he'd even done some decorating for her.

Two young people whose lives had been blighted by their parents. How unfair was that when she would have been happy to have had a houseful of children? Never mind, it was their loss, they were her blessings now.

Mrs Mac realised that her glass was empty. Should she have another one? It was her birthday after all. No-one had remembered though. No card from Australia, but that wasn't unusual. She was surprised that Carol hadn't remembered, she was always so good. The youngsters wouldn't have known as she wouldn't have dreamt of mentioning it. Where were they? They should have been back by now. They'd all decided they fancied a fish supper and they'd gone to the chippy. She had plates warming in the oven ready.

She was about to pour herself another bottle when she heard scuffling in the hall. All of a sudden the door opened and the room was full of people laughing and shouting "Happy birthday" and "Surprise". She beamed at them all: Bill, Carol, Carla, Karen, Mark, Gina and Darren. Her family – the family of her heart.

Bill laughingly pointed to the bottle in her hand, 'We know now why you're called Mrs Mac.'

Apart from the delicious-smelling packages of food they carried, they all bore cards and presents.

'I'm so sorry, Mrs Mac,' said Carol. 'I wanted to come here first thing this morning but I didn't have time before work and then, when I got back this lot wouldn't let me. They said you had to have a surprise birthday party.'

'How old are you, Mrs Mac?' asked Mark cheekily.

'Well!' she exclaimed laughing. 'What a question to ask a lady. I'm as old as my tongue and a little older than my teeth, young man.'

'Shall we eat first while the food is still hot and then you can open your presents. Don't bother with plates, we'll eat out of the paper.' The ever-hungry young lad showed clearly where his priorities lay.

'All right then. I suppose it won't do us any harm to be common just this once.' Mrs Mac relinquished her standards reluctantly.

What an evening it was. There weren't enough chairs for everyone so the youngsters sat on cushions on the floor. The fish and chips with salt and vinegar, eaten with fingers, were as good as any restaurant meal. Carol and Bill had brought a bottle of fizzy wine with them which they pretended was champagne. Afterwards Carol went out to the hall and brought back a cake with seven candles.

'There wasn't enough room for seventy,' she said.

'Aha!' Mark pointed out gleefully. 'No secret now!'

'Come on, blow them out and make a wish.' Carol held the cake for her.

Mrs Mac looked around her. 'I don't know what to wish for. I've got all I want and more.'

'There is something, isn't there? Wish for it and you might see him again soon, Australia's not that far away these days,' Carol said gently.

Mrs Mac blew out all the candles in one go. 'That's supposed to be lucky, isn't it,' she said proudly. 'I want to make some toast,' she went on, the others looked puzzled until she pointed at their glasses and they realised what she meant. 'I want wishes for you all too. I wish Gina luck in getting to be a nurse. I wish Carla and Darren good luck in finding a home. I wish Karen good luck in starting her own business now that she's a qualified hairdresser and I wish Mark good luck in his exams.'

'What about me Mrs Mac?' asked Bill. 'What's my wish?'

'For you and Carol, I wish you the best of everything.' They all raised their glasses but before they could speak she went on, 'I've got two more wishes left. I wish you'd let me open my presents and I wish you'd cut me a piece of my birthday cake.'

As she went to bed that night Mrs Mac looked at the photo of Paddy which was on her bedside table. She had felt him close all evening, as if he were sitting in the room sharing in her birthday party. She was sure he'd been watching as she'd opened her birthday presents: a cosy dressing gown from Carol and Bill, some slippers from Karen, chocolates from Mark, a slow cooker from Darren and Carla who must have remembered her remarking how handy it would be, and a watch from Gina. Greg and Charlie had even sent her a present: a pretty little brooch. Then there was that other present from them all. They had opened a bank account for her and had put some money in it and promised to add to it every month so that she could go to Australia to see her son. She hadn't said anything to them but thought it was ridiculous. It was so far away – as if she could travel all that distance at her age! But she was only seventy, that wasn't old at all really was it? How far was Australia anyway?

Chapter 39

Ellie fidgeted uncomfortably. She was lying in bed after promising Matt that she would stay there for a while. The house was quiet with Matt at work and the boys in school. Will, with his newfound independence as a result of passing his driving test, had taken Oscar and Hugo to school.

This pregnancy hadn't gone as smoothly as her others. Her morning sickness had lasted far longer than the usual few weeks and she was constantly tired; because of her age she assumed. She felt so old compared with the other mothers at the clinic. Her blood pressure was higher than it should have been too, hence Matt's insistence that she stay in bed this morning. Wriggling about in bed she struggled to sit up, her back aching. She was huge; almost as big as she was when she was carrying Oscar and Hugo but they assured her that she wasn't having twins this time. She put her hand on her tummy. 'Only a couple of weeks to go before we get to meet,' she spoke softly to her unborn child. 'I can't wait to see you.' She felt a slight movement and had the fanciful thought that the baby felt the same. She and Matt had decided against knowing the baby's sex. It would be welcome whatever it was. She was bored, she'd read her magazine, finished the tea that Matt had brought her and her feet were cold.

'Oh, blow this,' she muttered to herself. 'I'm getting up.'

Showered and dressed, Ellie made herself another cup of tea and sat at the kitchen table looking around critically. Matt was very good around the house and she was grateful for all that he did but she could see splashes on the tiles, crumbs on the worktop and stains in the sink. She thought she'd just have a little tidy round. Nothing strenuous, and if the kitchen was clean she knew she'd feel better. An hour later and it was gleaming. What can I do now, she wondered. Another cup of tea? No, she was in the loo often enough as it was. She'd just put those things away that were on the worktop. Matt was always leaving things out because he said he didn't know where they belonged. She opened the cupboard. What a mess! In no time at all she had taken everything out and washed the shelves. As she was putting things back she felt a slight twinge in her side. Regardless, she carried on. Task completed, Ellie felt pleased with her work and decided to start preparations for the evening meal. Half way through peeling the potatoes she felt another twinge, sharper this time. Was this it? She bit her lip. Surely she should know, this was her fourth pregnancy after all. The dull backache was worse now. Was it too soon to phone Matt? She'd promised she would so she dialled his mobile. As it connected she heard a phone ring and when she opened the door to the hall, there it was, on the hall table, the mobile phone upon which Matt had spent a fortune specifically for this purpose. Disconnecting the call she rang Matt's office and spoke to Amanda, his assistant.

'I'm afraid he's not here. He's taken a client out for lunch and I'm not sure where. Can I give him a message when he gets back?'

'Yes, just ask him to give me a call please,' she replied, telling herself there was plenty of time. Walking around the house, rubbing her back, she hoped there was, but as the minutes ticked by she was beginning to realise that there wasn't. Will sometimes came home from sixth form college early on the day he didn't have afternoon lectures. Think, she told herself. What day was it? What time are his lectures on a Wednesday? She was still trying to rack her brains when Will walked in.

'Will, I think the baby's coming,' she gasped just as her waters broke.

Will looked both horrified and scared at the same time. 'Oh! Mum, tell me what to do. Shall I call an ambulance?' he asked.

Ellie thought for a moment, took a deep breath and spoke with a calmness she didn't feel. 'I think you need to drive me to the hospital. Pop upstairs and fetch my suitcase while I call them.'

Will thought they'd never get to the hospital. Glancing at his mother with concern he saw that she was panting and breathing deeply alternately. He bit his lip as traffic lights turned to red as he approached them and he had to give way to cars on roundabouts, while all the time trying to drive as smoothly as possible. He was relieved to reach the maternity unit, Ellie's groans making him run in to call for help. With relief he handed her over to the calm staff who whipped her away in a wheelchair. He was sitting outside the labour ward when his father came rushing in.

'Where is she?' he panted. Matt had popped home to fetch his forgotten mobile phone to find the house empty and Ellie's hospital suitcase gone.

It was ten minutes later when a blue-clad nurse stuck her head around the door. 'Want to come and say hello to the new arrival?' she asked.

Nervously Will followed her inside. His mother was lying there smiling and his father, relieved to have arrived in time and dressed in a hospital gown, was cradling in his arms a tiny bundle with a mop of dark hair, that was making little mewing sounds.

'Come and meet your sister,' said Matt placing the baby in his arms.

Will looked at her and smiled. He touched her snub little nose. 'Hello, little one. Hey, she's looking right at me,' he said. 'She's beautiful, isn't she?' he looked at his parents in apparent wonderment. 'I thought newborn babies supposed to were ugly, but she isn't.'

Ellie and Matt exchanged glances and smiled. This was their son who had reacted with horror when Matt told him they were going to have another baby. He'd made Ellie promise not to go to any meetings or functions at the sixth form college he attended. It was only when Tom, on a brief visit home teased his parents by saying 'There's still life in the old dog, then' that it appeared to Ellie Will accepted the situation with good grace. And, to give him his due, he had, offering to help with chores and enthusiastically running errands, especially if they were by car, now that he could drive.

When Matt told the twins that they were to have a baby brother or sister their reaction was different again.

'A baby?' Hugo said. 'What for?'

'Yeah,' joined in Oscar. 'Why are we having a baby? It's a puppy we want, not a baby.'

'Well I'm sorry about that,' said Matt, 'but Mummy's having a baby, not a puppy, and it's growing in her tummy.'

The boys exchanged grimaces and turned back to what they were doing.

By the time the twins came home from school the following day, Ellie and the baby were home. She was fast asleep in a little crib in the lounge and both boys went to look at her.

'Do you want to hold her?' Ellie asked.

'No,' said Oscar, seeming to be puzzled at the question.

'What about you, Hugo. Do you want to hold her?'

'Why?' he seemed as puzzled as his brother.

'I thought you'd like to give your little sister a cuddle.'

He considered it for a moment. 'Maybe later. Can I have a biscuit please?' He gave the baby another glance. 'What's her name?'

'What name would you like her to have?'

'How about Princes Leia?' he suggested.

'If we'd had a dog we were going to call it Spot,' said Oscar, still a bit put out that they'd had a baby instead.

'Yes. Well, she's definitely not going to be called Spot,' smiled Matt and turning to Ellie he said. 'We are going to have to make a final decision aren't we darling?'

'I think I'd like to call her Angharad,' said Ellie. 'It's a lovely name and after all, she was made in Wales.'

'What? Made in Wales? Does it say so on her back?' Oscar was intrigued and a bit affronted when his parents roared with laughter.

'It means 'loved one'. And I'd like her second name to be Elizabeth, after my mum.'

'Angharad Elizabeth it is. They are beautiful names, just like our beautiful daughter.'

Angharad Elizabeth soon ruled the roost in Chestnut Grove. Her oldest brother, Tom, made a point of coming home to see her at the earliest opportunity but she was three months old before he had a chance. There was a race between him and Will to pick her up at the first hint of a cry.

'Can I have a turn now,' Tom asked when he walked into the room and found her in Will's arms. 'You can hold her any time. I've got to go back soon.'

He'd taken to his studies with enthusiasm and expanded his experience by working at the hospital in any capacity that he could during the holidays. As a result he had rarely been home since he left.

'What are the new neighbours like?' he asked his mother. 'It's awful about Ben. isn't it? I wonder how his mum and dad are coping. What about Gina? Did you ever hear what happened to her?'

'Which question would you like me to answer first,' smiled Ellie before trying to supply him with answers.

'I wish I knew what happened to Gina. You were fond of her, weren't you?'

Ellie watched her son's face suffuse with colour.

'Yes, Mum, more than a bit fond I think. I didn't realise how much until she went. I've been out with a few girls but I'm always thinking about Gina and I wish I could see her again.'

Ellie squeezed his arm gently and bit her lip, thinking this was another thing she felt guilty about.

When Oscar and Hugo saw how much interest their brothers took in the baby they started to take more notice of her too and they held her with great care. Before long, they considered themselves as her protectors, causing much amusement for their grandparents when they warned them to 'be gentle and watch her head'.

Mair had been delighted to hear of the birth and had sent them a card saying 'My husband and I were thrilled to hear of the birth of your daughter and that you have given her such a lovely Welsh name.'

'Just look at that!' Ellie had exclaimed to Matt, laughing. 'He's made an honest woman of her at last.' With the card there was a parcel of beautiful hand knitted jackets and a big stuffed Welsh dragon soft toy. 'I must phone and congratulate them straight away. And thank her for all these lovely gifts.'

Chapter 40

Throughout the year Greg and Charlie had lived their lives around the hole left when Ben died. For several months after, they had continued to visit the children's ward to see the young people they had got to know when Ben was a patient. They, and the other parents, shared a close bond that only people who have been thrown together by such tragic circumstances could ever know. Sadly, they grieved with some parents, knowing that there was nothing they could say to help but understanding their pain. More often than not, they rejoiced when a child returned home after a good recovery.

Both Greg and Charlie had thrown themselves into their work after Ben's death. For a time it seemed that they merely co-existed in the same space. They didn't seem able to connect. Charlie could understand how tragedy can break relationships. She grieved for Ben as if he had been her own son. She thought of how relationships are formed with people because they are connected to us through those that we love. This was the case with her and Ben, but because of the person he was, she had grown to love him just for being him. In the scale of things she had known him for such a short time, but he had changed her. She would never be the same person again after having let him into her heart.

For Greg the pain he felt at losing Ben seemed to swamp the love he felt for Charlie. He had been so angry at first. Angry that Ben would never follow that road signposted "The Future". He mourned the man he would have been. Angry that bad people had their lives and Ben didn't. There was so much that he wanted to share with him. He wanted to tell him how sorry he was that he had been such a useless father. Charlie had been so patient with him, sharing his grief, holding him when he cried.

'He'll always be with us, you know, even if he isn't alive,' she told him. And he would.

The crushing, overwhelming pain had faded over the past months to a dull ache as they lived their daily lives including Ben in as many ways as they could.

Charlie had designed a collection of furniture for a child's bedroom with pictures of a teddy bear surrounded by daisies. The co-ordinating fabric for bedding and curtains was printed with the same design. She had called it The Ben and Daisy Collection, by which she was able to acknowledge the kindness shown to Ben by his nurse. All the profits made from it were donated to the children's ward where Ben had been so lovingly cared for.

Despite the pain and sadness, the fact that Gina had come into their lives was a source of great delight to them both. As the months went by a close bond had developed. Greg and Gina seemed to take pleasure in each other's company as they got to know each other in a way they had never done before. Greg could barely believe that this beautiful, smart, intelligent young woman, with a wicked sense of humour, was his daughter. He was grateful for her kind and forgiving nature and knew he was fortunate to have been given a second chance. Gina and Charlie had become such good friends that they were almost like sisters.

The three of them enjoyed spending time together but it was more difficult now that Gina was a full-time student.

She had been lucky to get a place as a late entry to study nursing as a result of someone dropping out and she had now completed her first year at college. Greg admired her determination and her independence but he had insisted on giving her a car. She now drove down to see them when she could and they often went to Liverpool for the weekend.

One sunny, summer's evening, Charlie arrived home from work to hear Greg clattering around in the kitchen. His cooking skills had improved no end since they had been together and, as he was a better cook than she was, Charlie was quite happy to let him get on with it. Something was different today though: there was soft music playing and the table had been set with the best tableware.

Greg came rushing out of the kitchen and kissed her.

'What's going on? Have I forgotten something?' Charlie asked, looking puzzled.

'No, nothing at all,' Greg assured her. 'Off you go and freshen up then we can have a drink before dinner.'

She returned after a quick shower wearing a pretty dress to find Greg was waiting for her with a glass of champagne.

'You've got me really worried now,' she said. 'There must be something I've forgotten. I've looked at the date and nothing rings a bell. Tell me, what's special about today?'

'No, you haven't forgotten anything. It's just that it's two years since I moved in with you.'

'Is it really? I'm sorry I didn't remember.'

'Isn't life strange? In the past couple of years I've had to face one of the worst things anyone could go through and I wouldn't have been able to cope without you. Then Gina came into our lives. And, in you, I've found the woman I love and want to spend the rest of my life with.' From behind his back he brought out a single red rose and handed it to her with a kiss.

'Thank you,' she smiled at him. 'It's beautiful. I love you Greg.'

'I love you too, so very much,' he replied. 'Be careful of the rose in case there are thorns or insects or something else unexpected on it.'

She glanced down at the deep red bloom, so velvety that it almost seemed artificial. Then she did a double take and squealed. There, threaded on the stem was a diamond solitaire engagement ring.

'Oh Greg!... Oh Greg!' She slid the ring off and he took it from her and placed it on her finger. 'Oh Greg!...'

'I'm starting to get anxious now. Is it Oh Greg in a good way or a bad one?'

'Oh Greg!' she said again, 'It's lovely.'

'You do realise it's conditional, don't you?' he said putting his arms around her.

'Conditional on what?'

'That you'll definitely marry me, that you'll have lots of babies with me, that you'll help me find a lovely house for us to live in ... Oh! and that you'll stop putting your cold feet on me in bed.'

'Anything else?' she asked, raising an eyebrow ironically, leaning back in his arms.

'Yes, that we get a dog.'

She reached her face up to his and gave him a long, deep kiss before replying, 'Yes to nearly everything, maybe just not the feet!'

Greg insisted that she sat down while he served the meal he'd prepared. Charlie sat there turning her hand this way and that, watching the diamond glinting in the candlelight.

'The shop said you could change it if it isn't what you want or if the size is wrong.'

'It's perfect, just perfect.'

'It's been a long time coming, I know, but after Ben, it didn't seem right somehow.'

'I know,' she said. 'I know, my darling.'

'There was another reason too. Your parents are coming down next week and I was afraid that your father would think that I wasn't going to make an honest woman of you.'

The first thing they did was to get in touch with Gina who sounded sincerely happy for them on the phone.

'There's a bottle of champagne waiting here for when you get home,' Charlie giggled.

'Sounds to me as if you've been at the champagne already,' Gina said. 'Don't you dare open that other bottle without me.'

'Will you tell Mrs Mac and the others up there? We'll bring champagne for everybody when we come up next.'

Greg took the phone from Charlie and said 'Gina, are you really happy about us getting married?'

'What would you do if I said I wasn't?' she asked, taking the wind out of his sails for a moment. 'Dad, I'm joking,' she hastened to add when she heard silence down the phone. 'Of course I'm happy for you. I think Charlie is great and you make a lovely couple. I'm really thrilled for you. When's the big day?'

'Thank you, sweetheart. I don't know yet, you'd better ask Charlie.'

Charlie took the phone back. 'I don't know either. We'll talk about it when you come here. We'll see when you're free.'

Greg and Charlie spent the rest of the evening sipping their champagne and planning a future together, trying to decide how to make all their dreams come true. Charlie was still adamant that she didn't want a big fancy wedding and Greg didn't care. He just wanted to make her his.

Lying awake in bed that night Charlie wondered why being engaged made her so happy. She'd never been the sort of girl who hankered after a wedding ring. Friends had married but she'd never been envious. Some were happy, some were now divorced. Her parents remained happily married but she had never been a close witness to their marriage, they seemed like polite friends rather than a passionate couple. But they must have been – she'd come from somewhere hadn't she! She'd been independent from an early age and valued it. She wasn't one of those people who needed people, quite content on her own, she was used to it. So, why did the fact that she had a ring on her finger and was going to be Mrs Clark make her so happy? Had this love she felt been lying dormant inside her until Greg came along to rouse it? Greg had his flaws as she was well aware, but accepting his mistakes and his faults must mean that she loved him totally, and she did.

Chapter 41

It seemed to Ellie that no sooner had her little one come into their home than another of her children was leaving it. This time it was the turn of her second son to flee the nest. Will had done extremely well in his 'A' levels and had accepted a place to study Geography at Bangor University, North Wales. It was a beautiful area and he was full of plans to take part in all the outdoor activities the area was known for.

For the second time Ellie stood and waved a son off as he went, without her, to continue his education. This time she was staying behind because there was no room in the car for her and all the baby paraphernalia as well as Will and his belongings. Her parents had offered to come and stay but Angharad was teething and a bit fretful so she thought it best to stay behind. Will had been reluctant to leave and had come back several times to give Angharad 'one last kiss and cuddle'. He was absolutely besotted with her and seemed to have an affinity with her; she was always content when she was in his arms. Maybe it was the result of having held her within minutes of her birth.

Ellie wandered upstairs. The house seemed so empty without Will, even though he was the quietest, most self-contained of all her sons. His room smelled of him and she moved around picking up and putting down all those things that had seemed precious to him at some time or another but not important enough to take away with him: a shell from the beach in Glanaber, a fossil, a piece of rock. Will had turned out to be a gifted photographer and his bedroom walls were covered with examples of his talent. She saw that he had taken a couple of framed photos with him: one of them all outside the Tŷ Gwyn at Glanaber and one of a sweetly-smiling Angharad. Will had suggested that they turn his room into a nursery for the baby.

'Let's face it, Mum, it's unlikely that either Tom or I will come back home to live permanently again. Why don't you move my bed into his room and we'll share whenever we're home.'

His words had hurt at the time, she wasn't ready to let her boys go yet, but she supposed it was true. They were young men now, to all appearances, but they were still her little boys.

Chapter 42

Fiona was living the life she had always wanted. She lived in a beautiful house in its own grounds; it even had its own lake – well, bigger than a pond but not exactly Lake Windermere. And she had a wealthy husband. Was she happy? She sometimes wondered. She wasn't sure what being happy meant or how it was supposed to feel. Was happiness something you only recognised with hindsight?

She knew what sadness was. The loss of Ben hurt her more than anything in her life. In another way she had lost Gina too. Strangely, she rarely thought of her daughter. Did that make her a bad mother? She supposed it did. But motherhood was never something she sought – it was just visited upon her. She couldn't understand those women who craved motherhood and put themselves through so much to achieve it. How she regretted that foolish, throw-away remark she had made to Alistair about having a baby with him. She'd only said it to annoy Audrey but he kept going on about it. She hoped he wouldn't find the carefully hidden pills that would reveal her duplicity.

As a lover, Alistair was satisfying enough but she missed the conquests she had made when she was working. She'd always known when a man wanted more from her than her organisational skills. She would encourage them and then ignore them, making them wait until she decided the time was right – if they met with her approval that was. Yes, she missed the excitement and the feelings of wantonness and wickedness; the danger, and the power.

Fiona wasn't sad at the break-up of her marriage. Her initial fury at Greg had gone when she realised that she was better off without him, leaving her free to find someone better, someone richer. She didn't miss much from her old life. Funnily enough the one person she did miss was Ellie: kind, dependable Ellie. The thought had crossed her mind of getting in touch with her so that she could see where she was today but no, that final betrayal was too much. She was still amazed that Ellie had done such a thing.

Fiona realised that she was bored. Alistair loved his home and was content to stay in it. He enjoyed pottering in the grounds. It was a lovely house, beautifully and tastefully decorated and furnished by his late wife, Margaret. Sometimes she felt like changing something just for the hell of it. He would mumble uncomfortably that he liked it as it was because Margaret had done it. She would then put on her hurt face and say, 'But it's my home now and I'd like to do something different with it.'

He would hastily agree, 'Of course, my dear, I wasn't thinking. You must do as you want.'

That small victory was enough as she didn't change anything, recognising the late Margaret's taste and skill. She had always been house-proud but here, at The Grange, she didn't have any housework to do. That side of things was handled by Alistair's trusty ex-employee, Robert. Originally he had been employed at the engineering works but a road accident resulting in a head injury meant that the noise of the factory was too much for him. Alistair didn't want to lose the services of an honest, hard-working employee so he had offered him a job at The Grange. He was willing to turn his hand to anything and over the years Margaret and Robert had maintained the upkeep of the house and the grounds with the assistance of a small number of other workers.

When Margaret died he had taken a more prominent role in the care of the house and, together with a cleaner who came in a couple of times a week, Robert kept The Grange immaculate. He even did some cooking when necessary. Also, he had been a source of comfort to Alistair in those early days of his bereavement, often spending evenings with him playing chess, listening to him talk, or sitting in quiet reminiscence over a whisky. He was always unfailingly polite to Fiona, greeting her cordially when he arrived every day and asking her if there was anything specific she wanted him to do but she always had the feeling that he resented her. When she had sneeringly referred to him as "the daily male" Alistair had turned on her in fury.

'Don't you dare speak like that of Robert. He's a fine man and he's more than an employee – he's a friend of mine. You will not look down on him and you will treat him with respect. I'm disappointed in you, Fiona.' He looked directly into her eyes and spoke quietly but with a steely voice and, for the first time, Fiona saw a hint of the ruthlessness that had made him such a successful businessman.

Despite being the retired owner of a prestigious engineering company and having a Grade II listed home, Alistair didn't live the life of a rich man. He and Margaret had obviously led a quiet life. Fiona, however, had other ideas.

One of her hobbies was shopping. She had always had good taste in her own style and, rather than spend money on cheap shoes and handbags, she would wait until she could afford something classy, regularly window shopping and coveting what was out of her range. Now, she had a collection of designer handbags and matching shoes neatly lined up in her own dressing room. To her they were symbols of how far she had left her past behind. She was an attractive woman and always dressed smartly in expensive clothes. She loved tidying them and rearranging them in her dressing room, but where could she go to wear them? She no longer went out to work and she missed the envious looks of her colleagues. Fiona realised that she had no friends. Acquaintances, yes, but nobody she could call up and go shopping with or share a lunch with.

Several of Alistair's friends had fallen by the wayside, having been friends of his when he was part of a couple with Margaret. They felt he had married too quickly after her death. At first, they had been willing, almost eager, to accept invitations to dine at The Grange but they had merely been curious to meet the new Mrs Peak. When that curiosity had been satisfied they'd drifted away. Most of them were in the same age range as Alistair. So, apart from feeling bored, Fiona was also – lonely. She and Alistair had gone into their marriage without a shared basis of love or friendship. Their marriage had taken place too quickly for that, and it was taking a long time to build up, if it ever would. Sometimes she felt that he was drifting away from her and she certainly didn't want to lose Alistair and her comfortable lifestyle.

They had both developed a love of cruising holidays and had been away three times in the past year. Alistair was very interested in the countries they visited and took the opportunity to explore at every port of call. Fiona, however, preferred to lounge around on deck, dress up for the evening and have an occasional flutter in the casino. The countries they visited had all blended into one in her memory and she could only recall them according to what she had bought at the time.

She had eventually persuaded Alistair to buy her a new car and she loved zooming around in her little sports car. It had taken her several months of nagging but she persevered. She knew he would give in eventually but he wasn't as easy to twist around her little finger as she thought he would be.

It annoyed her that whenever she wanted to spend a large amount of money, Alistair always had to consult his solicitor or the bank manager. Surely, as a rich man, he shouldn't need to do this? She assumed that his money must be invested. He never discussed his finances with her but, as soon as they were married, he had set her up with her own bank account into which he transferred a monthly sum. Quite a meagre amount for a millionaire, in Fiona's opinion. She had invested her share of the money she had received after her divorce from Greg and she was constantly dipping into it when her spending exceeded what Alistair gave her.

Fiona often wondered if she had been wise in cutting herself off from Alistair's nieces and nephew. Perhaps she had been too hasty. Defensive from the start, she hadn't given them a chance to get to know her. They were closer to her age and she might have been able to make friends with them. They no longer came to the house and she knew Alistair was disappointed about that. He took them out for meals and although he was invited to their homes, the invitation never included Fiona. She knew it was her own fault and wondered if and how she could go about building bridges. It might make Alistair more generous if he saw that she was making an effort.

Then she had an idea which she knew would please him. It was Alistair's birthday in a couple of weeks. She would arrange a surprise party. First she needed to get Alistair's family on her side. He was out on the golf course so she would start immediately with Audrey.

Audrey sounded surprised when she heard Fiona's voice on the phone.

'Hello, Audrey. It's Fiona. I wonder if you would be kind enough to meet me over a cup of coffee so that we could have a chat about something. I don't want Alistair to know.'

'Er... I'm not sure. I wouldn't want to keep any secrets from Uncle Alistair.'

'Absolutely not. I know how fond you are of him, and him of you, but I would be grateful if you would just hear me out.'

'All right then. When?' said Audrey sounding ungracious, but clearly curious enough to agree.

'In the Coffee Pot in town in an hour?'

She rushed to get ready. What to wear? Nothing with a designer label or Audrey would think she was spending Alistair's money unnecessarily, so... smart casual.

Fiona was waiting at a table when Audrey walked in, looking around hesitantly. A bit frumpy, thought Fiona, needs a hairdo and some decent clothes but she waved with a smile on her face. She didn't get up to greet her with an air kiss, or a kiss of any kind, as that would have seemed a bit insincere. With coffee and cake ordered Fiona smiled and fidgeted with the little menu.

'I'm sure you were surprised to hear from me,' she said.

'You could say that.' Audrey sat back in her chair.

'I don't blame you.' Fiona wriggled around in her chair as if she didn't know how to go on. But she did, she had rehearsed this conversation in her head since phoning. 'Can I be perfectly honest with you?'

Audrey folded her arms and nodded, her body language indicating that she wasn't going to make this easy.

'When we first met, I was in a really bad place. Everything in my life had changed almost in the blink of an eye. First of all my husband left me, then my daughter ran away from home because she blamed me and now doesn't want anything to do with me. Then, the worst thing of all...' she took out her handkerchief and dabbed her eyes, '...Ben.'

'Yes, that must have been awful for you.' A mother herself, Fiona knew she would empathise with her. 'Jane and I wanted to help but you didn't seem to want anything to do with us.'

Fiona took a sip of coffee and pushed the plate of cakes towards Audrey. 'I know. You must all think I'm such a horrible person. But I'm not really,' she gave a tremulous smile. 'I was just so scared. Everything I had ever loved had gone. My husband left me for another woman, my daughter ran away, and I was so low. Then I met Alistair. He was wonderful. So kind. I was afraid to trust anyone and told myself that I didn't need a man in my life, but he gradually wore me down. Ben became ill and I didn't think I could cope. Then Alistair asked me to marry him and, because Ben was so ill, I didn't think it was fair for me to be so happy and I asked if we could have a quiet wedding. He really wanted you all there and it was my fault that you weren't. I'm so sorry. But you can see how things were for me, can't you?'

Audrey was now leaning forward at the table. 'Yes Uncle Alistair said you'd had a terrible time. But afterwards, you never seemed to want to have anything to do with us.'

'Again, you're right. I imagined that you thought I had married him for his money.'

Audrey couldn't lie. 'It did cross our minds. He said you had met when you were working in an hotel.'

'No, I was staying at the same hotel as him. I was an event organiser and I had been keeping an eye on a function there. It was only something I had taken up after the children were in school full time to keep myself occupied. My husband was the managing director of quite a prestigious company so I didn't need the money. The work kept me occupied.' Fiona was trying to sound as if she hadn't paid any heed to Alistair's wealth.

'We did try to be nice to you but you never wanted to know.' Audrey wasn't going to let her off easily.

'You're right. I just wanted Alistair for myself. I was so insecure after all I'd been through. It's taken me a while to see how silly I've been. Alistair thinks so much of you all. I wonder if we could start again? What I'd like to do is to arrange a surprise party for his birthday, in a couple of weeks, and invite you, Jane and Andrew and your families. I thought it would be more fun if it was a surprise for him.'

'I'll speak to Andrew and Jane, but as far as I'm concerned we can start planning now. You will let me help won't you?'

'Well, I'm the event organiser in the family,' Fiona wasn't ready to relinquish all her power just yet, 'but I'm sure there will be plenty to do and I would be grateful for your help.'

'I must dash now, but I'll give you a call over the next day or so.' Audrey rushed out, leaving Fiona at the table, sighing with relief. Pleased with her performance, she took out her powder compact and dabbed her face. *That went well,* she thought to herself, *and the truth fairy won't have too much to complain about, most of what I said was true; it's just down to perception.* Audrey had obviously been won over. Now it was up to her to persuade the others.

Fiona had shared the idea of a surprise birthday party with Robert and had roped him in to help. She had also issued him with an invitation to attend which, she knew, would please Alistair. He was more than willing to help but declined the invitation as he felt it was a familiarity too far. Fiona wasn't bothered, she had asked him and she would make sure Alistair knew. She had pulled a few strings with some old contacts and arranged caterers to prepare and serve the meal. That dratted Audrey had insisted on offering to do this and that so, in order to keep her quiet, Fiona had asked her to make some flower arrangements and arrange party packs which would keep the children quiet. Andrew had two, Audrey had three and Jane had one little toddler.

Fiona could never remember their names and vowed she would make an effort to learn them.

Jane had called round unexpectedly. She wasn't quite as easy to manipulate as Audrey had been and, although Fiona had given her the same sob story, she wasn't as sympathetic as she should have been, in Fiona's opinion.

As she left she said, 'Whatever the reason is behind this family get together, I'm prepared to go through with it for Uncle Alistair's sake.'

'What other reason could there possibly be apart from Alistair's birthday? And that we get to know each other a bit better as well,' Fiona said in surprise, with as sincere a smile as she could manage.

Andrew hadn't called but he had telephoned on a day when he knew Alistair was in a meeting on behalf of the company.

'Audrey has been in touch about this party,' he said. 'Why are you holding a family party for him? You've never shown any interest in Uncle Alistair's family before.'

Fiona guessed that her sob story wouldn't cut it with him so thought she would turn the tables and make it sound as if it was their fault. She said, 'Yes, and it has been very foolish of me. I felt that none of you liked me and thought I had ulterior motives for marrying him. I'm hoping that, by now, you can see we are happy and you are willing to accept me.'

'I'm sorry you felt like that when it was patently untrue. I'm willing to come to the party with my family and I won't mention it to Uncle Alistair. I hope he will enjoy the surprise.'

'Hmm,' mused Fiona as she put down the phone, 'what a gracious acceptance to a party.'

On the appointed day Fiona thought she was doomed to failure because Alistair had arranged to play golf with some friends. She insisted that they went shopping to a town about thirty miles away.

'Surely I get to decide what I want to do on my birthday?' he said petulantly. 'And shopping is something I don't want to do,' he added with emphasis.

Fiona pretended to be upset. 'That's so unkind of you, not wanting to share your birthday with me. And I especially wanted us to have lunch out and I wanted to buy you a special present. I've put so much effort in finding something I thought you'd like. I didn't think you could be so selfish. You can play golf at any time.'

The guilt trip she'd laid on him worked because he sighed and said reluctantly, 'All right. I'll phone the others to rearrange the golf.'

It wasn't with the best of grace that he joined her for the drive. However, Alistair was a good-natured man so his mood improved as the morning wore on, especially when their first port of call was to a specialist nursery. After consulting Robert, Fiona had ordered some trees and plants for his garden, with the proviso that Alistair gave his approval for the final selection. He was thrilled at her thoughtfulness and very impressed with the nursery and the expertise of the plant expert. He ended up ordering several more plants and arranged for everything to be delivered. He wanted to take Fiona out for a lavish lunch but, of course, she declined, suggesting that they ate in the little café at the nursery which served plain home-cooked food.

'I've booked a table for dinner this evening,' she said with a smile when he continued to try and persuade her, 'at somewhere rather nice but I'm not going to tell you where just yet.'

'You're spoiling me now, my darling. Thank you so much. You couldn't have given me a gift I would like more. You've been so thoughtful. Shall we pop into town after this so that you can do a bit of shopping and I can treat you to a little gift.'

'It's your birthday, not mine!' she exclaimed. 'There's no need to get anything for me. I'm so glad that you're pleased with my present.' And, perhaps for the first time, Fiona felt the joy of giving, even though, technically, it was Alistair's money that she had spent. She realised that she had become very fond of her husband, had even come to love him in her own way. She had watched him indulgently and noticed his pleasure in wandering around the plants and speaking to the experts and it brought her pleasure to see him so happy. 'Why don't you carry on strolling around for a bit longer? I'm quite content wandering around the gift shop here, they've got lots of pretty and unusual things and I can do some Christmas shopping. I'm not saying I definitely don't want to go into town,' she went on with a smile, thinking that her timing had to be accurate for the surprise to work.

The light was fading and it was time to go home. As they turned into the gates of The Grange, Fiona crossed her fingers, hoping that everything had gone to plan. They continued up the well-lit drive and when the house came into view the curtains of the reception room had been left open allowing the soft light to spill into the dark evening. The lamps on either side of the front door were lit making the house seem welcoming.

'I rather wish we were having an evening at home, my darling,' Alistair said. 'It would be nice to relax over a nice meal and decent bottle of burgundy.'

'If you want to stay home, then that is what we shall do, it is your birthday after all, so it's up to you,' Fiona said.

Robert was in the hall when they entered. Alistair shook his hand, saying 'I believe you and my wife have been in cahoots. Thank you very much. She wouldn't have known what to order but for you. You and I are going to have our work cut out when these plants are delivered.'

He gave Fiona an almost imperceptible nod and she said, 'Robert, we've decided to dine in after all instead of going out. I wonder if you would mind digging something out of the freezer for us. We'll just pop up and change. When we come down we'll come to the lounge so I wonder if you'll put out a bottle of champagne for us please.'

They had just changed and were about to go downstairs when Alistair turned to Fiona,

'Did you hear something? Is there someone here? I thought I heard voices.'

'I think Robert has the television on,' she replied. 'Come on, darling, let's go down.'

Just before they entered the lounge Alistair turned for the kitchen and said, 'I'll just remind Robert to decant the burgundy.'

'No, don't. He knows what to do and he'll be busy with the food.' Fiona tugged his arm and pushed him ahead of her into the sitting room.

As soon as the door opened, everyone shouted 'Happy birthday' and the children rushed over to Alistair. His face was a picture, and pleasure took over the astonishment in no time.

He turned to Fiona who stood back, 'Darling, is this your doing?'

Audrey came over and looped her arm through Fiona's. 'Yes, Uncle Alistair, it was all Fiona's idea.'

Fiona was quick to follow with what was expected. 'But I couldn't have done it without everyone's help, especially Audrey's. She's been marvellous.'

Alistair appeared delighted and thrilled that his family and wife were together at last. He turned to her and kissed her warmly. 'Thank you. Thank you so much. This has been such a wonderful birthday and to think I was grumpy because I couldn't play golf.'

Just then they were interrupted by Audrey's eldest daughter who presented Fiona with a beautiful bouquet of flowers. 'Thank you for having us,' she said shyly. 'This is from all the young ones.'

'How kind,' responded Fiona politely. 'You are making me feel like royalty now giving me such beautiful flowers. How pretty you are and what a lovely dress,' she added, making little Lucy blush to the roots of her blonde hair.

The evening was a resounding success. The caterers had excelled themselves with the food; every dish was delicious and beautifully presented and served. They had all sat around the large dining table with its pristine white cloth, gleaming silver and crystal glassware, candles flickering. Audrey made a point of fussing over Fiona and trying to include her in every conversation. Jane, on the other hand, was pleasant but more reserved. Their husbands were courteous enough to her, as was Andrew's wife. The children behaved themselves admirably, on the whole, and Fiona was successful in biting her lip when over-excitement had them running around until their parents regained control.

Alistair was as excited as a child, turning to Fiona and mouthing quietly every now and then, 'Thank you, darling.' When he was presented with his gifts, he asked the children, 'Who's going to help me open these?' to which they enthusiastically responded by tearing the paper off the beautifully-wrapped parcels.

Andrew seemed to avoid Fiona until later on in the evening. She was standing to one side at the far end of the room near the drinks cabinet and had just poured herself some wine. Glass in hand, she was observing the room. The children were amusing themselves with the bags of gifts that Audrey had provided, showing Alistair their efforts at colouring; the adults were chatting quietly. Andrew sauntered over to her. 'What are you up to?' he asked softly.

'What do you mean?' Fiona replied, turning her head to look directly at him.

'I know you're up to something. I'm afraid I just don't buy this happy family nonsense coming from you. You might have fooled Audrey but you haven't fooled me. There's some ulterior motive behind all this 'get together'.'

'If you can think of a motive, then please tell me. What have I got to gain from doing this, apart from making my husband happy?'

'At the moment, I don't know. But I'm keeping an eye open. You're in for a surprise if you think you can manipulate Alistair. He's more astute than you know.'

'Successful men usually are,' she smiled and left him standing there, moving to join Alistair.

When the children became fractious it was clear that it was time for the evening to end. Everyone thanked Fiona warmly for arranging the party and she stoically put up with being kissed by Audrey. Andrew hugged his uncle and gave Fiona a cool nod.

Alistair closed the front door behind them all and turning to Fiona he said, 'I thought you had given me the best birthday present this afternoon with all those plants, but this party has been better still. Thank you, darling, I'm so grateful to you. The more the family get to know you, the more they will love you as I do.'

She smiled, 'I'm so pleased you enjoyed yourself. I'm just going to check that everything is cleared in the kitchen and then I'm going to bed. I'm exhausted. Can I get you another drink?'

'It's all right, I'll do it. I think I'll just unwind with a small brandy. I have a bit of indigestion after that delicious meal but I won't be long. Goodnight, my darling.'

Fiona went through to the kitchen. The catering staff had cleared the dining room and the kitchen. Robert was there putting a few things away and tidying up.

'Why don't you leave that until tomorrow?' Fiona asked him.

'No, I'd prefer to come back to find everywhere tidy in the morning,' he replied. 'It will only take me another half hour or so.'

'Thank you again for your help. Alistair was delighted with the plants.' He nodded politely and Fiona went upstairs.

Fiona was just drifting off to sleep when there was a loud knocking on her door. She leapt out of bed to find a distraught Robert.

'Please come down now. It's Alistair. I've called an ambulance,' he said, almost in tears.

Grabbing her dressing gown she ran downstairs. At first she wondered why Robert was in such a state. Alistair was sitting in his chair, he'd obviously drifted off to sleep and he had a hint of a smile on his face. Then she noticed that the brandy glass was on its side on the floor.

'Alistair,' she said quietly, then more loudly, 'Alistair.' Shouting now, she rushed over to him and tried to shake him. 'Wake up,' she shouted.

Robert came over and took her by the shoulders. 'He won't wake up, Fiona,' he said sadly. 'He'll never wake up again.'

Over the next few hours Fiona realised why Alistair had thought so much of Robert. He dealt, in a calm, efficient manner with the police, the ambulance crew, the doctor, the undertaker. He had telephoned Andrew, Audrey and Jane who all returned immediately to The Grange. Throughout everything he took care of Fiona with great kindness.

She couldn't stop shivering so he made some tea and prepared a hot water bottle for her. Audrey asked the doctor for something to make Fiona sleep and insisted on spending the night with her at The Grange, despite Fiona's protests.

The following morning Fiona woke up with a dull, heavy headache and, glancing at the clock by her side, she realised she had slept late which was unlike her. Then the events of the previous evening came to her with a jolt. She had no sooner sat up in bed when there was a quiet knock on her door and Audrey came in with a cup of tea.

'It's true then. It wasn't just an awful nightmare,' Fiona said.

'No, I only wish it was,' Audrey said sympathetically. Her eyes were puffy and red.

'How are you?'

'I don't know,' replied Fiona honestly. 'I can't believe it. Alistair wasn't an old man. What happened?'

'The doctor thinks it was a massive heart attack but there will have to be a post mortem.'

'I must get up,' Fiona started to push the bedclothes away. 'There must be so much to do.'

'No, you stay where you are and try and get some rest. Andrew's downstairs and he will handle everything.'

'No, really, I must get up. Someone gave me a tablet last night and I've slept heavily and I still feel a bit drugged. There must be something I should be doing ...' she tailed off 'but I don't know what.'

'Andrew's downstairs in the study. He'll make all the arrangements, don't worry yourself about it.'

After her shower Fiona stood in her dressing room trying to decide how to present herself. She opted for something plain, suitable for a newly-bereaved widow. Widow, she thought to herself. That was what she was now. A widow.

She looked at herself in the mirror. She didn't think the family would deem it suitable for her to wear make-up so she satisfied herself with the smallest hint of foundation. She supposed that she ought to be crying, but apart from the initial shock she could find no tears inside her. Was she upset? Obviously Alistair wasn't the love of her life and she had been very fond of him, but she wasn't broken-hearted. She realised she had to be careful if she wanted the help of his family. There would be so much to do, she surmised, and it would be nice to have someone else to do it for her. She went downstairs to Alistair's study and found Andrew going through the drawers.

He stood up and shook her hand formally. 'Please accept my condolences. What an awful shock for you.'

'Yes, it was. Especially as we had had such a lovely day for his birthday and he was thrilled to have had all of you here for his party. Perhaps it was my fault; perhaps the whole thing was too much for him.' Fiona looked up at Andrew with genuine shock at the thought.

'I don't think so. If it was a massive heart attack as the doctor thinks it was, it could have happened at any time.'

'What are you doing?' asked Fiona. 'Is there something I should be doing?'

'No, it's all right. I'll handle everything – with your agreement,' he added as an afterthought. 'I'm just going through Alistair's papers in case he left any instructions regarding his funeral. Do you know of any?'

'No, we never even discussed death or funerals. We thought there was so much time to enjoy living.'

Over the next few days, as news of Alistair's death percolated through to everyone, Fiona was glad that Andrew, Audrey and Jane were around to deal with the callers and telephone calls. They were from people she hardly knew anyway. She was happy to leave most of the arrangements to them all as she sat in the drawing room listening to them planning his funeral. When she heard them say that they would have one big wreath on the coffin, with yellow and white flowers from the gardens, she sat up and said 'No' sharply. The others looked at her in surprise as she burst into tears, the first time that any of them had seen her cry.

'Please, no,' she said, 'anything but yellow and white. Those were the colour of the flowers on Ben's coffin. Anything but that.'

Audrey leapt up to comfort her. 'Of course we won't in that case. Tell us what you would like.'

'Alistair loved Christmas colours. Could we have something red, and maybe some lilies? You choose, Audrey. You're so good with flowers. Would you excuse me please, I think I'll just take a walk before it gets too dark.'

Fiona, wrapped up warmly against the winter chill, walked down as far as the lake. She turned and looked up at the house, the mellow stone and the windows reflecting the warm colours of the setting sun. She felt a worm of excitement wriggle inside her. Just the funeral to get through and then... What lay ahead for a rich widow? What indeed.

Chapter 43

I had absolutely no regrets about choosing a nursing career. Now, in my second year, I was coping fairly comfortable with the academic side but I loved the practical side of things when I had contact with the patients. The only thing that I disliked was when I was constantly chivvied on by the staff nurse or sister because I spent too much time on each patient.

I was at a different hospital from Elaine, Sarah and Nicola so I never came across them at work but I maintained a close friendship with them. When Nicola decided to move in with her boyfriend they tried to persuade me to take her place but I was happy with Mrs Mac and, even though it was further to travel to and from work, I preferred to stay there. They welcomed me to stay over whenever there was a party or when we all went out together. It didn't happen often, I wasn't really a party person and I wasn't looking for a boyfriend. Tom still filled my thoughts in a pipe dream sort of way. When one of the girls mentioned that they had met a medical student from the north east named Tom, who had been on a study seminar, my heart fluttered briefly but I mentally shrugged at the impossible coincidence of it being my Tom. My Tom! I couldn't help a wry smile to myself at the irony. I had become friendly with a fellow student, an Irish girl called Aoife, when we were both nervous first year students. She was a year younger than I and very homesick at first but soon settled down, enjoying her choice of career as much as I did. When I mentioned the flat-share vacancy, Aoife jumped at the chance of moving in and had, by now, become firm friends with the other girls.

Much to my surprise, Henrietta had left me a sum of money in her will. When the letter came from the solicitor with the cheque for £5,000 I couldn't believe my eyes. There was also a note enclosed from Henrietta's daughter, again thanking me for caring for her mother and wishing me well. I hoped she realised what a friend Henrietta had been to me. I thought back to the last time Henrietta and I had spoken and I remembered exactly what she had said: 'the rest of your life is in your hands, it will be what you make of it.' I wished she had lived long enough to see me on the path of my chosen career. There had been such a connection between us, proving that age doesn't govern a friendship.

The damp, foggy December weather was making me look forward to Christmas. It was going to be a very different Christmas for me this year. Dad and Charlie were getting married in Barbados. They were having a beach wedding and I was to be a bridesmaid for the second time in as many months. I was honoured to be asked to be bridesmaid in Carla and Darren's wedding and delighted to have been able to share their happy day. Mrs Mac warned me that I mustn't agree to being a bridesmaid again.

Why on earth not?' I asked

'Three times a bridesmaid, never a bride. That's what they say.'

'You and your superstitions!' I scoffed whilst thinking I would never be a bride unless I settled for second best.

When I told Mrs Mac about Dad and Charlie marrying on the beach she was astonished at such a thing, from the look on her face I might have well have said they were getting married on the moon! She very much doubted that it was right in the eyes of the Lord.

'On the beach! Is that legal? Oh! My goodness.' She thought for a bit before going on, 'How will her father walk her down the aisle? Where will all the guests sit? Everyone will get sand in their shoes. What about the hymns?'

The questions and comments came thick and fast and I tried to paint a simple picture for her.

'The wedding will take place at sunset. On the beach there will be a small area prepared for us and Dad and Charlie will walk up to the priest and he'll marry them. Her parents will be there and I will be, and that's all. Afterwards they will be Mr and Mrs Clark and we'll all go and have a nice meal.'

'Well...' said Mrs Mac astounded at the whole thing. 'It sounds very strange to me but I'm a bit old-fashioned, I suppose. I'm sure they know what they're doing.'

I promised to take lots of photos and to deliver the wedding gift she had bought them.

I was due to drive down to their flat in a day or so and had been trying to pack but it was difficult to think that I only needed to put summer clothes in my suitcase when it was so cold outside. Charlie had asked me what sort of dress I wanted but I had told her to choose, confident in Charlie's taste that she would select something that I was bound to like. Dad had asked if I wanted to take someone with me for company but I was happy to go alone.

A warm welcome awaited me when I arrived at Dad and Charlie's. Charlie was bouncing with excitement and couldn't wait to show the dress she had bought for me as well as her own wedding dress. I loved them and told Charlie how honoured I was to be sharing their happy day.

'The only thing that concerns me is that I'm going to be such a gooseberry in sharing your honeymoon. But I promise I'll keep out of your way. I'm absolutely exhausted so all I want to do is relax in the sun,' I smiled at the bride-to-be.

'Don't be so silly. We're thrilled that you are going to be there. We don't see enough of you,' Charlie reassured me.

Dad had a thick file of particulars of houses he wanted to show me. 'I was hoping you could help us choose our new home. I want it to be a home for all three of us.' he said.

'Dad, that's really lovely of you. But you don't need to consider me. It's never going to be my home really, is it?' His face fell as I went on. 'I'm happy living on Merseyside and that is where my life is. That's not to say I won't come down and see you as often as I can.'

'I just want you to know that, whatever happens in your life, you'll always have a home here with two people who love you very much.'

I gave him a big hug. 'Thanks, Dad. I love you too, very much, and Charlie.'

I started to appreciate the kind of upbringing Charlie had had when we stepped out into the heat of the airport in Barbados. A limousine was waiting and drove us past corrugated shacks and small houses up into the hills where the homes became larger and grander. As we wound up a curving drive with a manicured lawn, Philip and Susan waited on the veranda of their beautiful villa and greeted us warmly. Two beaming members of the house staff were hovering in the background, excited to see Charlie. She threw her arms around them and hugged them both, asking after their children and families.

Then came the day of the wedding. It was perfect. Charlie looked beautiful in a slim-fitting white lace gown, elegant and simple, with pearls and crystals embroidered on the bodice. She wore tropical flowers in her hair and carried a small bouquet of colourful matching blooms, Dad wore a white suit and I wore the elegant dress selected by Charlie. It shaded gradually from a pale blue bodice to a deep aquamarine at the hem. I felt like a mermaid who had just stepped out of the deep blue sea. The setting sun tinted the sky with shades ranging from duck egg to peach and then finally orange and red. Gentle waves whispered, guitars played and singers sang. Inevitably Susan cried, and my eyes watered as well, when Dad and Charlie faced each other and made their vows in the company of their loved ones, half a dozen family friends and several ghost crabs. They both looked so happy and I felt a surge of love for my dad and this young woman who had turned him into the loving man he now was.

Afterwards Philip and Susan hosted a small reception at an hotel and, despite the wedding being so informal, they couldn't dispense with the traditional speeches from the bride's father and the groom.

Dad and Charlie spent a couple of days a few miles down the coast at a beach bungalow loaned by some friends of Philip's. I stayed with Philip and Susan who were delighted to show me the island where they had made their home and made me feel welcome. They took me into Bridgetown to see the red and green Christmas decorations and lights, the roundabouts were decorated to portray various Christmas themes. It was odd to hear the radios playing songs about snow and winter weather when the sun was blazing down. I enjoyed a relaxing few days before Dad and Charlie returned for Christmas. They joined in the tradition of strolling around Queen's Park in Bridgetown on Christmas morning wearing their finery. I was amazed at the enormous baobab tree that is said to be over a thousand years old. The rest of the day, as is usual everywhere, was based around family, friends and food and we all enjoyed the traditional baked ham, jug jug – which was a bit like haggis – and fruit cake.

It was soon time for Mr and Mrs Clark and me to catch the flight home. I had enjoyed my holiday, despite my initial reservations about encroaching on Dad and Charlie's honeymoon. Everyone had made me so welcome and I was returning to my studies in a relaxed frame of mind.

Charlie kissed her parents warmly saying, 'Mother, Father, thank you so much for everything. I've had the perfect wedding day and I'm so glad you're happy for me.'

'We can see that Greg has made you happy and I trust him to look after you,' replied Philip, giving Dad a semi-mock stern look.

'That's one thing of which you can be absolutely certain,' he said shaking hands with his father-in-law and giving his mother-in-law a kiss on her cheek.

'We'll see you again before too long,' Susan said. 'We're coming to see the aunts in a few weeks or they'll never forgive us. Dotty and Dissy might be getting on but they always remind us when we're due to visit, bless them.'

The limousine was waiting to take them to the airport but I just had to take 'one last photograph' several times.

'Come on, or we'll miss the flight,' chivvied Charlie as yet another photo was taken.

'Yes, Mummy,' I replied jumping into the car, leaving Philip and Susan with the sound of laughter echoing in their ears as the car moved slowly down the drive.

Chapter 44

Matt and Ellie had the busiest but best Christmas ever. The boys came home, bringing new friends to stay and inviting old friends over at various points during the holiday. Angharad, was a bonny little baby who had her brothers in the palm of her chubby little hands – the two oldest that is, they played with her patiently, handing her toys which she promptly threw down with a giggle. The twins, who saw her daily weren't quite so patient!

Tom and Will's friends were also patient with the little girl. Tom's friend, Arun, was from India and didn't have enough time to go home for the holiday so Tom had invited him to spend the holiday with them. He was a quiet, polite young man with dark chocolate eyes. Angharad had taken quite a shine to him despite his shy manner. She sat on his lap and stuck her thumb in her mouth and rested her head against his chest and he spoke softly to her telling stories of his childhood as if she understood every word. A paediatrician if ever I saw one, thought Ellie.

Will, too, had brought a friend home for the holiday. She was also studying at Bangor. Her name was Louise and Ellie had wondered if romance was in the air, but Will assured his parents that they were just friends, muttering that she was having parent problems. She was tiny and only looked about fourteen with her slim figure and urchin haircut, but Will said she was extremely bright and as fit and strong as any of them when they went on field trips. He mentioned casually that the two of them might spend some time travelling after their degree as neither had taken a gap year before university as they had intended. The Band Aid hit of the season 'Do They Know It's Christmas' had had a profound effect on them and, apart from raising money at uni, they wanted to do more. When Louise first held out her arms Angharad twisted her body and reached out to Arun instead.

'That's put me in my place,' laughed Louise.

Despite having the house full of people Ellie wasn't rushed off her feet as everyone was so ready to help and, in true Ellie fashion, she had been preparing for weeks so the pantry and larder were full.

One morning she crept down to the kitchen to make the first cup of tea of the day and found Louise sitting there with a cup in front of her.

'You don't mind, do you ...?' she asked hesitantly.

'Of course not. I told you to make yourself at home,' Ellie assured her pouring herself a cup. They sipped companionably for a while.

'You're awfully kind to have me here at such a busy time,' said Louise.

Ellie shrugged, 'The more the merrier. As long as you take us as you find us, that is.'

'My parents wouldn't be so accommodating,' she sighed.

Ellie wasn't sure what to say so simply remarked, 'Everyone's home is different, I suppose.'

'Home? I couldn't wait to leave home. That's why I studied so hard.'

Ellie said nothing, sipping her tea quietly, suspecting that Louise had more to say. When she appeared to be blinking away tears Ellie took a chance and put her hand over Louise's comfortingly. This opened the floodgates.

'My parents divorced this year – at long last. It was a bitter divorce and I was fed up with being stuck in the middle. They both wanted me to go to them for Christmas. Can you imagine that? Expecting me to choose so that one could score points off the other. No way. I've had enough of that over the years. So they're both on their own and it serves them right.' Ellie sensed the hurt and sadness and stood up to give the young girl a hug. 'Will is so lucky to have parents like you,' her words muffled into Ellie's shoulder.

Ellie closed her eyes tightly and thought that she was the lucky one.

Chapter 45

Four thousand miles away from the blue skies and sunshine of Barbados, the grey, drizzly December day reflected the mood of the mourners at Alistair's funeral. There were so many people expected that they used the church hall next door as an overflow location and had fitted it out with speakers so that everyone could take part in the service. It was a measure of the man that so many turned up to pay their respects. The factory was closed for the holiday period and most of those who worked there turned to say farewell to the man who had given them their livelihood and treated them so fairly throughout their time with Peak Engineering.

Fiona had maintained a quiet dignity throughout the days following Alistair's death and the funeral. She had allowed Andrew, Audrey and Jane a free hand in arranging the service. They had consulted her over everything and had chosen well. The hymns were familiar and the church was filled with the voices of the congregation; the readings were read with sincerity by the vicar and Robert, who asked if he could take part in the ceremony even though it was clearly a strain for him; Andrew paid a moving tribute to his uncle which brought tears to everyone eyes, including Fiona's.

The only hint of awkwardness had been about where to bury Alistair. Andrew and his sisters had been very hesitant in broaching the subject and Audrey had been the one to bring the matter up.

'Had Uncle Alistair ever mentioned to you where he would like to be buried?' she asked gently.

'No. It isn't something we ever discussed. I know he was older than I but we both thought we were a long way from dying. Did he say anything to you?' replied Fiona.

Audrey looked a bit uncomfortable. 'Not lately but...'

'But?' Fiona questioned.

'Well he always said that he wanted to be buried with Aunty Margaret. But that was before he met you of course,' she went on hastily.

'Oh.' Fiona reflected for a moment and then looked at the three of them. 'Is that what you would like?'

'How do you feel about it?' Audrey asked.

'I know that Margaret was the love of his life and from what I've gathered he was hers. They had a long and happy marriage which was ended too soon. Alistair and I loved each other too, but it was a different kind of love. We didn't have enough time...' she broke off, and then gathering herself together she went on, 'if you think that is what Alistair would have wanted please arrange for him to be buried with Margaret.'

Fiona knew that her words has surprised them all, especially Andrew and she wondered if they were starting to think that they had misjudged her all along.

In the days leading up to the funeral Fiona had hidden her irritation with Audrey's well-meant visits.

'Please come and spend Christmas Day with us,' she said. 'We have to have some kind of a Christmas for the children's sake even though it will be a bit more low-key than usual.'

Fiona shuddered at the thought but replied graciously enough that she would prefer to be on her own.

What had irritated Fiona more than anything was Andrew's constant presence at The Grange. She knew he was an executor of the will and he said he was going through

Alistair's papers but, for goodness' sake, how many papers were there? It was true that he spent most of the time in the study and Fiona took him a cup of coffee occasionally. She felt that he was constantly scrutinising her, sometimes she caught an odd expression on his face, a slightly supercilious smirk perhaps. But maybe she was just imagining it. Then she guessed what it was. Had Alistair left the factory to Andrew? That was highly likely, she decided. What did she care? She couldn't run a factory anyway and wasn't the slightest bit interested in doing so. No, she would be quite happy with the house and the money. The first thing she would do would be to reorganise the study. It was such a pleasant room, looking out on to the grounds at the back of the house and it caught the afternoon and evening sunshine. She would turn it into a small sitting room for herself.

Following the funeral Fiona had agreed that a small reception be held at The Grange. How glad she would be when everything was over. The past few days had been such a strain but she felt she had acquitted herself well as the shocked and grieving young widow, not that she had been play acting entirely, of course.

After the reception when everyone had left and the caterers had cleared, only Robert remained, tidying around, drawing curtains, locking doors and windows before he left for the evening.

'Robert,' Fiona said. 'I would just like to thank you for reading at the funeral. I know how difficult it must have been. And thank you too for everything over the last few days. I don't know what I would have done without you.'

Robert looked at her in surprise. She had never shown any appreciation in the past for anything that he did. 'You're welcome. It's only what Alistair would have wanted me to do.'

'I do hope you will stay on now that he is no longer here. I doubt The Grange would survive without you,' she said ruefully.

'We'll see, shall we, Mrs Peak. Let's not think of that for now.'

When he left, Fiona sat down in one of the comfortable chairs in the drawing room and kicked off her shoes. There wasn't a sound. Of course there wasn't, there was nobody else here. She realised that this was the first time she had ever been alone in the house. For a moment she felt swamped by the loneliness that had crept up on her during the last few months of her marriage. Would she stay at The Grange? It was a huge house, far too big for one. And worth a fortune. She sat there in the silence. An owl hooted outside the window and she shuddered.

A few days later, with the beginning of a new decade only a couple of days away, the solicitor arranged to come to The Grange for the reading of the will. Fiona hadn't expected this as she thought it was the sort of practice one only saw in films but Andrew had arranged everything. Mr Tumbril from Tumbril, Tumbril and Finch presented himself at the appointed time. Fiona was expecting an elderly gentleman but it was a young, smartly-suited man who shook Fiona's hand. She showed him through to the drawing room where Andrew, Audrey and Jane were sitting and also Robert. Andrew had insisted on his presence so Fiona guessed that there might be a bequest for him.

Fiona listened as Mr Tumbril went through the formalities. The will was dated before his marriage to Fiona and he said that, as no other will had come to light, this was declared the last will and testament of Alistair Peak Fiona listened with a twinge of anxiety as Mr Tumbril read out a list of bequests, some small and some more substantial. Then Robert's name was mentioned. Alistair had left him the cottage in which he lived, just outside the grounds. Overcome with emotion Robert took out his handkerchief and blew his nose. Fiona didn't even know Alistair owned it. She was thinking how little she knew about Alistair's wealth; he must have been very rich if he was able to make all these bequests. She was finding it difficult to concentrate as she wondered what to do with all her money. Then she realised Mr Tumbril was gathering his papers together and Andrew was looking at her with a condescending expression. Audrey and Jane merely looked at her in shock.

'What...?' she asked confused.

'You did understand, didn't you?' Andrew said.

'No, I'm sorry, I didn't.' Fiona replied.

'There's nothing for you,' Andrew said bluntly, and she detected a hint of satisfaction in his voice.

'The factory, the house, the cars, everything... It was all left to the trust. After Margaret died Alistair set up a trust which gave him the right to draw out an income for life. Upon his death the trust is shared between Audrey, Jane and me. So, I'm afraid that all you are entitled to is any personal items and any money he had in his personal bank account – and whatever gifts he made to you, of course.'

'That can't be right. No, no. We were married. I was his next of kin.' Fiona's voice rose into a shriek.

With exaggerated calmness, Andrew turned to his sisters, 'Let's give Fiona a few minutes in private with Mr Tumbril so that he can explain everything properly to her.'

When Mr Tumbril left, Andrew and his sisters returned to the drawing room to find Fiona sitting in shock. Audrey rushed over and tried to put her arms around her but Fiona pushed her away.

'Get off me. You knew, you all knew,' she shouted.

'No, no, I promise I didn't,' protested Audrey.

'Neither did I,' added Jane.

'Well I did, of course,' said Andrew smugly, 'and I was just hoping that Alistair hadn't changed his will or made another one. You see, marriage doesn't invalidate a trust made before that marriage.'

'So you let me think... Why do you hate me so much?'

'You didn't fool me for one minute. I'm not as gullible as Audrey. I know you only married Alistair for his money and I didn't buy all this family reunion business for his birthday. At one point, the thought even crossed my mind that you had something to do with his death.'

'What?' Fiona stepped back in shock.

'Andrew, you're going too far now.' Audrey made a move to put her arm around Fiona but she pushed her away.

'Get off me, for Pete's sake. I'm sick of your pathetic sympathy and constant interfering.'

'You bitch,' said Jane reaching out to her sister. 'Audrey has done nothing but try to be kind to you.'

'Get out the lot of you. I'm going to contest this will and I'll take it to the highest court in the land,' Fiona screeched.

'You can contest it all you want – if you have the money that is, but I can assure you that it's watertight. And as for telling us to get out, I rather think that it's the other way around, don't you? You don't own this house or anything in it apart from what you brought with you and I don't think that's very much, do you?' Andrew's calmness infuriated her even more. 'But, we're not heartless and none of us want to turn you out into the cold, winter night so I'm sure my sisters and I would be happy enough for you to stay over the New Year but we want you out as soon as possible after that. Shall we say by mid January?'

Jane went through to fetch their coats while Fiona fumed.

'We'll see ourselves out shall we?' asked Andrew.

'You haven't heard the last of this,' Fiona shouted, following them into the hall.

'By the way, don't even think of removing or destroying anything,' Andrew said. 'I've taken photographs of every room and given it to the solicitor and he has the latest inventory of all the valuables in the house.' Andrew ushered his sisters out of the door, shutting it behind them.

Fiona screamed and picked up a huge Chinese vase which stood on the hall console and threw it against the front door, shattering it into hundreds of pieces, 'So sue me then,' she shouted in the empty house.

Chapter 46

No sooner was Christmas over and the New Year warmly welcomed in than Mrs Mac started to think about spring cleaning. When the days started to lengthen she began. There was a lot to do this year but Darren had promised that he would do all the painting and that on no account was she to go on a stepladder. She had reluctantly agreed but thought the poor lad had enough to do so she would just start to prepare in order to make things easier for him.

Darren and Carla had married in November. They had bought a house in the next street so they weren't far away. It had belonged to old Florrie Scott who had died aged over ninety. It hadn't seen a paintbrush for years and was in desperate need of modernising so the youngsters had been able to negotiate a good price. For weeks they had worked very hard, roping in anyone they knew to help. Mrs Mac had been banned until it was finished and then they had put a ribbon across the front door which she was ceremoniously invited to cut and declare the house a home. Then they proudly showed her what they had done. She had joked that she felt just like the queen must do. The house was basically like hers but she couldn't believe how different it looked with an extension at the back and a wall knocked down between two rooms. Some of the décor wasn't to her taste but they were youngsters and braver than her with their choice of colour.

Carol and Bill had told Carla and Darren that they would pay for a smart wedding or, if they preferred a smaller wedding, they would give them the money towards the house. Sensibly they opted for the latter and put the money towards furnishing their new home. In any event they had a lovely wedding and it was such a happy day. Carla had bought a second- hand wedding dress which Carol and Mrs Mac had altered between them, changing the neckline and sewing crystals on the bodice. Karen and Gina were bridesmaids and they had insisted on paying for their own dresses as they chose garments they could wear again and they looked stunning. They had hired the function room of the pub and Carol and Mrs Mac had prepared a lovely buffet. Carol had made an amazing three-tier wedding cake. Karen had been in charge of everyone's hair and Carla had been able to use her staff discount not only for her mother's dress but Mrs Mac's as well. There was no-one present from Darren's side of the family and she was honoured that he asked her to sit at the top table in place of his mother. For the life of her Mrs Mac couldn't think of a single thing which would have made the day go better. She had a photograph of the young couple gazing into each other's eyes on her sideboard and it made her smile every time she looked at it, they looked so happy and in love.

She had known that she would miss Darren when he left, and she did, but it was nice to have some peace and quiet too. They only lived around the corner after all, and they came round for supper once in a while and invited her there. Carla's culinary skills did not match those of her mother's but they would improve with practice. Darren had told poor Carla not to bother learning how to make scones as no-one would ever make any better than Mrs Mac's so she was obliged to bake a batch whenever she was invited round there.

But now it was spring cleaning time again so she thought she would make a start on Darren's bedroom and strip the wallpaper. She had to work around Gina and her studying and she didn't want to do anything to jeopardise the young girl's prospects, she was putting so much into her career and would make a dedicated nurse. In a way Mrs Mac was not looking forward to her qualifying as she had a feeling that she would move away, after all she was now reunited with her father. She knew she would miss her dreadfully. They had become incredibly close over the past few years and, although she was a quiet girl, the house wouldn't be the same without her. When the time came, as it would some day, she would smile and give her blessing. She'd manage and she knew that Gina would always remain true to her. After all she had managed when Peter went away. Peter, her dear son Peter. How soon would she be able to see him again? The savings account was building up slowly and the money box was getting heavier. She felt a quiver running through her body. Was she excited – or scared? Maybe a bit of both, she thought as she tore the next strip of wallpaper from the wall.

Chapter 47

It was with a great sense of excitement that I said goodbye to Mrs Mac, giving her a peck on the cheek.

'Off you go and have a lovely holiday. You deserve it after all your hard work. It's time you relaxed for a bit.' The old lady waved me off.

Aoife and I had worked hard and passed our exams and we were now qualified enrolled nurses. There were big changes taking place in the nursing profession and we both intended to stay on to gain further qualifications. But for now we felt it was time to take a much-needed holiday. Some of the girls in our group were going to Spain for sun, sea and sangria but I was going to Ireland with Aoife. She'd invited me several times but I hadn't been able to accept previously due to family commitments of my own.

It was a beautiful day as we boarded the *Isle of Innisfree* at Holyhead. The sky was cloudless and the calm sea was a deep blue. We watched as the ship pulled out of port and turned to sail behind the long breakwater with the square lighthouse at the end, protecting its picturesque harbour. We sailed past the small mountain with another lighthouse below it on a little island. As it became smaller and smaller we went to find a seat for the three-hour journey.

'We couldn't have had a better day for the crossing,' said Aoife. 'It's so calm. Do you get seasick?'

'I don't know. I've never been on a ship before. I don't suppose the ferry across the Mersey counts, does it?' I laughed with her.

'Thanks for coming with me. I'm looking forward to showing you my part of the world.'

We found a couple of seats and Aoife went to fetch coffees. I sat back and looked around at my fellow passengers. A group of young men passed by, laughing noisily, obviously teasing one in their midst. One of them glanced in my direction and, for a second, my eyes met his. As he went on his way, I caught my breath. It was as if I had forgotten how to breathe. I could feel myself go cold. My stomach flipped and I felt dizzy. I became aware of Aoife standing in front of me bearing two paper cups.

'Quick, take one, it's hot,' she said. I stared at her blankly, as if she was speaking a foreign language. 'What's the matter?' asked Aoife looking concerned. 'Are you seasick? Although how anyone could feel seasick when it's like a duck pond out there...'

I pulled myself together. 'No, I'm absolutely fine. I just went a bit dizzy for a minute. I didn't sleep much last night – too excited.' I smiled and took the hot coffee.

'Drink your coffee and eat this.' Aoife fished a chocolate biscuit out of her pocket 'Then you can put your head back and have a snooze. We've ages to go yet.'

I sipped slowly, barely taking in Aoife's chatter. I'd heard the term *coup de foudre* before but surely this feeling wasn't that. I was wondering if my eyes had deceived me, but I knew they hadn't. It was *him*. I'd recognise him anywhere. He hadn't recognised me though. I had changed so much. I wasn't the girl I was four years ago. I really wasn't. And I wasn't only thinking of the way I looked. I wanted to tell him that but I couldn't. Tom probably hated me and I didn't blame him. I didn't even have the courage to find him to apologise. I had probably ruined his family so I'd be the last person he'd want to see. I sighed deeply. I'd have to pretend I hadn't seen him to get him out of my mind – but how?

The young men sat in a corner of the ship's lounge and, despite it being just past breakfast time, they all had a pint of beer in front of them except one – and he nursed a half pint.

'Hey, Will, is your brother a bit of a lightweight?' laughed one of them.

'No,' said Tom. 'I'm just pacing myself. It's going to be a long day.'

'Well, you're not making me feel guilty by being the older sensible brother. I'll have a bacon sarnie to mop up the beer later.'

'Ooh, bacon sarnies,' said another. 'Let's go and get some.' Off went the other four leaving Tom and Will to save their seats.

'It's great that you came with us,' Will said. 'And it'll do you good. All that studying isn't healthy.'

Will had persuaded Tom to visit him in Bangor before they went down to Glanaber to join the rest of the family for a few days. Will had been roped in to attend the stag party of Sam, one of the technicians at university with whom he was friendly. They were heading for Dublin to the Temple Bar area and Tom had been invited along too. For some reason Sam's fiancée, Iola, had decided that Will was the most sensible of the group and had put him in charge of Sam and warned him to make sure that he brought him back in good working order.

'I half expected to find that Louise would be on this stag do as well,' remarked Tom.

'She's such a game girl and almost one of the lads that she nearly came – until Iola heard about it and put her foot down,' replied Will.

'You still see her then?'

'Oh yes. We're mates. Good mates. We're still planning on going travelling after we graduate. What about you. Any girlfriends on the scene?'

'A few dates here and there but nobody special,' said Tom. For some reason his mind went back to the girl he had passed earlier. She'd looked strangely familiar; perhaps she was an actress or something. She was certainly a beauty.

The ship was nearing Ireland when an announcement came over the Tannoy that the gift shop would soon be closing. I left Aoife in charge of the bags while I went to look for something for my hosts. There was a queue at the till waiting to pay and a couple of young men were laughing at the funny captions on the T-shirts they were buying. One stepped back without looking, treading on my foot. He immediately turned to apologise and as he turned away his head twisted back, looking at me searchingly. Then we both recognised each other.

'Gina?'

'Will!'

Will's friend nudged him. The cashier was waiting to serve them.

'You go ahead, I'll be after you in a moment.'

He drew her out of the queue. 'How are you? You're looking great, I almost didn't recognise you.'

'I'm fine,' I replied, feeling the heat in my cheeks. 'It's been a long time.'

'Yes. What are you doing with yourself these days?'

'I'm a nurse.' I was trying to edge away but Will seemed so pleased to see me.

'Wow, that's great. Tom's here and he's a doctor – or nearly. He'll be thrilled to see you. He tried for ages to find out where you'd gone and he still asks around when he goes home.'

'Does he?' I couldn't hide my surprise but tried to remain cool while my stomach flipped and my heart seemed to miss a beat.

'Yeah. Come on. He'll kill me if I don't take you to him.' They paid for their goods and I had no choice but to follow him to the group of young men who cheered when they reached them.

'Look, Will's pulled already!' they shouted.

'Shut up, you lot. Gina's an old friend.'

Tom leapt to his feet and before I had a chance to do anything he had enveloped me in a huge hug. 'Gina. How fantastic to see you. How've you been? What are you up to these days? No-one knew where you'd gone so I couldn't get in touch.'

'Tom, it's lovely to see you too.' I had barely started to tell him that I was nursing and living on the Wirral, when a voice again came on the Tannoy announcing our arrival in Ireland. Before I rushed away to re-join Aoife Tom asked for my telephone number and address, promising to get in touch soon.

Chapter 48

I followed Aoife until we were eventually on the bus that would take us to Ballyvale, Aoife's village. It was as if I was in a trance.

Aoife looked at me with some concern. 'Are you okay?' she asked.

'Yes, a bit tired that's all.'

What could I tell her? That I'd just bumped into the man I'd loved since he was a boy?

I still felt breathless. My thoughts drifted back to the ship. Tom seemed pleased to see me but perhaps that was just the surprise of bumping into each other. What were the chances of that? I remembered searching his sweet, handsome face as he spoke to me, looking for signs of anger. Say something, I told myself or he's going to think you're an idiot. It was as if my body was floating like a balloon and my brain was working in slow motion. Eventually my brain reconnected to my body and told my mouth to work. Had he really said that he would get in touch? Would he, I wondered, hoping against hope that he would. It was only later that I realised that he hadn't given me his telephone number so he'd left himself an escape route in case he thought better of contacting me. As I sat looking out of the bus window I felt as if I were looking through crystal glass. The skies seemed bluer than ever, the fields a sharp green. Even the cattle stood out as if they were in a 3D film.

'You're looking better,' smiled Aoife eventually. 'It must be the Irish air and you've only been here for two minutes. Just think what you'll be like after the long weekend. I thought you were going to be seasick back there.'

'That would have been embarrassing wouldn't it, with the sea so calm.' I laughed. 'I'm looking forward to meeting your family.'

'Wasn't it a coincidence bumping into someone you knew?'

'Yes. I was in school with them,' I said vaguely, not wanting to elaborate. I wanted to relive the meeting again in private and recall how pleased the boys seemed to be at seeing me.

I already knew that Aoife's father was a farmer and her mother a part-time teacher. I also knew that her two brothers, Sean and Brendan, worked on the farm. If I had envisaged their home, it would have been something rural, obviously, and a bit bucolic maybe. When the bus stopped at a pair of wrought iron gates and Aoife said, 'Come on, we're here,' my jaw dropped in surprise. The gates opened into a long fence-lined drive, at the end of which stood a large modern house. A couple of horses looked over the fence twitching their tails occasionally.

'This is lovely,' I exclaimed. 'It doesn't look like a farmhouse.'

'What were you expecting – a stone bothy?' laughed Aoife. 'Those are the farm buildings over there,' she said, pointing across a field to some huge modern sheds. 'The original farmhouse is over there too. My grandparents used to live there but since they died it's let out to visitors now. Mum and Dad built this house about ten years ago.'

They hadn't quite reached the end of the drive when the door opened and a woman came rushing out with her arms open wide.

'Aoife, my baby, you're here.' Aoife was duly kissed and hugged and then she turned to me, shaking my hand warmly. 'And you must be Gina. Welcome or céad míle fáilte as we say over here.'

I saw an older version of Aoife. They had the same green eyes, dark hair and flawless skin. Aoife's mother wore her hair at shoulder length and they both had the same habit of running their fingers through it. She led the way into the house, talking non-stop, giving me a chance to take in my surroundings. It was a beautiful house, modern and immaculately tidy. I was shown to my room so that I could freshen up before going downstairs to the kitchen for a cup of tea.

'My room is lovely. Thank you very much for having me, Mrs Donnelly,' I said.

'Oh call me Maeve. And you're welcome here. I hope you'll make yourself at home. Now tuck into these scones, not that I made them, mind you. I'm no domestic fairy! The local baker didn't teach my children and I don't bake his scones, so all's well in our worlds,' she laughed. 'These will keep us going until later and we thought we'd have a barbecue.'

Later that day I was soaking in the bath, daydreaming about Tom and listening to the voices coming from the patio area behind the house. There seemed to be a lot of laughing as the preparations for the barbecue were underway. I had just finished dressing when there was a gentle knock on the door. It was Aoife.

'I've just come to see if you're coming down. Don't be shy. The boys are dying to meet you.'

Aoife's father, Joe, and her brothers greeted me, shaking my hand politely. They were very friendly and polite but before long they were teasing me as much as they teased their little sister. Joe and Sean were tall and dark-haired with blue eyes but Brendan was short with the green eyes of his mother and sister and a mop of red curly hair. They were a handsome family and obviously very close.

'Now that you're qualified when are you coming home to treat the sick of Ireland?' asked Joe.

'Kill them off, more like,' said Brendan. 'I remember when I was little and had a sore throat once, she put a plaster on it. Taking it off hurt more than the sore throat!'

'Yes and do you remember our old dog Donny? Whenever he saw a bandage he'd disappear because Aoife practised so much on him,' Sean joined in the reminiscing.

'It will be great to have you back home, my love,' said Maeve.

'Stop it, all of you,' snapped Aoife. 'Give me a chance; we've only just passed our exams and I want to go further with my studies. What makes you think I want to come back here? I don't know yet where I want to work.'

'Of course you don't sweetheart, but wherever it is, we'll always be here for you,' soothed her mother.

Everyone exchanged glances before Brendan said, 'Who's for another sausage?' and Sean topped up everyone's wine glasses to defuse the tension. Once again I was reminded that I had missed out on having a loving family like this. Aoife didn't know how lucky she was. I vowed that if ever I was to have a child, he or she would be so very loved.

Later that evening Aoife and I went for a stroll down to the paddock.

'Sorry about earlier,' she muttered. 'Didn't mean to create an atmosphere. But they just want to rule my life. They want me to come back, work at the local hospital and marry a local boy and it would be as if I'd never been away. I'm not sure I want to do that,' she sighed, frustrated. 'Sometimes I think I'll just stay in Liverpool or wherever I decide to go and not come home again.

We leant against the wooden rail.

'Listen to me, Aoife. You really mustn't do that. You would hurt your family so much if you did.'

'I don't care. I just wish they'd leave me alone.'

'Believe me, you don't. You are loved Aoife – by your parents and your brothers. I know you. You couldn't live with yourself if you hurt them. I know I sound like an old woman but being loved brings responsibility towards the people who love you. When you love someone you just want the best for them and that is what your parents want for you. You are lucky because they might be disappointed if you don't come back here to work but they'll accept it because it's right for you.'

'When did you get to be so wise?' Aoife smiled sadly.

The holiday seemed to pass so slowly. Everyone was kind, taking me on picnics and outings, the highlight being the beautiful Glendalough. I felt guilty at wishing to be back home in case Tom rang. Had I told him how long I would be away for?

On the evening of our last full day in Ballyvale I was wandering around the garden on my own when Brendan joined me.

'Hello,' he said. 'Have you enjoyed your first taste of Ireland?'

'Yes. It's lovely here, so beautiful, and you've all been so kind to me.'

'Perhaps we could meet up again. I wouldn't mind coming over to Liverpool,' he said.

I looked at him and knew I couldn't take advantage of his niceness. My head was still full of Tom and sometimes I thought I'd dreamt our meeting. Maybe he would get in touch with me again and maybe not but I wasn't ready for a relationship with anyone else, perhaps I never would be.

'Brendan,' I said gently, 'I've always wished I had a big brother just like you. You are good and kind and I would love it if I could share you with Aoife. I'm looking forward to starting my nursing career when I get back to Liverpool and whenever you come over and see Aoife, I hope to see you too.'

'Thanks, that would be grand. But it's a bit hard to get away from the farm, you know.'

'I know,' I said, and we both understood.

On our last day I was up early. I quietly made myself a cup of tea and took it out to the garden. I was surprised to see Maeve sitting on the bench in her dressing gown. She moved to make room for me.

'I'd always hoped she would live close by. She's such a precious daughter and I thought we'd share so much. And now she'll probably live far away and I'll only see her now and again.' Maeve dabbed at her eyes.

'You have such a strong bond that you don't need to worry. She might not be living on your doorstep but you'll never be far apart. You're so lucky, the two of you. In a way I'm jealous. I wish I'd been lucky enough to have a mother like you.' Maeve looked at me in surprise and was about to ask a question when I went on, 'Oh there is someone who gave birth to me somewhere. But a mother? No.'

The silence between us was broken by a call from the house.

'Mum, where's my—'

Then it was time to go. The entire Donnelly family waited with Aoife and me at the gate until the bus came. The driver showed no sign of impatience as the second round of hugs, kisses and goodbyes were being made.

Two excited young girls boarded the *Isle of Innisfree* at Dun Laoghaire – one to return to her nursing career and the other to await a phone call.

I was sipping a cup of tea listening to Mrs Mac exclaiming at the traditional gifts I had brought her from Ireland – an Aran cardigan, a shamrock brooch and a little lucky leprechaun.

'Tell me all about it. I've never been back to the old country, not that I remember it at all. Just the odd little thing seems to strike a chord somewhere in the back of my mind – the smell of wood smoke or, funnily enough, the smell of jacket potatoes. I think my mam used to put them in the embers of the fire to cook.'

'Why did you and your husband never go back for a visit?'

'Paddy never wanted to. His memories weren't good ones and he always thought of Liverpool as his true home.' She was in the middle of bringing me up to date about Carol and Bill and their family, as if I had been away for a month instead of a week, when she said suddenly, 'Oh, I nearly forgot. A man phoned wanting to talk to you.'

My mind, which had been wandering previously, jumped to attention. 'Who was it?'

'He said his name was Tom something. I've written it down by the phone. He asked when you were coming home but I didn't know who he was, so I wouldn't tell him.'

'Did he say anything else?' I asked.

'Yes, he made me take his telephone number down and read it back to him and he said would you please phone him back.'

My emotional pendulum now swung the other way as I leapt up to the phone and, trying to speak casually, said, 'I'll try ringing him now.'

Picking up the note by the phone I dialled carefully, each number etching itself on my brain as I did so. The phone rang and rang. I was about to put it down when a man who wasn't Tom answered.

'He's away in Wales until tomorrow,' said the sleepy voice.

'Thanks. It sounds as if I've woken you up. Sorry,' I said.

'It's a good thing you did. I'm on duty in an hour.'

'Will you tell him that I called please? My name is Gina.'

I had an early night but, although I was tired, I couldn't sleep. I was envisioning myself in various situations featuring Tom. We could start seeing each other, or not. We could have a relationship, or not. Whatever I thought of, I reached a point when I knew they could go no further. Tom's parents and my father could never meet again and it was all my fault. Perhaps it would be best if Tom and I didn't see each other at all. Yes, that would be the best thing, so I wouldn't take things any further even if he wanted to, even if it broke my heart. I was still dithering as the sun rose. I pulled the pillow over my head and told myself that, even if we did meet again, we mightn't even like each other. He mightn't like me but I knew, with absolute certainty, that Tom was the love of my life, whether or not he was part of it.

The following day Carla and Darren invited me for a cup of coffee to show me the latest bit of work on their house and Carol invited Mrs Mac and me for lunch. I feigned a headache and said I had slept badly which Mrs Mac confirmed, telling Carol that I did indeed look a bit peaky and me just having been on holiday.

I didn't put on the radio and did my chores quietly. Every sound in the house seemed magnified and with the windows open to allow in the fresh air the sounds from outside seemed unusually loud. When the phone did eventually ring, later in the afternoon, I nearly jumped out of my skin and, although I rushed to answer it, I tried to sound casual as I said 'Hello'.

'Hi Gina, it's Tom. How are you?' For a moment I was overwhelmed. 'Hello?' he said. 'Are you there?'

'Hi Tom. Yes, I'm here. How nice to hear from you.'

'Did you have a good time in Ireland? I wasn't sure when you were coming home.'

'Yes. Brilliant. You?'

The stilted conversation continued for a while but eventually we both relaxed as our mutual nervousness disappeared. I don't know for how long we had been talking but I was still on the phone when Mrs Mac returned from her lunch. We concluded our call by arranging to meet the following weekend.

'Was that the fellow who rang before?' Mrs Mac asked.

'Yes,' I smiled.

'Well, he's certainly perked you up,' the old lady commented.

Months later I was to look back and wonder why I had been so nervous about meeting Tom.

Our first date was when he came over to Liverpool one weekend. I was so excited I was almost ill. He had been delighted to see me and the time we spent together flew by. He told me he had been to Liverpool on a study seminar and had a date with a nurse called Nicola while there. I couldn't believe the coincidence – it must have been my friend Nicola. If only I'd gone to that party! When it was time for him to go home he leaned down to kiss me. Was it merely going to be a goodbye kiss from one friend to another? But no, his lips gently sought mine and I could feel him tremble, or was it me? The first gentle kiss turned into another, deeper one, then another. He looked into my eyes and I hoped he could read what I felt in them. I think he could, because we kissed again and again. We hugged tightly, and he was as reluctant to let me go as I was him. He almost missed the train! After that, we met up whenever we could, taking turns to visit Durham or Liverpool, both of us falling deeper in love every time we met. Sometimes we met half way and these were the best times as we stayed in an hotel. I thought I'd be nervous the first time we slept together because I'd never slept with anyone else but it was magical. I felt so safe in Tom's arms and so very loved. It was difficult to say goodbye to him when we parted. The only fly in the ointment was the fact that I had to keep our relationship a secret. I had made Tom promise to do the same and it was only with great reluctance that he had agreed. Mrs Mac, Carol and Carla could all tell that something was going on in my life and I knew I was evasive. I felt guilty at hiding something so huge in my life from people who had taught me to trust again.

And so the months passed. I loved my work and it seemed that if I wasn't working I was seeing Tom. But our work patterns were making it more and more difficult. One weekend I was at home, tired having had a busy week and feeling a bit melancholy. I was sitting curled up on the sofa staring into the flickering fire. Mrs Mac came in and put a cup of tea for me down on the nearby table. Normally I would have thanked her but I just picked it up and sipped slowly, lost in my own little world.

'Gina, love,' said Mrs Mac, 'you know I'm not one to pry but I'm getting a little worried about you. We all are. One minute you're up and full of the joys of spring and the next you seem to have the worries of the world on your shoulders.'

I turned my head. 'I'm sorry, Mrs Mac. Have I been difficult to live with?'

'No, it isn't that. I've hardly seen you. Is it to do with this man you're seeing?'

'Yes, it is.'

'Do you want to tell me about it?'

'Oh! Mrs Mac. I've been dying to tell you. I love him so much and I wanted to bring him here to show him to you and for him to get to know you and love you as I do.'

'Well, why haven't you then?'

'Two reasons. One – it can't go on. I'm going to have to stop seeing him no matter how I feel about him and, two – because I don't want to put you in a difficult position, that's why.' Mrs Mac looked at her, mystified. 'It's Tom, you see,' said Gina.

'And...'

'Tom, who I used to live next door to. It was on his birthday that I left home...'

'Oh!' said Mrs Mac. 'I see.'

'I didn't want to ask you to keep it from Dad and Charlie whenever you see them; that wouldn't be fair. I don't know what to do.'

'You poor girl. I think it's time for two tinks, don't you? Carol might have some ideas.'

Shortly after the coded message Carol appeared and Mrs Mac handed her a cup of tea, explaining everything.

'Phew,' Carol sat back in her chair. 'What a difficult situation. And none of it is your fault.'

'It is really. If I hadn't blurted things out like I did, the fling Dad and Aunty Ellie had mightn't have gone any further and no-one would have known.'

'Yes, and it might have gone on and there would have been two family breakups,' said Carol.

'What does Tom say about this?' asked Mrs Mac.

'He says that I'm overreacting and that his parents will be okay about it. He's promised not to say anything to them until I agree. But now he says that as soon as he graduates, he wants us to find a place together and we'll have to tell our parents and that's that. What they do about it is up to them.'

'Maybe he does have a point? Okay, it might mean that in future you have to have separate family gatherings but, surely, if you love your child enough you want them to be happy and you'd do anything for that. They'll just have to make the effort.'

'I suppose you're right. I feel so much better for having told you. I don't like secrets between us but you do understand why I couldn't say anything don't you? I don't want anything to upset Tom now, just before his exams, but as soon as they are over he must tell his parents and I'll tell Dad at the same time.'

Chapter 49

A suntanned Fiona went round her apartment opening the windows despite the frosty December weather. The apartment smelled stale and needed airing after having been shut up for several weeks. Rather than staying at home she had decided to spend as much time as she could cruising the world. She found that many widows seemed to do the same, except that most of them were sad to have lost a partner.

Any sadness she had felt at Alistair's death had quickly dissipated when the circumstances of her financial situation had come to light, and just when she was getting used to living in the way she felt was her due. Unfortunately for him and his stupid sisters, Andrew hadn't been quick enough to cancel her credit card so, before she left The Grange for good, she had put it to good use and, as she had left no forwarding address, she hadn't heard anything from them. She had emptied their joint bank account as she was entitled to do and she had cleared The Grange of everything she and Alistair had bought as a couple. Plus one or two other things which appeared to be of value. Together with the jewellery Alistair had given her Fiona had amassed a tidy sum. There was also the money from her divorce from Greg, what little there was left of it. She had been able to buy a small apartment in a smart block not far from the town centre with a charming view of the river. There was enough money for her to take the luxury holidays she enjoyed – to begin with. She would soon have to economise. Perhaps.

It was on one of the cruises that she met John Grant. He was a tall good-looking middle-aged man who exuded charm and politeness and yet, there was a hint of vulnerability about him. Fiona watched the gilded widows fluttering over him, hair dyed and lacquered, crepe-skinned necks adorned with diamonds and the wings of their upper arms hidden by elbow-length sleeves. Fiona kept her distance and used her charm on those men who came seeking her company. It was true to say that Fiona wasn't a woman's woman – in fact the only female friend she had ever felt close to was Ellie who had hardly respected their friendship. No, she was definitely a man's woman – and not just any man, preferably a rich one. There were several who sought her out but she didn't keep herself exclusively to one man: no, she needed to find out more about them first.

Fiona was, without doubt, a striking woman who always made the best of herself and, as she was the youngest by far of the widows on board the luxury liner, she had the choice of the lonely widowers seeking company. It didn't take John Grant long to join Fiona's circle and before they were halfway through the cruise John was spending nights as well as days with her. He was generous too, often buying her little surprise gifts.

Towards the end of the holiday Fiona and John stood on deck at the stern of the ship watching the moonlit path reaching along the sea.

He kissed her gently and said, 'Fiona, when I came on this holiday it was the bravest thing I had done. I was bruised and in pain after losing my wife. I never expected to have feelings for anyone else. But you – you've healed me and now I don't think I want to live without you. It's ridiculously early in a relationship to say something like that, but it's true.'

'I know, John. You've just swept me away,' she replied breathlessly.

'You know what they say about shipboard romances but it won't be true in our case.' John was adamant.

'I wish you were flying home with me tomorrow,' sighed Fiona. 'I can't believe that I'll be home leaving all this behind. It's been like a dream.' She laid her head on John's shoulder. 'I wish you were on the same flight.'

'So do I, my dearest but I'm meeting someone in Miami and there are another five days before I fly home, but I'll come straight to you from the airport.'

Fiona put her hand on his cheek, 'I'll be waiting,' she sighed. 'I suppose it will give us a few days to put things in perspective. Everything's happened so quickly.'

'I know. I suppose we shouldn't rush into things. But I want to. I can't wait to be with you again. I want to show you my home, take you out on my boat and I just want to share my life with you.' Fiona felt a frisson of excitement run through her body. Was this too good to be true? She had fallen in love at last and, as an added bonus, he was a rich man. 'I couldn't bear not to hear from you so let me give you details of where I'll be staying for the next few days.' He reached into his pocket for his wallet and somehow or other it slipped out of his hands into the sea, far below. 'Oh! Damn.' he exclaimed. 'My wallet.' He turned to Fiona in distress. 'It's got everything in it. My credit cards, bank card, money – everything.'

'Don't panic. Your passport is safe isn't it? I can lend you some money until you can get things sorted.'

'Oh! Damn,' he said again. 'What a fool you must think I am. Thank you, sweetheart. I'm so grateful.'

'We disembark tomorrow so we'd better go down and sort things now,' smiled Fiona. 'I'll just fetch my credit card from the safe. I've already settled my account.'

When they went downstairs to the Admin Desk there was a long queue of people waiting to settle their accounts. Eventually Fiona was able to withdraw some cash which would keep John going for a while. They both went to their cabins to finalise their packing for the morning but John had promised to come and say a final goodnight as they were disembarking at different times.

Fiona answered his gentle knock to see him standing there with a bottle of champagne and two flutes. They stood on her balcony and raised their glasses.

'To our first goodbye and may it be short-lived,' said John. 'By the way, here is your credit card. They handed it to me instead of you after we withdrew the money.'

'Thanks,' she said. 'It's a good thing you're honest – I hadn't missed it.'

Although she was up early the following morning Fiona didn't see John as she joined the queue for her transport to the airport, despite craning her neck for a tall, prematurely-greying man with blue eyes which crinkled at the corners.

'Pull yourself together,' she told herself firmly. 'You'll soon be home and he'll follow on before you know it.'

She was humming as she opened the windows of the stuffy flat. She was thinking of John and looking forward to seeing him. Not long to wait now. And she waited... and waited ... until her credit card bill arrived. Then she was sick.

Chapter 50

It seemed like no time at all since Greg and Charlie had married and yet their first anniversary had been and gone. The skies were just as blue as last year but instead of the warm sun and azure seas of Barbados the grass was frosted white in the winter chill. Their Christmas had been a quiet one this year with Gina electing to stay on the Wirral. She had promised to come down in January as soon as she had the phone call to say that her baby brother or sister had arrived. Charlie had been a bit anxious about Gina's reaction to her pregnancy but Gina was delighted as she had guessed that Charlie wanted a child. Greg had been a bit embarrassed but thrilled at the same time.

Charlie had blossomed over the past few months and had worked until Christmas but had given in to Greg's persuasions that she give up work in the New Year and take life a bit easier. She found it difficult, however, and although she was happy to put her feet up, her sketch pad was never far from her hand. Predictably all her designs were now nursery-related and once she passed them on to her staff at Charlie Taylor Design they developed them further and prepared them for production.

She was currently working on a collection from a very unusual source. During their Christmas visit to her great-aunts, Dissy had presented her with a box of baby clothes which she had knitted. Initially, when she opened the box

Charlie was speechless, first at the kindness and all the hard work that Dissy had put in to produce the little garments and, secondly, at the unusual colour choice. Her quirky aunt had decided that lime green, purple and brown were suitable colours for a little baby. The more that Charlie looked at them the more she thought that, for some reason, the colours worked. They were different, that was certain, and excitedly Charlie realised that there was a place for something bold and different in the baby market as young mothers moved away from the traditional pastel baby colours.

Taking her inspiration from the striped blanket and baby jackets, Charlie had spent ages toning down the shades and experimenting with the width of the stripes, until she was happy with the design which she had called The Dissy Collection. She was now playing with the same colour scheme but, instead of stripes, she was using dots on toning background colours. This she intended to become The Dotty Collection. She hoped her aunts would be pleased.

The telephone rang and Charlie put down her sketchpad and struggled to her feet. This would be Greg, she guessed, as he always rang at some point during the day to see how she was. As she lumbered towards the telephone she ran her hands over her belly. She was huge.

'Please come soon my little man,' she whispered. Although they had both decided against finding out the sex of the baby in the scan because they didn't mind either way, Charlie was convinced she was carrying a boy.

After reassuring Greg that yes, she was fine and no, she wasn't doing too much, Charlie wandered restlessly around the flat. They had spent much of the past year looking for a suitable house before finding one which they thought would be ideal. Unfortunately the sale had fallen through at the last minute so they had decided to stay where they were until the baby arrived. Although the flat was spacious, Charlie realised, as she looked around, that they would soon need more space. All of a sudden she felt a sharp pain. Gasping she held her side. Was this it? Was she soon to meet her son? Feeling scared and excited she picked up the phone to ring Greg.

When Gina arrived home each day she was absolutely exhausted. She and Aoife were only a few months away from their final exams. They were now close friends. She had invited Gina to go back with her to Ireland to spend Christmas with her family but she had wanted to celebrate the festive season with Mrs Mac and the rest of her Wirral family and because Charlie was so close to giving birth. More than that, she was hoping that she and Tom would be able to meet up at some point.

Gina was thrilled when the long-awaited telephone call came to say that the baby had arrived safely and weighed 8 lbs 2 oz and that mother and baby were well. On her first day off she set off to meet the new arrival with a suitcase packed with delicate knitted matinee jackets and gifts from Mrs Mac and Carol.

Arriving at the flat Greg opened the door to Gina. She gave him a brief hug and said, 'Congratulations, Dad,' before pushing past him. 'Where are they?'

Charlie picked up a little pink-cheeked bundle from a Moses basket in the lounge and handed it to Gina. 'Meet your little brother, James,' she said with a proud smile. Gina took him in her arms and sat down, gazing at the sleeping child with delight.

'He's absolutely beautiful,' she said in wonder. Tears blurred her eyes as she looked up at Greg and Charlie. 'You called him James,' she said.

'Yes, he's James Taylor Clark,' said Greg, his voice breaking with emotion.

'Thank you, Charlie.' Gina smiled at her stepmother.

'You don't have to thank me. I loved Ben too and I'm happy that your new brother carries one of his names.'

Gina studied the little boy. 'He looks a bit like Ben. I remember when you and Mum brought him home from hospital. He's definitely got Ben's nose.'

It was just as well that James was the most placid baby ever because, for the entire weekend, the three adults in his life vied with each other to pick him up, to cuddle him and to photograph him.

'It's a good thing I'm breast-feeding him,' smiled Charlie. 'It means I can hold him sometimes!

The new parents could tell that it was with great reluctance that Gina left to return to her studies after the weekend with promises that she would soon return.

Chapter 51

I felt that most of my life was spent on a train. I was either going to see baby James or meeting up with Tom. Tom was getting fed up with my insistence of not telling our families that we were seeing each other. Tom's open character and honesty made it difficult to hide things from his parents and he told me how difficult it was to remain non-committal when they asked if he was seeing anyone. I felt that Charlie and Greg had enough to cope with as life with a new baby is always hard and I didn't want them to have to face anything that would spoil their happiness. I was also working towards my nursing registration so, between everything I felt stressed and under pressure.

One weekend we were sitting in a pub having a drink and Tom said, 'Look, Gina, this has gone far enough now, and it's getting a bit silly. It really is time to tell our parents. I'm finding it harder and harder and I feel I'm being dishonest with Mum and Dad.'

'Are you giving me an ultimatum?' I jumped up nudging the table enough to spill some of our drinks.

'Of course not.'

'If you loved me you wouldn't put pressure on me like this.'

'And if you loved me, you would see that there really is only one way forward.'

'No, there is another way. Let's end it and there'll be no problem.'

And that was it. The great love affair over.

What an awful thing pride can be but somehow it found a place in both our lives. Our lives did go on, one lived on the east coast and the other lived on the west. I did think Tom would make an effort to get in touch with me and I suppose he thought the same.

When my nursing registration came through Dad and Charlie came up to take everyone out for a celebratory meal, but Mrs Mac preferred to babysit James with Carol's help. Little James was absolutely adorable and charmed everyone with his toothy grin. I thought I had put a brave face on things but I noticed Charlie looking closely at me once or twice.

As I was going to bed that evening Mrs Mac said, 'Charlie was asking me if you're alright. She said you had lost weight and there was no spark in you. She asked if you were having boyfriend trouble.'

'What did you say?'

'I felt very uncomfortable, Gina. You know how I feel about people lying, so I just answered the last part and said I didn't know.'

'Well you won't have to worry any more Mrs Mac. I don't have a boyfriend.'

And I turned and went to my room before I said anything else.

I worked very hard for the next few months and when I went to visit James, and his parents of course, I was able to appear as if life was wonderful but that I was tired after taking on new responsibilities at work. That stopped them from asking anything else. They asked me if I would like to join them for James's first Christmas but I was working. I didn't tell them that I had volunteered to do so.

There's no time to think of yourself on a hospital ward on Christmas Day. No-one was ill by choice so a brave face is a must and the day passed quickly enough and those patients that were able seemed to appreciate our silly fancy dresses and special little gifts. As I was leaving for home I heard someone call my name and when I turned there he was, by the entrance. He held his arms out and without hesitation I ran to him. I relished the feel of his arms around me, holding me tight.

'I'm sorry,' we both said, almost simultaneously.

'How did you know I was working?'

'I asked Mrs Mac and, bless her, she couldn't cope with the cross-examination I gave her so she told me everything. I'm guessing you missed me as much as I missed you.'

'Come back home with me and meet her.'

'I wish I could, my love, but I'm working again tomorrow so I've got to get back.'

Goodness! It was hard for us to part but we did in the certain knowledge that nothing would ever keep us apart again and I felt like the most important girl in the world.

Tom told me he would go back to his studies with renewed vigour to ensure our future and I got him to agree to wait until after his graduation before we spoke to our parents.

Chapter 52

A few months later Ellie and Matt had two graduation ceremonies to attend. That of Dr Thomas Harris at Newcastle, the medical school linked to Durham University, and William Harris who attained a 2:1 degree in Geography at Bangor. No parents could have been more proud. They whipped out the camera at every opportunity, asking anyone who was near to take a photo of the smiling family. There was one photo which would haunt poor Angharad for ever. It was one of her standing with her arms folded and a furious expression on her face because, for once, she was not the centre of attention. The rest of the family were laughing at her antics. There was another of her in Tom's arms wearing his mortar board and a big smile. Eventually Ellie and Matt framed this as a partner to the official portraits of their sons.

In Bangor, Louise had also attained a 2:1 and both her parents were present. There were a few photos taken of her with her mother, others of her with her father, but not one photo was taken of the three of them together. Matt and Ellie were introduced to them both and what a miserable, bitter pair they seemed. It was no wonder that Louise had left home. They said they weren't sure that they were happy with their daughter taking a year out to travel with Will, but it was difficult to imagine anything that they would be happy about. Will still insisted that they were just mates but Ellie, watching them watching each other, and finishing each other's sentences, felt that, with time, they would be more than that. And, if they were, she would be happy for them. Louise was a lovely girl.

Tom was another matter. Her normally open, honest son had seemed to be avoiding them lately. Matt said it was just exam stress and not to press him. She'd asked Will if he knew if there was anything bothering him, such as woman trouble and he seemed to clam up and said nothing. The anxiety of examinations might be over for Tom but he still had another stressful two years as a junior doctor to contend with. He was coming home for a week at the end of the month. She'd do her best to spoil him.

When Ellie answered the phone a few days later she expressed her delight at hearing from him and hoped he wasn't phoning to cancel his long-awaited visit.

'No, Mum. I'm still coming home but I'll be bringing someone with me, not that she'll be staying with us.'

'Well, she's welcome to stay if she wants to, as all your friends are.'

'It's Gina, Mum, Gina Clark from next door. We've been seeing each other.'

There was a long silence as Ellie absorbed the information. 'I knew there was a woman in your life but I didn't expect this.'

'I'm sorry if you don't like it but we love each other. It isn't some passing thing, we want to move in together and I fully intend to marry her at some point, if she'll have me.'

'Hang on. I never said I didn't like it. I was just surprised, that's all. After all these years of wondering what happened to her and you've been seeing her all along!'

'No, it wasn't like that. We met about a couple of years ago – a pure fluke – and we tried to take it gradually but we both knew. I wanted to tell you straight away but Gina made me promise not to until we were sure of how we felt about each other, because of what happened all those years ago. She didn't want to hurt you all over again. She's so sorry you know, Mum. And her life was so hard after that day and she didn't deserve all that happened to her. She's great, Mum, and I love her so much. I always have done really.'

'Tell her I can't wait to see her. If she's the girl for you then I couldn't be happier.'

'You know that means that you and her father will have to come face to face at some point? How will Dad feel?'

'That isn't your problem. And it isn't a problem as far as I'm concerned either, and I'm sure it won't be for your dad. It's something that happened a long time ago and maybe it's not forgotten, but it's certainly not even thought about any more. Don't even give it another thought.'

'Thanks, Mum. Can't wait to see you. I feel as if a ton has lifted from my shoulders.'

Ellie put the phone down. Her poor son, having to feel like that all because of her momentary aberration all that time ago. What was that saying about the sins of the fathers? She went to speak to Matt with whom she was so in tune these days, and she knew he would take it in his stride as well.

Chapter 53

I had taken a week off to go home with Tom, as I'd promised, and the night before we left I made the call I was dreading, hoping for a reaction as good as the one Tom had had from his parents.

With a deep sigh I picked up the phone and dialled. Charlie answered and when I asked to speak to Dad she picked up on the tension in my voice and asked, 'Is everything all right?'

'I've got something to tell Dad and he won't like it.'

'Okay, come back to me if I can do anything to help.'

Dad had overheard and took the phone. 'Hi Gina. What's the problem? Are you okay?'

'Yes, Dad, except that I've got something to tell you and you're not going to like it.'

'Go on.'

'I've been seeing somebody and we're in love and we're hoping to move in together.'

'What part of that do you think I'm not going to like? I'm delighted that you've met someone to love and I've got no problems with you moving in together.'

'It's Tom Harris.'

'Who?'

'Tom Harris, who used to live next door to us.'

'Oh! I see.' There was a brief silence. 'Well, I'm okay with that. How does he feel about me?'

'Are you? Are you really? Tom's absolutely fine with it. You don't think it will make it awkward for you with Tom's mum and dad?'

'It might be a bit embarrassing to begin with but a lot of water's gone under the bridge since then.'

'Oh, Dad, thank you. I've been so worried. I've been afraid to tell you.'

'You silly girl! I'd do anything for you, Gina, my love. If Tom's the man for you and you love each other, then I'm happy for you both. Bring him to see us when you come home, though I don't expect it will be easy for him.

Tom pulled up outside the house in Chestnut Grove. I glanced towards my old home, someone else had put their stamp on it now but Uncle Matt and Aunty Ellie's house looked the same. Neither of us got out of the car because we were having a row. Not a row exactly as we almost never argued, but Tom was running his fingers through his hair in frustration.

'You're being ridiculous. You can't stay in the car,' he said.

'Well I can't come in either!'

'You're just being silly. They said they're looking forward to seeing you again.'

'They said that for your sake.'

'I'll just go in first and say you're feeling a bit nervous but you're really being stupid. We're here now after all and they know you're here,' Tom snapped getting out of the car and going in the house.

A few minutes later the front door opened and Aunty Ellie walked down the path and sat in the driver's seat. 'Tom tells me that you're afraid to come in. What on earth are you afraid of? We're dying to see you again and hear all about what you've been up to. You wouldn't recognise the twins any more. They've grown up so much.'

'Aunty Ellie, I'm so sorry for what happened. I honestly didn't think of the consequences of my actions and how it would affect everyone. It's haunted me ever since, the way I hurt you when you'd always been so kind to me.' I couldn't stop my tears.

'Please don't cry. You've nothing to be sorry about,' Ellie said.

'That's what everyone says but I've never believed that.'

'Well it's time you did. Your dad and I are the ones who should be sorry. I am, and I'm sure he is. It should never have happened but it's behind us now. We've moved on. Who knows, if it hadn't happened Matt and I might never have had that little nosy parker who is dying to meet you.' Ellie pointed towards Angharad who was swinging on the gate waiting for her mum.

Aunty Ellie took me inside where everyone was waiting for her. Tom kissed and hugged me, saying 'Thanks, Mum' over my head. Uncle Matt also took me in his arms and kissed me. The twins greeted me briefly but, curiosity satisfied, they politely asked to be excused to carry on with whatever they were doing. Angharad inserted herself on the sofa between Tom and me.

Chapter 54

There was another difficult meeting that needed to take place. Ellie and Matt were invited to the new house that Charlie and Greg had moved into a few months previously. Greg, Charlie and James were waiting at the door to greet them. Charlie kissed Ellie on the cheek as she took the proffered flowers and ushered everyone inside.

'How's things?' asked Matt.

'Great thanks. This little chap keeps us busy,' Greg replied, indicating a fidgeting James in his arms, grateful to be holding him as he wondered whether he should shake hands with Matt or not, but Matt had not proffered his hand. 'Ellie,' he continued, nodding at her, 'welcome.'

It was a lovely day and Charlie had put chairs out in the garden with toys for the children to play with. Angharad promptly took charge of James and pushed and pulled patiently according to what toy he wanted. He jabbered away in his toddler language issuing orders which only she seemed to understand.

Ellie fidgeted constantly, wiping Angharad's hands or fussing with her hair. Greg meant absolutely nothing to her but she was considering Matt's feelings. She knew how hard this must be for him, and she admired his dignity as she flicked a glance over to him from time to time. She made a point of keeping as far away from Greg as she could and only spoke to him when he asked a question or included her in the conversation. She was charmed by Charlie who was so pleasant and relaxed but must have known how difficult the circumstances were for everyone else.

Greg, who she and Matt hadn't seen since that fateful day, was clearly nervous and he looked as if he was going to say something but what could he say? Ellie hoped he wasn't going to mention the past. She watched him playing the part of attentive host.

Matt sat back, sipping his cold beer. He didn't particularly want to be here, but he knew that he had no choice. The happiness of his son was paramount, and if it took being in the same place as Greg Clark, then he would do it. This was the first of many occasions at which he would be forced to share his company now that he was going to be indirectly part of the family. He sensed Greg's anxiety but said nothing. Things had obviously turned out well for him and, if Matt was honest, he had a vague feeling of resentment about it. Then he remembered the loss of Ben and he felt guilty. Looking at his own children, no-one should ever have to suffer that, he thought to himself. He caught Ellie's glance from time to time and he wanted to tell her not to worry. He sent her a mental message to say everything was all right. And he realised it was. Greg had made his life difficult for a while but he hadn't come between him and Ellie in the end and, in a strange way, their relationship had been strengthened, so nothing would ever come between them again. There was, therefore, no point in being bitter as this would affect him and his family, but most of all his eldest son. Tom and Gina were clearly nervous to start with, both being artificially bright and polite but, as time passed, they relaxed.

Charlie had prepared a light snack and, gradually, everyone started to unwind. As the afternoon wore on, everyone seemed to get along so well that Charlie suggested an impromptu supper. Greg and Matt masked any reluctance they might have felt to reinforce their assurances to Tom and Gina that all would be well and to help them lay a foundation for their future. Angharad and James were given special dispensation to stay up late. Oscar and Hugo were entrusted with cooking the sausages on the barbecue and Ellie helped Charlie in the kitchen, leaving Greg and Matt sitting side by side in the garden chairs. They sat in silence, looking towards their eldest children who were leaning against an old apple tree laughing at something before exchanging a kiss. Their two youngest children were kicking a ball between them.

'Matt...' Greg turned to say something but Matt held up his hand.

'Don't say anything. You've got nothing to say that I want to hear. Let's face it, we're only here because of our children. So, for their sake, I'll always be civil towards you but we're never going to be friends,' he said still looking at their children. He didn't tell Greg that he was happier than he'd ever been but went on, 'All actions have consequences – but not all of them are bad.'

EPILOGUE
A YEAR LATER

If there was ever a wedding that could be described as perfect, this was it. It was a day filled with tears, smiles and laughter: tears of joy, smiles of love and the laughter of happiness.

It was a beautiful late summer day, the sun's rays shining through the stained-glass created a myriad of patterns on the whispering congregation, like a child's kaleidoscope. The perfume of flowers filled the little church with their rich scent from the vases set out at various points: cream and pink roses, lilac freesias, blue forget-me-nots, stephanotis and baby's breath tumbled out of their containers.

The door of the church opened. The organist came to the end of the gentle music she had been playing. From the moment the bride walked down the aisle on the arm of her father to Handel's 'Arrival of the Queen of Sheba', the handkerchiefs came out to dab eyes which were to test the efficacy of waterproof mascara. Gina seemed to glide along as she smiled from behind her veil at the guests in the pews. Every bride looks radiant on her wedding day but Gina looked breathtaking. Her ivory silk dress was a study of elegance as she moved towards the man who was waiting at the altar. Their eyes met and he felt that the breath had been knocked out of him. Greg walked slowly by Gina's side carefully measuring his tread as they had rehearsed and Aoife followed, shimmering in a column of blue silk.

Behind her, full of importance, came Angharad, wearing a pale pink dress which wasn't the kind of Barbie pink she had been hoping for but, nevertheless, she was quite happy with. Alongside Angharad walked a very shy little James, carrying a cushion onto which the wedding rings had been tied. He looked sweet in his little suit complete with bow tie.

When they reached the front of the church and took their places, the best man relieved little James of his cushion and Angharad waited to take his hand to go and sit down with his mum. James, however, was having none of it.

'Where's my tractor?' he asked, his voice echoing clearly in the silence of the church. For a second no-one said anything and he started to cry. 'I want my tractor. You said!' he turned accusingly to his mother who was rushing to pick him up. The rest of the congregation laughed, realising that his bribe had yet to be honoured.

'Shh, sweetheart,' said Charlie. 'I have it here. Come on,' instantly quelling the tears, and he was quiet throughout the service as he nursed his promised red tractor.

The handkerchiefs came into play again as Gina and Tom made their vows with all the conviction and promise of their shared love. While the register was being signed a tenor sang the song 'Sunrise, Sunset' from Fiddler on the Roof and even Greg and Matt couldn't hide their emotion. When Dr and Mrs Tom Harris left the church to Mendelssohn's glorious 'Wedding March' they seemed to float on a cloud of happiness.

Before they left for the reception Gina excused herself and went to place her bouquet on a little grave. 'There you are, Ben, you're part of our special day and you'll always be part of my life. I love and miss you so much.'

At the reception, as the speeches came to an end Gina looked around her at all those who loved her and whom she held dear. For the second time in her life, Mrs Mac was sitting at the top table. This time it was in the place reserved for the mother of the bride, and never was there a more proud surrogate mother. She was as nervous of the honour accorded this time as she had been at Darren and Carla's wedding but, on one side of her was Matt and on the other was Will, and between them they took great care of her. Mrs Mac was quite a woman of the world now, having made her long-anticipated visit to Australia earlier in the year to see her son Peter.

Gina had insisted that Charlie also sat at the top table. Gina was incredibly fond of her and she had become a dear friend as well as a stepmother, a title which still made them both laugh. It was with Charlie's assistance that Gina had chosen such a beautiful wedding dress and she had done so much to help with the organisation of the wedding, despite being pregnant again.

Greg had been nervous throughout the day. He kept kissing Gina's hand in the car on the way to the church and could say no more than, 'Oh Gina, my beautiful girl.' He hadn't relaxed until he'd made his speech in which he had openly thanked all those who had helped Gina when he had failed. He spoke sincerely about second chances and of his gratitude at having a daughter like Gina. He also said how lucky he was in having an extended family in Mrs Mac, Carol and Bill and their children, and he publicly thanked Charlie for making him the man he had become. There was barely a dry eye when he came to the toast.

Bill had insisted on making a speech, despite being nervous, because he couldn't let the occasion pass without wishing "our Gina" all the luck in the world. As always, his reference to her as "our Gina" touched her heart. Carla and Darren sat with them. When Gina had asked her if she would be a bridesmaid she had been disappointed when Carla refused but, when she explained the reason, Gina was thrilled for her. After trying so hard and having two miscarriages, she was pregnant and glowing as she proudly displayed her baby bump.

Philip and Susan, Charlie's parents were also present. Sadly, Philip's aunts, Dotty and Dissy, had died a few months earlier. Separated at birth by two minutes they were separated at death by two days.

There were several guests who were important to Tom and his family who Gina was looking forward to getting to know better. Mair and Idris had presented them with a beautifully-carved wooden love spoon and she was looking forward to learning more about this Welsh tradition.

Tom had been so pleased that Will had been able to come back home to be his best man but Adam, his old school friend, had been on stand-by. Will and Louise had both been working abroad on a conservation project. Much to their surprise, but to no-one else's, they had discovered that they were in love with each other but they had no plans to marry in the near future – or so they said at the moment.

Louise was sitting at a table with Elaine, Sarah, Nicola and Tracy and Gina hoped she wasn't being led astray by them. They were the girls that Gina had so serendipitously met on the train all those years ago. They roared with laughter when they saw Gina and Tom's wedding cake. There, on the top, was the bride and groom ornament that Nicola had pinched from the top of the cake at the wedding they had attended that day. The one which she had drunkenly, but with great ceremony, presented to Gina as a gift. The day her new life began. Was it only six years ago? Gina cast her mind back to life with her mother and asked herself if she missed her? Was there a faint pang of longing for her presence? She answered herself honestly. No. She looked around the room once more, then at her husband, and felt complete.

The churchyard was quiet now that the wedding guests had departed but one or two people wandered around the cemetery visiting their loved ones, confetti drifting on a gentle breeze. A woman walked along her familiar route to lay her little posy of yellow and white roses on a grave but, to her surprise, there were some flowers already there, a large fresh bouquet of cream and pink roses, lilac freesias, blue forget-me-nots and stephanotis – a bridal bouquet. She picked it up thoughtfully and came to the obvious conclusion. She sat in the churchyard for a while. *I wonder where the wedding reception is being held. It shouldn't be difficult to find out,* she thought. With that, her high heels clacked as she hurried along the path.

Fiona parked her car outside the hotel and made her way to the reception desk to make enquiries. She was astounded to hear that it was the wedding of Dr and Mrs Tom Harris. Had she made a mistake? Perhaps it was Ellie who had put the bouquet on the grave. Surely Gina and Tom wouldn't have got married! How could she find out? She moved to a corner of the foyer and had just sat down wondering what to do next when a group of people accompanied by a bride went past towards the front door. It wasn't Gina! Or was it? This girl was slim and beautiful. She could hear the conversation.

'Carla, thank you so much for coming in your advanced state,' said the bride patting the pregnant girl's stomach. 'Take care of my little niece or nephew.'

Perhaps it wasn't Gina then. The bride put her arms around the girl and gave her a hug. 'Meeting you was one of the best things that ever happened to me. You've been like a sister to me for the past few years.'

Ah! So it was her. Fiona wondered what to do but before she had a chance to do anything, the bride turned in her direction and started to go back to the reception. She then caught Fiona's eye and stopped, her mouth gaped open.

'What are you doing here? You weren't invited and I don't want you here. If you have come to spoil my day let me just tell you, there's absolutely no way that you could do that.'

'I haven't come to spoil anything.'

'Why are you here then?'

'I don't know,' she shrugged. 'Curiosity, I suppose.'

'Curiosity! That's all I am to you. A matter of curiosity!'

'No. That came out badly. I often wondered what had happened to you.'

'Did you really?' I'll tell you then shall I? After leaving your house I eventually found a home with the most wonderful people in the world. They love me and I love them. I've been happier with them than I ever was with you. With their support I have a career that I love and today, I've married a man who makes me happier than ever and I can't wait to spend the rest of my life with him. Everyone who loves me and whom I love is here with me today and there's no room here for you. Please leave.'

'I'm glad things have turned out well for you. Truly I am. I'm sorry I wasn't a better mother to you.'

Gina rolled her eyes. 'I've often wondered why you disliked me so much. Even as a small child I sensed that you never wanted me around.'

'Sit down for a minute.'

'No, I have a husband and family to get back to.' Gina gathered up the skirt of her dress and prepared to turn away.

'Please. Just five minutes and then I'll go.'

Gina perched on the edge of the chair opposite Fiona. 'Five minutes then,' she said, knowing that anything Fiona said now would never upset her again. She no longer cared.

'I was very young when I had you, I was just seventeen.'

'Yes, I know. Is that your excuse? Being seventeen precludes you from loving your child?'

'No, no. Please let me go on. I was terribly unhappy at home. I hated my stepfather, he was a monster. He had been molesting me since I was a child and he was cruel. He said that if I told anyone he would hurt my mother. I believed him. As I got older and prettier the abuse got worse and he hated the fact that I went out with boys. I'd just started going out with Greg and I think he was jealous. One night he raped me; he was violent. I told my mother. She hit me and said it was my fault for flaunting myself.' Fiona scrabbled in her bag for a handkerchief. Gina looked at her, shocked, feeling sorry for her despite herself.

'Not long after I found I was pregnant. I told Greg that he was the father but I don't know if that was true. I still don't. I've never said a word to anyone.' The glamorous Fiona was openly crying, uncaring about the make-up running down her face. No-one could have failed to be moved by what she had just said. Gina put out her hand and Fiona grasped it.

'So when Ben came along he was easier to love than I was,' Gina said quietly.

'He was my lovely boy,' Fiona said sadly. 'I was so sorry I hadn't felt that way about you.'

'That's why you said that I could have saved him after Dad wasn't a bone marrow match for him. I wish I'd known. Truly I do. I loved my little brother very much.'

'Greg wasn't Ben's father, that's why he wasn't a match for him.'

Shocked, Gina snatched her hand away. 'What? What do you mean?'

Fiona shrugged. 'What can I say? I hoped he was but when I saw those lovely chocolate brown eyes of his I knew deep inside. They say that two blue-eyed parents can't have a brown-eyed child, don't they? I never wanted him to find out though so I prayed no-one else would figure that out.' Her breath caught in her throat. 'You know everything now.'

Gina was stunned. She sat there looking at her mother with a mixture of sadness and disgust. She hoped her father would never know. It would break his heart to think that neither of his children might actually be his. 'And you thought today was a suitable day to come and tell me that I might be the child of a rapist and that my brother was my half-brother? Your timing is impeccable!"

'No, I didn't mean it to happen like this. I was at Ben's grave and saw the flowers and I wondered if they were from you. I'm not completely heartless, you know.'

Gina heard someone call her name and there was Tom, coming towards her with a loving smile on his face. 'I wondered where you'd got to.' He turned to Fiona and when he realised who it was the smile slid from his face immediately. 'What are you doing here?' Turning to Gina, 'Has she upset you?'

Gina stood up. 'No, we've just been tying up a few loose ends. She's leaving now.'

'Goodbye,' she said to Fiona. 'I'm glad we've had this little chat and I'm genuinely sorry about everything that happened to you, but none of it was my fault was it? I don't expect we'll be seeing each other again.'

'Come on husband,' she smiled up at Tom before looking back at Fiona at saying pointedly, 'let's go back inside. My dad will be wondering where I am.'

About The Author

Edwina Jones, a fluent Welsh-speaker, was born on Ynys Môn (Anglesey) and, despite having travelled widely, she has never found anywhere else she would prefer to be.

She started work for the local authority where she met her husband and eventually she spent many years working in a school office. They have two children, grandchildren and great-grandchildren.

Edwina was on the team that organised the first writing festival in Anglesey and has had several pieces of work published in anthologies by local writers.

When she was a primary school pupil she remembers being so engrossed in writing her essays that she was oblivious to play-time. Mrs Crawford, her teacher at the time, asked her what she wanted to do when she grew up. She replied that she wanted to write a book and her teacher told her that she would one day. Well Mrs Crawford, she did!